SHERLOCK HOLMES
AND THE KING OF CLUBS

Sherlock Holmes has retired to Sussex to keep bees, and Dr Watson, now a widower, has returned to general practice. Desperate for distraction, the doctor agrees to accompany his old friend to Vienna to visit the eminent neurologist Sigmund Freud. But it is not long before the pair are pulled back into the murky world of ruthless villainy. For a shadowy terrorist group, the Black Hand, plagues the city — and when the tentacles of a crime committed in England reach into Europe to coil around Harry Houdini, the Great Detective and his Boswell must rise to the occasion once more . . .

STEVE HAYES AND
DAVID WHITEHEAD

———◆———

SHERLOCK HOLMES
AND THE
KING OF CLUBS

Complete and Unabridged

ULVERSCROFT
Leicester

First published in Great Britain in 2014 by
Robert Hale Limited
London

First Large Print Edition
published 2015
by arrangement with
Robert Hale Limited
London

A catalogue record for this book is available
from the British Library.

ISBN 978–1–4448–2506–0

Published by
F. A. Thorpe (Publishing)
Anstey, Leicestershire

Set by Words & Graphics Ltd.
Anstey, Leicestershire
Printed and bound in Great Britain by
T. J. International Ltd., Padstow, Cornwall

This book is printed on acid-free paper

For Robbin and Janet
This King for Two Queens

1

Unlucky for Some

That morning's auction had gone just like a thousand auctions before it, until it came to Lot Thirteen.

Then, knowing that this was what the overwhelming majority of his audience had been waiting for, the auctioneer allowed himself a dramatic pause, leaned forward over the podium and scanned his congregation through a pair of small, rolled-gold pince-nez.

More than a hundred expectant faces peered back at him, then turned almost as one when an elderly porter in a buttoned brown warehouse coat entered the room through a door in the left-hand wall. He shuffled to one of six polished-oak plan chests that stood side by side along the rear wall.

The room fell quiet but for the squeak of his boots on the parquet floor and the odd expectant turning of a catalogue page.

The porter pulled out the first large, shallow drawer and carefully set it down on one of three trestle tables in front of the auctioneer's podium. Heads immediately craned forward to get a closer look at its dog-eared contents.

Eventually all six drawers from the first plan chest were placed almost reverently side-by-side.

The audience watched in respectful silence; the only movement among the predominantly male audience came from the pipe and cigarette smoke that curled slowly toward the ornate, nicotine-stained ceiling.

At last the auctioneer spoke, his cultured voice echoing around the wood-panelled room. 'Gentlemen — '

He broke off, almost immediately, in order to acknowledge the only female in the audience: a tall, slender spinster in a beige two-piece woollen walking suit. Though her face was hidden beneath the veil that hung from the brim of a torque hat adorned with two ostrich plumes, she inclined her head in thanks.

'Lady and gentlemen,' he continued with an indulgent smile, 'we now come to Lot Thirteen, the first of thirty such lots being auctioned here today on behalf of the widow of the late and much-respected architect, Sir Andrew Montefiore.

'The architecture of the Habsburg Empire, with its eclectic mixture of baroque, Renaissance, neo-Gothic and Romanesque, is of course of tremendous interest to scholars, historians, architects and aesthetes alike. It was particularly fascinating to Sir Andrew, whose collection of ephemera upon the subject is considered by many to be among the finest in the world.

'Like its subject, the Montefiore collection is also of a somewhat eclectic nature. It includes personal papers, monographs, sketches, prints, maps, plans and cyanotypes relating to a wide variety of building projects undertaken during the period in question. A conservative estimate suggests that, *in toto*, the collection contains some 75,000 separate items relating to the lives and works of such luminaries as Filiberto Luchese, Johann Lukas von Hildebrandt, Ludovico Burnacini, Joseph Emanuel Fischer von Erlach and, in particular, Joseph's father, Johann Bernhard Fischer von Erlach.

'As is well known, Fischer the elder began his architectural career in 1687, and during his lifetime undertook major commissions from Joseph I, Charles VI and the Archbishop of Salzburg among others. His instructions were not only to replace many of the buildings damaged during the Great Turkish War, but also to represent through the medium of architecture the absolute power of the monarch Leopold I, as well as that of the Roman Catholic clergy.

3

'Thus, he was responsible for such buildings as the Schönbrunn Palace, Schloss Klessheim, the Glam-Gallas Palace, the Dreifaltigkeitskirche, the Kollegienkirche, and the Winter Palace of Prince Eugene of Savoy. Additionally, he made a most notable contribution to the Imperial Palace of Hofburg in Vienna.

'An original manuscript of Fischer's book on architecture, *Entwurf einer Historischen Architektur*, dating back to 1721, is being offered separately in Lot Forty-Two of today's proceedings. Lot Forty-Three consists of an additional 25,000 glass plate negatives produced by George Washington Wilson and Company which date from the 1860s.'

He gave his audience a moment to absorb his introduction, then said: 'In Lot Thirteen, you will be bidding upon the cornerstone of the collection, a selection of — '

Before he could go any further, however, there was a sudden commotion at the rear of the room. Two men who had been seated in the back row sprang up, one of them pulling a handkerchief up over the lower half of his face as he shouted, 'Don't move, any of you!'

Naturally everyone moved. As the gathering turned in their seats, there were demands to know what was happening.

By then both men had stepped into the

aisle. The taller, leaner of the two, his features also hidden behind a crude handkerchief mask, ran to the door, where he stood holding a Webley Mk IV revolver. The cries of protest quickly faded when the audience saw the gun.

The man's shorter, fatter and older companion also produced a weapon — an ugly, angular, self-cocking Webley-Fosbury — and hurried to the front of the room, the glittering eyes above his mask seemingly looking everywhere at once.

'What is the meaning of this, sir?' the auctioneer demanded.

'Shut up!' the fat man hissed. He, like his companion, was dressed in a nondescript black suit, white shirt and black tie, and had donned the hat previously resting in his lap to make further identification more difficult. What the auctioneer could see of his face looked very pale, almost sickly. He wore glasses — small round lenses set in tortoiseshell frames — and the eyes behind them were cold and spiteful, the colour of chocolate.

'Do as I say and you will live!' he told everyone. 'Cross me and you will regret it!'

His English was excellent, but the auction-eer sensed that it was not his first language. It was too clipped and precise, and allowed for no trace of the vernacular.

A strained, uneasy silence descended over the room. The auctioneer exchanged a helpless look with the scribe seated at a roll-top desk behind him, who had been faithfully recording the sales of the day. The elderly porter looked equally at a loss as to what to do.

Stuffing the revolver into his waistband, the fat man quickly rifled through the contents of the first of the six plan chest drawers. The dry, urgent crackle of old paper was now the only sound in the room.

Clearly he was searching for something specific.

When he did not find it in the first drawer, he went to the second and again searched it quickly but efficiently. Uneasy murmurs came from the trapped audience behind him.

When the fat man searched the third drawer he found what he was after. He took a folded sack from his pocket, opened it and began filling it with the contents of the drawer.

'Now see here . . . ' protested the auctioneer.

The fat man silenced him with a warning glance. He continued filling the sack until he had everything he wanted, and then turned to the audience.

'We are leaving now,' he announced, his glasses reflecting the watery October daylight filtering in through the tall sash windows. 'And lest one of you 'gentlemen' get the urge to follow us or sound the alarm before we are safely gone, we shall be taking one of you with us as a hostage.'

Instantly there were cries of indignation. The fat man grabbed his Webley and aimed it at the audience, silencing everyone.

'*You*,' he said softly to the only woman in the room.

She looked around, as if thinking he was addressing her by mistake. Then, realizing that he wasn't, her dark hazel eyes grew alarmed and she gave a tiny gasp of fear.

At once the elderly gentleman seated beside her stood up, saying, 'You *cad!* How dare you intimidate this poor woman — '

The fat man sprang forward and struck him viciously on the head with the butt of his gun. The elderly gentleman collapsed in his seat, bleeding from his forehead.

Though horrified, the woman bravely turned to aid the injured gentleman.

'Leave him!' the fat man ordered. 'Just get out here — *now.*'

She glared at him, her veiled expression a mixture of fear and defiance. Then, realizing she had no real choice in the matter, she stood up, clutched her tapestry purse more tightly, and with as much dignity as she could muster stepped into the aisle.

The fat man grabbed her by the arm and turned to the audience. 'All of you, listen to me. No harm will come to this woman as long as you do as I say.' He glanced at the old yellow-faced clock on the wall. The time was a minute past eleven. 'If you have any concern for her welfare, you will make no attempt to raise the alarm until half-past the hour. I have men watching this building. If they see anything to suggest that you have not given us the time we require to make our getaway, I will shoot this woman, and her death will be upon the conscience of every man here. Do you understand me?'

There came a few grudging affirmatives.

'Do you understand me?' the fat man repeated loudly.

'Yes, we understand,' the auctioneer replied grimly. 'I will make sure you have the time you need. But I promise you this: when you are brought to book it will be my great pleasure to testify against you.'

But the robbers and their hostage were already hurrying to the door through which the porter had entered, and all the audience could do was watch helplessly as one after the other they disappeared into the bowels of the building.

Impulsively the auctioneer called out,

'Have courage, madam!'

The last he saw of her was the woman looking back at him, her expression one of abject terror.

It was the last time anyone would ever see the tall, slender spinster again.

2

Special Delivery

One week later

It was a little after six o'clock in the evening when Dr John H. Watson saw the day's final patient out of his office. In her sixties, the poor woman wasn't much older than he, and yet there was a world of difference between them. Aside from his gammy leg and a modest thickening at the waist, Watson still retained his straight-backed, square-shouldered military bearing, and continued to enjoy almost rude good health. Mrs Levy, by contrast, was short and overweight, and suffered with recurring nausea and stomach pain, the pain predominantly over the right quarter of her considerable abdomen.

While Watson examined her, she explained nervously that she had put off visiting him for as long as she could in the hope that the problem, whatever it was, would clear up of its own accord. But when the pain grew worse instead of better . . . well, she had gone to see the local apothecary, who had recommended she seek the opinion of a physician. Beside herself with worry, she had done precisely that.

The woman's history, coupled with the yellow pigmentation that was visible in the whites of her eyes, was enough for Watson to make a preliminary diagnosis — that she had developed jaundice, probably due to one or more gallstones obstructing her bile duct. An X-ray would be required to confirm this — but such a prospect, when he mentioned it, had thoroughly alarmed his patient.

'Do I have to have one, doctor?' she asked fearfully.

'You don't *have* to,' he replied. He finished writing his referral and slipped it into an envelope, which he then licked, sealed and addressed. 'I cannot *make* you attend your appointment, Mrs Levy. But I must impress upon you the need for clarity in this matter.'

She considered that, then enquired anxiously, 'Will it hurt?'

He smoothed his small, neatly-clipped moustache. The X-ray had been a vital diagnostic tool now for almost two decades, and yet still the so-called 'ordinary man in the street'' harboured a distinct sense of unease when subjected to it. 'No, Mrs Levy,' he assured her gently, 'I promise you it will not hurt.'

11

'But it *is* important, you say?'

'Vitally so. We have to know the exact nature of your ailment before we can address it, don't we?'

'Yes, I suppose so . . . All right, doctor,' she agreed reluctantly. 'I suppose you know best. Is there anything I can do in the meantime? You know, just to feel better, like?'

'Firstly, I would advise you not to worry unduly.' He handed her the referral and helped her up. 'And for your own sake, I recommend that you try to reduce your weight.'

'Would that I could, doctor. But it ain't easy. Not after eighteen children, anyway.'

'Nevertheless you must try, Mrs Levy. You will feel a considerable benefit.'

'I will, sir,' she promised. 'You've been so kind, settin' me nerves at rest like this.' She hesitated, then cocked her head and studied him for a moment. 'I tell you what, sir. I'll make you a bread puddin' and drop it round. A special one, with currants and all sorts in it.'

'There's no need for that.'

'It'll be my pleasure, sir. Kindness given should see kindness returned.'

Watson didn't press the point. She obviously wanted to show her appreciation . . . and he *was* rather partial to bread pudding. 'Well . . . thank you.'

The surgery occupied two lower-ground-floor rooms in a tall, narrow house that overlooked the south bank of the River Thames. Watson escorted Mrs Levy outside and across the stark waiting room to the curtained glass doors.

As she stepped outside into the chilly Deptford dusk, Mrs Levy looked at him once more. She gave him an appreciative smile that revealed two missing teeth and then struggled awkwardly up the worn cement steps toward the street.

Watson locked the door after her, switched off the gas mantels — electric lighting had yet to reach this impoverished part of the city — and returned to his office to finish making notes on the woman's card.

He had been attending the Bacton Street surgery in the capacity of a locum for two weeks now, having more or less retired from medical practice upon his sixtieth birthday, the year before. Although medicine had become increasingly secondary to his career as a writer, he had happily accepted the request to stand in for a medical colleague who had been laid low with a viral illness.

He had enjoyed his return to practice, and Watson was surprised by just how much he had missed it.

The pleasure he derived from returning to work was especially heartening because some months earlier his life had been turned upside-down by the unexpected death of Grace, his wife of almost ten years. And in the dark months that followed, he had thought never to derive satisfaction from anything ever again.

But in all respects, Watson was recovering far better than he could have hoped. His life was getting back on an even keel — until, that was, he heard a soft, sibilant sound and looked up just as a folded sheet of paper was slipped beneath his closed office door.

Startled, he limped hurriedly across the room. Not bothering to pick up the note, he opened the door, determined to confront whoever had broken into the locked surgery to deliver it.

The dark waiting room was empty.

The room was lit only by the bluish glow of the streetlamps outside. It was sparsely furnished, offering no place to hide, and Watson crossed the outer room and checked the front door. It was still locked.

Puzzled, he bolted the doors, top and bottom. Then, his sense of unease only increasing, he limped back to his office, stooping to pick up the note before closing the inner door behind him.

Unfolding the note, he held it up to the light and read:

MRS HASTINGS IS NOT WHAT YOU THINK SHE IS. IF YOU DO NOT BELIEVE ME, BE AT BECKWORTH PARK ROAD, NW, TONIGHT, NO LATER THAN NINE. THERE IS GOOD COVER DIRECTLY ACROSS FROM THE SHIELLS HOTEL FROM WHICH YOU MAY DISCOVER THE TRUTH FOR YOURSELF.

The note was not signed.

Angry now, for Irene Hastings — undoubtedly the Mrs Hastings of the anonymous note — was a dear personal friend, Watson went to his desk and set the note on his blotter so he could study it more closely. It yielded no clues. Of course, if Holmes had been there he would discover all manner of hints and indications during his first examination. But, though Watson had grown familiar with his companion's methods over their years together, he still lacked the expertise to use them to the fullest.

Though a casual observer might have found it hard to believe, Watson had once lived an adventurous life, first with the Fifth Northumberland Fusiliers, and later the

Berkshires, as an assistant surgeon. He had served in the Second Afghan War and been wounded at the Battle of Maiwand. While recovering at a hospital in Peshawar he had contracted enteric fever and, severely weakened, been invalided out of the army and sent back to England.

It was during this unhappy period that his fortunes had turned. Unable to survive as comfortably as he would have liked on an army pension of eleven and sixpence a day, he had decided to seek a companion with whom to share the expenses of living in central London. It was then that a mutual friend named Stamford had introduced him to Sherlock Holmes.

That had been in 1881 — a little over three decades ago.

Their subsequent years together had been eventful, to say the least. But like all good things, they had finally come to an end. Watson had married for the third time in 1903, and though he and Holmes had continued to see each other regularly for the next year or so, they had finally gone their separate ways. Holmes had retired in 1909 to keep bees in his beloved Sussex, and written a highly regarded book upon the subject called *Practical Handbook of Bee Culture, with Some Observations upon the Segregation of the* Queen. Watson had seen him even less frequently thereafter. Indeed, the last time had been at the funeral of his beloved Grace.

His thoughts returned to Irene Hastings. How *dare* the writer of the note try to defame her! The woman had been a tower of strength to him in the months following Grace's death. Watson doubted that he could have survived that period without her.

They had met by chance at a restaurant where she was dining with her brother, Robert. He was a pleasant, jocular fellow, and Irene and Grace had got along famously until their friendship had been cut short by Grace's sudden death.

Irene and Robert had immediately offered Watson their support. Irene had been widowed for several years, and knew perhaps better than most how Grace's death had devastated him. It was inevitable, he supposed, that he should eventually develop certain . . . *feelings* for her. Tall and willowy, with fair hair that hinted at Nordic ancestry and eyes as clear and bright as the finest diamonds, she turned heads wherever she went. Robert, sensing Watson's attraction for his sister — and the awkwardness of it coming so soon after his bereavement — had deliberately made himself scarce so that their relationship might flourish with some degree of privacy.

Watson now looked at the address on the note again: The Shiells Hotel, Beckworth Park Road, NW. The address was not familiar to him and he wondered if the note was part of a plan to lure him into danger. He and Holmes had made no shortage of enemies during their years together. Yet somehow he did not think it likely. He and Holmes had not worked together for almost a decade, and as far as Watson was aware, Holmes himself had not engaged in any professional cases since the murder of Fitzroy McPherson in 1907.

So what was the intention of the anonymous note-writer? A practical joke? If so, it was a decidedly unfunny one, as the perpetrator would soon discover. For if Watson did go to Beckworth Park Road, he would take his loaded service revolver with him.

But of course, there was no *if* about it. He *would* go, if only to satisfy his curiosity.

He scowled at the wall-clock. It was now twenty minutes past six. Time enough to return to his lodgings in Queen Anne Street and prepare for whatever events this dark autumn evening had in store.

3

Appearances are Deceptive

The night was cold, and a biting wind brought with it a miserable, slanting drizzle. For a moment, as Watson peered out into the darkness, he was tempted to dismiss the note as a ridiculous prank and simply stay at home. He found himself wondering again, though, how the messenger had passed through a locked door in order to deliver it. And why he — or she — had chosen to libel Irene Hastings, of all people.

These questions required answers and Watson knew he could not rest until he had them.

He turned from the window, checked his Webley Mk II, and tucked the gun into his Chesterfield overcoat. After buttoning the garment, he tugged his grey herringbone cap down over his thinning sandy hair and went outside to hail a cab.

The hansom took him north across London, past the dark, countrified sprawl of Regent's Park and on through the urban maze of Chalk Hill until it reached Belsize

Park. Here the driver stopped, as directed, at the corner of Beckworth Park Road. Watson climbed down into the wintry night, hooked his cane over one arm and paid the driver.

As the coach drove off, Watson surveyed his surroundings. The street was largely residential. A row of stuccoed terraced houses curved away from him. The front door of each house was flanked by whitewashed Doric columns. Each had a cast-iron balcony on the second floor, but over the years the neighbourhood had fallen into decay and was now nowhere near as grand nor fashionable as it had once been.

Watson took out his pocket watch and saw that it was just after 8.30. Good. He had deliberately planned to arrive early. Squaring his shoulders, he limped along Beckworth Park Road, keeping to the shadows between the streetlamps lest he already be under observation. The sound of his footsteps and the click of his cane on the pavement mingled with the noise of the wind and pattering rain.

One of the houses ahead of him had been converted into a dismal bed-and-breakfast establishment. The sign hanging above the entrance identified the place as THE SHIELLS HOTEL. Lamplight showed in its white-framed windows and a lantern swung over the closed front door, causing flickering shadows in the puddles on the pavement.

Watson took one final look around, then ducked into the darkness under the trees bordering the park. There he realized that the note-writer had been right about one thing — his present vantage offered him an excellent view of the hotel while he himself was practically invisible to anyone on the street.

Various emotions warred within him: unease, anxiety, indignation for Irene and a concern that he had been the victim of a practical joke after all.

It was the longest half-hour Watson had ever spent. Cold and uncomfortable, he had decided to wait for ten more minutes when he heard the distinctive sound of a motorized taxicab approaching.

Moments later a green Panhard Levassor appeared, its yellow wheels splashing through puddles, its oil lamps casting a mustard glow in the rainy darkness ahead.

Immediately, Watson ducked further behind a tree.

The cab came closer, slowing as it neared the hotel. He held his breath as he waited to see who would alight.

A man in his late fifties stepped down first, wearing a top hat and carrying a stick. The fellow did not look familiar. He had a thin face and a grey pencil moustache — otherwise, he was quite unremarkable. Watson was certain he had never seen him before.

The man made to help his companion from the cab. Watson felt a sinking feeling in his stomach as he sensed who this would be yet was loath to believe it.

Sure enough, a woman climbed out of the cab, and she was without any doubt Irene Hastings.

She stumbled against her companion. Her laughter carried across the street to Watson; it was a delightful sound, one he had enjoyed many times during their meetings. Yet he hated it now as it implied an intimacy between the two from which he was excluded.

Immediately Watson chastized himself. He had no right to feel jealous. He and Mrs Hastings were friends — *good* friends — but he had no claim upon her. And yet he had believed there existed between them an unspoken agreement. She had done nothing to disabuse him of that belief.

Now, though, he realized that he had been mistaken.

The man in the top hat paid the driver. He seemed in good humour, for Watson heard the driver thank him profusely for what he assumed was a generous tip.

The cabbie then turned his vehicle slowly

to return the way he had come. As the head-lamps swept across the park, Watson moved back even further so that he was quite hidden behind the tree. A moment later, once more covered by the darkness, Watson peered around the trunk in time to see Irene Hastings and her . . . her *gentleman friend* . . . entering the hotel.

Watson's heart sank. He realized there was only one possible interpretation. Irene Hastings had given him the distinct impression that their friendship would ultimately lead to a more permanent state of affairs. She had indicated that they had an understanding and with such sincerity that he had almost convinced himself that he was falling in love with her.

Still, he had maintained a discreet distance, unwilling to commit himself to another relationship so soon after Grace's death. But he had always enjoyed the company of women and had never been happier than when married. And when her brother's business ran into financial difficulties, Watson had been only too willing to loan him money . . .

An alarming thought occurred to him, and suddenly the phrase used in the note rang in his ears.

MRS HASTINGS IS NOT WHAT YOU THINK SHE IS.

Were his fledgling suspicions right, then? That her only interest in him had been his money? He didn't want to acknowledge the possibility, but now that he thought about it there had been numerous occasions when he had offered to help Irene and Robert financially. There were the shares he had bought in the Dartford Shipping Company. Robert, claiming insider knowledge, had assured him that its stock would rise within six months to double its present worth, and so Watson had invested heavily — or rather, Robert had taken his money and invested it upon his behalf.

Then there had been the solicitor's fees to pay for the transaction, and a loan to pay one of Robert's more pressing business debts.

Suddenly Watson saw that he had been played for a fool and his usually mild temper flared. There was only one way to settle this thing, and that was to go over there now and confront her.

But even as he stepped out from behind the tree, the curved handle of another walking stick hooked his arm a familiar voice said, 'Hold hard, Watson. Not so fast.'

Stunned, Watson turned and faced a tall, spare silhouette.

'H-Holmes . . . ?'

The figure stepped forward and unhooked

his cane from Watson's arm. 'Forgive the somewhat dramatic nature of my entrance, old friend,' he said, removing a kid glove in order to shake Watson's hand. 'I am sorry that we should meet again under these circumstances.'

Watson, confused, shook his head. 'What circumstances, Holmes?' And then: 'By God, it was *your* note that brought me here, wasn't it?'

Holmes's silence confirmed that it was.

'What do you know about Mrs Hastings?' Watson demanded. 'And why did you have to be so damnably mysterious about it?'

Holmes glanced across the road at the hotel. Dressed in an immaculate, double-breasted frock coat and a beaver top hat, he looked as tall and gaunt as ever, with his high, pale forehead and oiled, backswept hair that was now the colour of steel. 'Come,' Holmes said briskly. 'We have some letters to post.'

'Letters? What the deuce are you talking about?'

Holmes didn't reply. He stepped out of the trees, onto the pavement, and walked quickly back along the street until he reached the postbox on the corner. It was all Watson could do to keep pace with him.

Upon reaching the box, Holmes took out a thin stack of envelopes and stuffed them into the slot. As Watson studied his friend's profile he was momentarily transported back in time, for it seemed just then that the years had hardly touched Holmes. Age had done nothing to reduce his more than six feet; his grey eyes appeared as incisive as ever; his nose still as thin and hawklike; his chin as square and prominent as it had ever been.

Then Holmes started across the road. Watson hurried after him, realizing that time had left something else about Holmes unchanged — his ability to be as insufferably cryptic as ever.

They climbed the steps to the Shiells Hotel. Without pausing, Holmes pushed open the door and entered a hallway with a counter along the left-hand wall. Behind it sat a scruffy-looking clerk of about thirty, dressed in a white shirt, maroon tie and a food-stained navy waistcoat. Looking up from the paper he'd been reading, he greeted Holmes and Watson.

''Evenin', sirs. 'Ow can I help you?'

Holmes glanced at the register. Reading the most recent entry, he said to Watson, 'Mr and Mrs Haslemere, Room Seven.' Then, fixing the clerk with a penetrating stare he snapped, 'The pass-key, if you will.'

'P-pass-key?'

'I have yet to meet the lock I cannot

master,' Holmes replied, 'but the pass-key will make my job here tonight considerably easier.'

'You're talking in riddles, mate. Are you drunk? You'd better 'op it.'

Holmes stood his ground. 'As an accomplice in blackmail, you presently occupy a very precarious legal position. Were I you, I should look to distance myself from the prime movers in this sordid enterprise and cooperate before the authorities get involved.'

Watson watched the blood drain from the clerk's face. 'I dunno . . . ' he began.

'Then I suggest you summon a policeman at once, for part of your premises is presently being used for a highly immoral purpose.'

The clerk grew surly. 'I know nothing 'bout that, guv.'

'Then give me the pass-key and don't interfere,' ordered Holmes.

Grudgingly the clerk obeyed. 'Remember now, I don't want no trouble.'

Ignoring him, Holmes climbed the stairs to the first floor. Labouring behind him, Watson said, 'B-blackmail? Holmes — what is this all about?'

'Very soon now,' Holmes replied grimly, 'you will see for yourself.'

4

The Badger Game

At the head of the stairs, Holmes looked firstly left, then right. The narrow hallway was lit by a single, flickering gaslight. Spying room seven, he went to the door and swiftly unlocked it. With a still-baffled Watson at his heels, he entered a spacious gaslit room that was furnished with a double bed, a chest of drawers and two armchairs. A six-fold Coromandel lacquered screen stood in the far corner, presumably masking an area where one might make one's ablutions, or use the chamber set.

Though clothed, Irene Hastings and her companion sat, embracing, on the edge of the bed. On seeing Holmes, they sprang apart, shocked by his sudden entrance. The man looked horrified to have been caught in such a compromising situation and immediately began to bluster.

Irene, astonished to see Watson at Holmes's elbow, managed a hasty but undeniably hollow-sounding, 'John! Thank goodness you're here! This man — '

Holmes cut her off, saying, ' — has just had a very narrow escape . . . *Mrs Channing.*'

Struggling to straighten his tie, the man frowned, confused. 'Chan — ? What the deuce do you mean . . . ?'

'It is quite elementary, sir,' said Holmes bluntly. 'You have been seduced by your companion, as have many others before you. And having allowed your vanity to get the better of you, you have left yourself open to blackmail.'

The man gaped. *'What?'*

'You have been the mark in what is known as the badger game,' said Holmes. 'A curious expression, I grant you, but one that hails from Wisconsin, the so-called Badger State, wherein the 'trick' itself originated.

'Put simply, the idea was to lure you into a compromising position, after which a witness — the desk clerk, perhaps, or the woman's 'brother' — would have burst in and caught you *in flagrante delicto.* If you refused to pay for their silence they would have threatened to expose your infidelity unless their demands for cash were met.'

The man paled at the suggestion. 'You can't mean that!'

'I'm afraid I do, sir. Of course, you could always have called their bluff, informed them that it was merely their word against yours.

That might have made them back down. But in this modern age, with such impressive advances in photography . . . '

Without warning he suddenly struck the lacquered screen with his cane. It teetered and then toppled forward onto the carpet, revealing —

'Robert!' croaked Watson.

For the man standing beside a Triple Victo camera on a wood-and-brass tripod was the person he believed to be Irene Hastings's — or rather Mrs Channing's — brother.

' . . . the results would have been undeniable,' Holmes concluded.

Recovering himself, Robert dropped the magnesium-filled flashpan he was holding and clambered forward over the fallen screens, fists clenched, his expression contorted with pure hatred. For an instant Watson feared for Holmes, knowing that he was no longer a young man. But he had forgotten that Holmes was a master of the Japanese martial art *baritsu*.

Crouching, Holmes used his cane like a billiard cue, using his right hand to thrust it up through the fingers of his left, slamming it into his attacker's solar plexus.

Winded, Robert fell back against the camera. The tripod and camera crashed to the floor. Its glass photographic plate popped out and shattered into pieces.

As Robert tried to extricate himself from the broken tripod, Holmes barked: 'Stay where you are!'

Intimidated by Holmes's tone, Robert grudgingly obeyed.

Watson saw it all then — a tiny peephole artfully worked into the flowers painted on the lacquered screen and done in such a way as to be almost invisible. Behind the peephole the camera had been set up to photograph the couple on the bed, providing irrefutable proof as to the man's infidelity. Irene's victim would have had no idea what was about to befall him until the flashpan ignited and the damning picture was taken.

Her present victim saw as much for himself, and cried, 'Oh dear God, I am ruined!'

'On the contrary,' Holmes said. 'You have been given a second chance and one I hope you will take to its full advantage.'

The man who had signed the register as 'Mr Haslemere' nodded. 'I will,' he assured Holmes earnestly. 'This shall serve as a . . . a sobering lesson.'

'Then I suggest you leave now as a wiser man than when you arrived.'

'But what about . . . ' The man gestured toward Irene, who had crossed the room to help the still-seething Robert get to his feet.

'Never fear,' said Holmes. 'This woman and her companion are finished.'

The man needed no second urging. Greatly relieved, he grabbed his scarf and topper and ran from the room.

After the sound of his departing steps had faded, silence again filled the room. The woman Watson knew as Irene Hastings said, 'John, this isn't what it looks like.'

Watson almost laughed. 'Then please explain it to my satisfaction. That, I think, would be *quite* a feat.'

Before she could answer, Robert, having finally extricated himself from the broken tripod, grabbed her by the arm and pushed her toward the door. 'We're leaving,' he snarled at Holmes. 'And you'd better not try and stop us!'

Instinctively, Watson moved to bar their escape. But Holmes shook his head. 'Let them go, old friend. We have done our bit.'

Watson disagreed, but he trusted Holmes and if he said the matter was finished, then he must have a good reason for doing so.

Irene Hastings — Watson still couldn't think of her as anyone else — and her brother brushed past him. At the door she gave Watson one final look, and then she was gone.

5

A Second Chance

The disappointment of it all suddenly caught up with Watson and he sagged. 'I have been a fool, haven't I?' he said, sitting on the edge of the bed.

'You have been *human*, old friend, and heir to all the failings of that species,' Holmes replied. 'And if you *have* been a fool, then so have a great many other men of similar station before you. But in your case . . . '

Watson looked up sharply. 'What?'

'Well, let us say there were . . . extenuating circumstances . . . where you were concerned. At the outset, Mrs Channing and her husband — the man you were led to believe was her brother — identified you as a mark for the badger game. After your wife died so unexpectedly, however, they realized there was no one to whom they could expose you.

'But they are of agile intellect, those two, and it soon occurred to them that no man is easier to manipulate and beguile than one thoroughly preoccupied by his grief. You were lonely and the attention of 'Mrs Hastings', as she called herself, was a soothing balm, a pleasant comfort. But all the time it was just a pretence to take more and more of your money. And she did, didn't she?'

Watson nodded, ashamed. 'But why did you not come to me directly, and sooner?' he asked.

'Would you have believed me, Watson? Or more correctly, would your *heart* have allowed you to believe me? No, my friend, it was better for you to see the truth with your own eyes. Besides, I had to make absolutely sure of my facts first.'

'But how did you know? I mean . . . what first put you onto her?'

'That, my dear fellow, was simple,' Holmes said, idly inspecting the shattered remains of the camera. 'As you know, I have an excellent eye for detail and a keen memory for faces. And even though I am now retired, I still continue to read the *Police Gazette* with great interest.

'You will remember that I met Mrs Hastings when I attended your wife's funeral. She was and indeed remains a handsome woman, but I noticed at the time that she overuses her rice make-up in two places, one at the left corner of her mouth, the other on her forehead, between her eyebrows up to her hairline. I confess I did not make much of it at the time, and of course there was no reason why I should. But I am afraid I have lost none of my mistrust of women. It was only upon reading a report in the *Police Gazette* about a certain Mrs Violet Channing that I connected the two events.'

He paused and regarded Watson keenly. 'I need hardly explain the term *naevus flammeus* to you.'

Watson scowled. 'A port-wine stain?'

'Indeed. As you know, they are much less common than the so-called 'salmon patches' which usually occur in newborns and fade with time. The *naevus flammeus* remains and as the years progress the mark or marks tend to become somewhat uneven. This is what Mrs Channing was attempting to disguise with the overuse of powder.'

'There is no crime in that.'

'None at all. Indeed, for what it is worth, the poor woman has my sympathy for the condition. But Mrs Channing was reported to have the self-same affliction, Watson. And so I took it upon myself to investigate her a little more closely.'

'Ever the detective, eh, Holmes?' Watson said with a hint of bitterness.

Holmes smiled wryly. 'Let us say that, even if there was the faintest chance that your Mrs Hastings was in reality the larcenous

Mrs Channing, I could not allow you to be taken in, as had so many men before you. And I dearly wish I had been mistaken, Watson, but unfortunately I was not. The facts I was able to unearth regarding 'Mrs Hastings' were suspiciously few. Indeed, as near as I could ascertain, she seemed to have appeared out of thin air, some months after Mrs Channing, on the run from the police, went to ground. From there it was a small matter to keep the woman under observance until her own actions condemned her.'

'Then we must report her, Holmes! We cannot allow her to continue with such an abhorrent business!'

'There is, I believe, no need for that. To bring them to book now might only cause the very embarrassment and exposure that their victims were hoping to avoid. Besides, after tonight's little encounter, I fancy they will go to ground once more.'

'Then they will have got away with it.'

'Perhaps,' Holmes replied enigmatically.

'What does that mean?'

'It means that upon reaching their lodgings in Tooting, the Channings will pack their bags and leave the city for pastures new. But as they gather their belongings, they will discover three curious things. One — the notebooks in which they recorded all the sordid details

36

of their victims will have mysteriously disappeared. Two — so will the vile collection of
photographs they used in their demands for
payment. And three — all the paperwork relating to their several well-stocked bank accounts
will have been destroyed, rendering them all
but penniless; for to make any attempt to
reclaim those accounts may well invite close
scrutiny of their somewhat questionable finances
— firstly from the banks themselves, and then,
in due course, from the police.'

'You have well and truly ruined them, then?'

'Let us just say that I have lost none of my
skill at breaking and entering.'

Watson snapped his fingers as something
else suddenly became clear to him. 'And those
letters you posted earlier this evening . . . ?'

'Were all addressed to those same victims,
informing them — anonymously, of course
— that they have nothing further to fear from
their blackmailer, and suggesting they learn a
salutary lesson from the experience.'

'So there *is* some justice, then.'

'There is nearly always *some* justice, old
friend,' Holmes agreed softly.

'And there is no fool like an old fool,'
Watson grumbled. 'And I will be perfectly
honest with you, Holmes: I doubt that I have
ever felt so old or so foolish.'

Unexpectedly Holmes smiled, and the light

of good humour entered his grey eyes. 'Then allow me to give you a second chance to recapture your salad days.'

'Salad? You've lost me, Holmes.'

'I must confess, as much as I enjoy my life in Sussex and my study of bees, it falls far short of the adventurous life you and I once enjoyed in Baker Street. It is, as Browning would have it, 'That's the wise thrush; he sings each song twice over, lest you should think he never could recapture the first fine careless rapture!''

'You are, as usual, speaking in riddles and displaying a knowledge of verse that I never before suspected.'

'Then I will say it plainly,' Holmes replied. 'We cannot go back, Watson. But we may go forward. I have recently been thinking of travel . . . but where is the pleasure in travelling alone?'

'Where were you thinking of going?'

'Austria,' came the startling reply.

'Austria!'

'Yes. For some time now I have been corresponding with the neurologist, Dr Freud. He appears to be a most fascinating man and one I will enjoy meeting, for I am keen to discuss at greater length a diagnostic technique he calls *psychoanalysis*. What do you say, old friend?'

'I am hardly enamoured of Freud's theories,' Watson said. 'Indeed, I heartily disapprove of some.'

'But *Vienna*, man!'

Watson could hardly deny the temptation. But still he hesitated. 'When do you plan to leave, Holmes? I mean, I have my duties as a locum to consider . . . '

'Then first thing tomorrow morning,' Holmes said, clapping him on the arm, 'arrange for a replacement, and I will take care of everything else. Within forty-eight hours, my friend, we will be on our way — and who knows? Once again, if we are lucky, the game may well be afoot!'

6

There is No Trick to It

The following day Watson dutifully arranged for a locum to take over the practice in Deptford. Holmes, meanwhile, who was staying at the Goring, less than two miles from their old stamping ground in Baker Street, began arranging every detail of their trip. Thus it was that they departed from Charing Cross aboard the Ostend-Vienna Express promptly at ten o'clock two mornings later.

Watson had mixed feelings about the trip — and with good cause. The Summer Olympics, held in Sweden earlier in the year, had brought together competitors from almost thirty countries and encouraged overseas travel as never before. Austria, though, was still a suspect destination for most. Although four years had passed since Emperor Franz Joseph I had annexed Bosnia and Herzegovina, there still lingered considerable ill-feeling among the three million Serbs who, quite rightly, objected to Austria's bullish attempt at empire-building.

The Serbs were not alone in these objections. For some time now, Italy had been threatening military action against Austria as a consequence; while Russia, taking advantage of the unrest, had been inciting a revolution throughout the Balkan states. The situation had become so dire that the leader of the German Catholic Centre Party had warned that any Austrian retaliation against Serbia would inevitably draw Russia even further into the conflict, and that in turn could lead to a European war.

When Watson mentioned his misgivings, however, Holmes only filled his favourite clay pipe with his usual acerbic blend of shag and replied that, with Vienna presently such a hotbed of intrigue, there was little chance of their having a boring holiday.

An hour and forty minutes after leaving Charing Cross, they reached Dover, where they caught a steamer to Ostend. From this Belgian municipality they made their next connection easily and continued their train journey through Brussels, Aix-la-Chapelle, Cologne and Bonn.

In all, the thirty-two-hour trek proved to be a pleasant one, although Watson was not sorry when they'd left Passau behind them; and the train steamed into Vienna three hours later.

A fifth set of tracks was being added to the terminus. More building work was being carried out to the two towers that flanked the station entrance and the roof. In consequence the din was tremendous and so — as they climbed down from their carriage and Watson tried to shake some life back into his gammy leg — they were startled to hear a brass band suddenly break into the Austro-Hungarian national anthem, *Land der Berge, Land am Strome.*

Watson turned toward the far end of the platform where the band was playing and could see a group of dignitaries as well as several journalists from the Austrian press.

'Good Lord,' he said above the noise. 'They must have found out you were coming, Holmes.'

Holmes gave a sardonic chuckle. 'I fear the greeting is not for me.'

'Really? You mean, they greet *all* their new arrivals this way?'

'I doubt it. No, my friend, this is in honour of someone *else.*'

He paused as a number of the passengers broke into spontaneous applause.

He and Watson turned just as a short, stocky man in his mid-thirties led his entourage off the train and began to work his way up the platform, waving and smiling as the crowd parted to make way for him.

Watson squinted at him. He was well dressed in a suit of grey serge, with a heavy winter overcoat slung over one arm. He looked vaguely familiar, but Watson couldn't put a name to the fellow. Finally he gave up and asked, 'Who is that man, Holmes?'

'That, my friend, is Mr Erik Weisz.'

Watson sniffed. 'Never heard of him.'

'Then perhaps you will know him better by his stage name,' said Holmes. 'For he is none other than the escapologist Harry Houdini.'

The name, of course, was instantly recognizable. And how could it be otherwise? Houdini was a legend. The son of a rabbi, he was a Hungarian Jew whose family had emigrated to the United States when Houdini himself was four years old. Moving to New York from Wisconsin — the home of the badger game, Watson reminded himself sourly — the young Weisz had eventually changed his name in tribute to Jean-Eugene Robert-Houdin, the French magician he so admired, and went into showbusiness.

From vaudeville, where he had mostly performed card tricks, he had gone on to tour the world as an escapologist extraordinaire. No gaol could hold him, no straitjacket restrain him, no set of shackles bind him. He had escaped from all manner of prisons, was an accomplished safe-cracker and a year earlier had astounded audiences with what he called his Chinese Water-Torture Cell, escaping from chains and padlocks whilst being suspended upside-down in a glass case filled with water.

It seemed impossible to believe that this man, who stood five feet, five inches on bowed legs, was the person who had performed so many wondrous acts. At a distance he seemed almost nondescript. And yet here was someone who could walk a tightrope; untie knots with his toes; dislocate his shoulders at will; climb skyscrapers; and hold his breath for more than three minutes at a time. He was an inventor, businessman, a scientist of sorts, philanthropist, magazine publisher, newspaper columnist and author.

As Houdini passed Holmes and Watson he happened to glance in their direction. The next time he looked at them it was with a frown. He took two more steps, then suddenly turned and came back. His entourage stopped at a respectful distance to watch, but the two women flanking him continued to accompany him as he approached Holmes and Watson.

'It's Holmes, isn't it?' Houdini asked as he came up. 'Sherlock Holmes?'

'You are, I perceive, a reader of the American edition of the *Strand*,' Holmes replied.

Houdini looked surprised. He had dark, wiry hair that was parted in the middle, angular features, sharp cheekbones, and vivid blue eyes.

'I am indeed,' he replied with a boyish grin. 'But how did you know that? Do I have some distinctive type of printer's ink on my fingertips? Or a myopic squint that indicates that I've spent more than my fair share of time poring over the *Strand*'s small type?'

'Far simpler than that,' said Holmes, shaking Houdini's outstretched hand. 'Since I make it a practice to keep as low a profile as possible, it is highly unlikely that you have seen a photograph of me. The late Mr Sidney Paget popularized a spurious version of my appearance as an Inverness-wearing pipe-smoker in a deer-stalker. He did, however, capture my physiognomy reasonably accurately. Subsequent artists employed by the *Strand*, such as H. M. Brock and Joseph Simpson, have maintained it.'

Houdini chuckled. 'Well, I'm sure glad we cleared *that* up.' Suddenly remembering his companions, he added: 'Oh, say, let me present my wife, Bess, and my assistant, Miss Frances Lane.'

A petite woman with dark, curly hair and an impish tilt to her nose stood forward; Bess Houdini was of a similar age to her husband

and though homely, she had fine, dark brows, large, well-spaced eyes that showed a sense of humour, a strong chin and a smooth complexion.

Frances Lane was her complete opposite. She was taller by several inches, slimmer and more elegant-looking in a well-tailored, military-style grey coat with a fur hem. Beneath her fetching purple velvet hat, her copper-coloured hair shone richly. Her eyes were sea-green, with a curious upward slant at the corners, and beneath them her cheekbones were high and well defined.

'How do you do, gentlemen,' she said, her voice deep and confident.

With introductions out of the way, Houdini — seemingly unaware that he was keeping his welcoming committee waiting — said, 'So, what brings you to Austria, Mr Holmes?'

'We are here on holiday.'

'Not business, then?'

'I no longer practise as a consulting detective, Mr Houdini.'

'Too bad. It might have been fun to watch you in action.'

'Alas, sir, my skills are not meant to entertain, merely to clarify and resolve. But you, I see, are here in your capacity as an entertainer.'

'Uh-huh. I've toured Europe before, of

course, but that was years ago. And now I've got a whole new set of wonders to show the folks.'

'I hope we may be able to come and see you, Mr Houdini,' said Watson. 'Where are you performing?'

'The, ah . . . what-you-call-it, the — '

'The Theater an der Burg,' Frances Lane said with a smile.

'That's it.' Houdini turned to her, adding, 'Say, Frankie, can we get some tickets for Mr Holmes and Dr Watson? Best seats in the house, naturally.'

'I believe we can manage that,' she said. 'Where are you staying, gentlemen?'

'At the Grand,' Holmes replied. 'On the Kaerntner Ring.'

'I'll have opening-night tickets delivered to you first thing tomorrow morning,' she promised.

'That is most generous of you.'

'Generous, shmenerous,' said Houdini dismissively. 'You being the Great Detective and all, I'm surprised you haven't already guessed my ulterior motive.'

'I confess, sir, it appears to have escaped me.'

'Well, I've read Dr Watson's stories for years now, never miss 'em. And my gut feeling is that you have some sort of *schtick*,

Mr Holmes, but for the life of me I've never yet managed to figure out how it is that you do what you do.'

Embarrassed, Bess squeezed her husband's arm. 'Harry!'

Ignoring her, Houdini continued, 'After tomorrow night's performance maybe we can have a late supper, and I can pick your brains.'

'There is no trick to it, I assure you,' Holmes said stiffly. 'It is all based upon simple observation.'

'OK,' said Houdini. 'So tell me something about myself. Right here, right now.'

'Please, Mr Holmes, pay him no mind,' Bess apologied. Her voice was gentle, her manner somewhat retiring. 'I'm afraid Harry's notorious when it comes to challenging those who question his own illusions and he's always keen to learn from others.'

'I quite understand,' Holmes said. 'However, I do not deal in illusion.'

'Prove it,' said Houdini, but the good humour in his eyes softened the challenge.

By now the brass band had stopped playing, and the waiting dignitaries were beginning to chatter irritably among themselves, irked by the poor manners of these visiting *Amerikaners*. Directly behind Houdini, the rest of his entourage moved a little closer, eager to hear Holmes's response.

He did not keep them waiting.

'I perceive that you were sleeping when the train arrived and woke suddenly at the very last moment. Furthermore, for this last stage of the journey you sat with your back to the engine. Though you were not born ambidextrous, you have worked diligently to become so. In your time you have also held a position in tailoring. Oh, and may I congratulate you on giving up the habit of biting your fingernails two weeks ago.'

Houdini stared at him in amazement. 'My God, Holmes, what the . . . I mean, how the heck do you do that?'

'Am I correct?'

'In every detail. But . . . how?'

'I have already told you, Mr Houdini — simple observation. There is a tiny flake of *rheum*, more commonly referred to as 'sleep' or 'sleep sugar', in the corner of your right eye. Almost certainly you would have washed it away during your morning ablutions. That you did not implies that you slept for some time *after* you washed this morning. Had you not woken suddenly when the train arrived, you would almost certainly have had the chance to 'freshen up', as you Americans say, or your wife would have pointed it out before you met your public.'

Reaching up to rub at his right eye, Houdini said, 'And the fact that I slept with my back to the engine?'

'You cradled your head in your right hand while you slept. I can still just detect the faintest impression of your fingertips against your right temple. It is far more likely that your right arm in turn was resting against the wall of your compartment as you slept — which would have you seated facing the way we had just come, and thus with your back to the engine.'

'I don't believe this,' Houdini said. 'But what about the tailoring?'

'If one is sufficiently receptive there is an inordinate amount of information one may obtain from the hands,' Holmes replied soberly. 'In your case I noted when we first shook that your right hand carried a ring of noticeably calloused skin around the base of your thumb and between your index and middle fingers, very close to the knuckles. This suggested to me the act of holding and using scissors for long periods of time. The most likely cause for this would not, as one might expect, be associated with the hair-dressing trade, but rather with the tailoring industry.'

Houdini chuckled. 'I started off as a necktie cutter, if you must know. And the business about biting my nails?'

'Again, when we first shook hands I observed that your fingernails are somewhat uneven, and have not, as one would expect, been clipped into the usual uniform ellipsis. From this I could only surmise that you have recently given up the habit of biting your nails and have allowed them to grow out before cutting them.'

Houdini exchanged glances with his wife.

'You . . . you're absolutely right again,' she said. 'But how did you know Harry had only given up in the past two weeks?'

'The same way I knew that he had trained himself to be ambidextrous, Mrs Houdini. Fingernails grow at a rate of just less than a millimetre a week, slightly quicker on the dominant hand. By estimating the length of the faster-growing nails on your dominant hand from the distal nail fold to its edge, I was able to reach a figure of roughly fourteen days. Since there was barely any difference between the rate of growth upon the nails of your left hand, I concluded that you had taught yourself to use both with equal facility.'

Houdini grinned admiringly. 'I *still* say it's a trick. But it's a darned good one.' He stuck out his hand and they shook once more. 'Now, if it's OK with you, Mr Holmes, I'd better get a move on. My audience awaits, as they say. Oh, and by the way,' he added as an afterthought, 'if by some unlikely chance you should figure out how I perform the impossible . . . keep it to yourself, will you?'

'My lips shall remain sealed, Mr Houdini.'

With a theatrical flourish Houdini and his entourage continued on their way along the centre of the platform toward the waiting dignitaries and reporters, and seeing him approach, the band once again struck up *Land der Berge, Land am Strome.*

7

Kunstmaler

Houdini was greeted like the celebrity he was. Cameras clicked and flash-pans ignited. Dignitaries accorded him as much deference as they would visiting royalty, and story-seeking reporters yelled questions at him in broken English. Diplomatically, Frances Lane stepped to one side, allowing Houdini and Bess to take centre stage and promise all kinds of wonders for his new run at the Theater an der Burg.

Holmes and Watson skirted the ever-swelling crowd and left the station unobserved. A row of Bersey cabs were lined up outside. As they got into the first one, Holmes called their destination up to the driver, who was perched on his exposed seat above and in front of the cab. Moments later the mechanized taxi whirred out into the broad thoroughfare known as the Ringstrasse.

As the cab took them toward the Kaerntner Ring and the Grand Hotel, Watson consulted the paperwork relating to their holiday. 'I say, Holmes,' he concluded enthusiastically, 'you have certainly done us proud. The Grand is one of the finest hotels in the city, if not *the* finest. It says here they have close to four hundred rooms, all heated with hot-water radiators, and half of them fitted with telephones!'

Holmes scowled. He had used telephones in the past — they were rapidly becoming a necessary evil — but had never been enthusiastic about them.

'And see here,' Watson continued. 'It boasts its own steam-powered lift *and* its own telegraph office. The dining room even holds two concerts *every day*, one during afternoon tea at five, and another at eight, so that guests may listen to fine music while they eat.'

But Holmes was now busy studying the city itself.

Vienna was magnificent. And when Watson finally slipped their paperwork away and settled back to enjoy the ride to their hotel, it seemed to him as if every one of the capital's two million inhabitants had descended upon its major shopping routes, the Kaerntner Strasse, the Graben and Stephansplatz. Posted everywhere were colourful posters promoting Houdini's run at the Theater an der Burg, while beside them were anti-government notices urging a quick change of regime.

At length they reached the Grand Hotel, a vast, majestic building that exuded old-world charm and more than lived up to its name. While Watson booked them in, Holmes purchased a street-map of Vienna. He then scribbled a message and asked that it be sent immediately, via telegram, to Dr Sigmund Freud at Bergstrasse 19.

As they crossed the lobby to the lift, Holmes told Watson that he had just informed Freud of their safe arrival, and were looking forward to meeting him at the earliest opportunity.

Watson's good humour abruptly vanished. 'Well,' he remarked stiffly, 'I am sure that *you* are, at any rate.'

Holmes waited until they were in the lift and heading up to their suite before saying, 'What is that supposed to mean?'

'I told you at the outset, Holmes, that Freud has certain . . . theories . . . of which I heartily disapprove.'

'Specifically?'

'It is hardly important.'

'On the contrary, your behaviour suggests that it is *highly* important.'

'Well, since you insist, may I remind you that Freud, like yourself, is a proponent of cocaine. I've read his papers upon the subject. He claims that cocaine has beneficial effects in that it can stimulate the senses and relieve pain.'

'And you do not agree?'

'No, I most certainly do not! Furthermore, I worry that you may take Freud's rather cavalier approach to the drug as a reason to use it all the more.'

'I can assure you that I will not.'

Watson offered a sad smile. 'Your word has always been good enough for me in the past, Holmes. But as a doctor, I have learned that the word of an addict should always be taken lightly.'

'Are you still suggesting I am an addict?'

'Are you still suggesting you are *not*? After all these years?'

The lift jerked to a halt and they stepped out onto the opulent fourth floor. As the attendant closed the doors behind them, Holmes said, 'I see you have lost none of your mother hen qualities, Watson.' Then before Watson could take offence, he added softly, 'And it is good to have someone fretting over my health once more.'

Watson shrugged self-consciously. 'I don't mean to preach — '

'But if you *do*,' Holmes interrupted, 'it is only with the best of intentions. And though I may not be good at showing it, your concern is *greatly* appreciated. As for my addiction, I assure you that you need not fear any relapse on my behalf. Age has brought with it a degree of . . . perspective. I no longer dread the mundanity of everyday life as I once did and neither do I crave constant stimulation.' He offered his hand. 'You have my word on it — whether you care to accept it or not.'

'Of course I accept it,' said Watson.

They shook.

For a moment Watson was tempted to ask Holmes if he regretted his bachelor existence. After all, he was approaching sixty, and to face one's declining years alone was, in Watson's mind at least, a daunting prospect. But though he sensed that time had softened Holmes, Watson did not believe he had softened *that* much. The only thing Holmes would ever regret was that he might not use his amazing abilities to observe and deduce to their fullest extent. He would have removed anything from his life that stopped him doing that, clinically and efficiently. For as fine a man as he was, he did not think in terms of love and companionship as other men do. Although, mused Watson, he might once have, had he not met his match in the opera singer and sometime-courtesan, Irene Adler.

'It has been a long and tiring journey,' Holmes said, breaking Watson's train of thought. 'Rest, my friend, and await the arrival of your luggage, which I daresay will be along shortly. Then we will meet again for supper, do a little sightseeing and retire early, so as to be fully refreshed for the morrow.'

★ ★ ★

The following morning, as they were entering the dining room for breakfast, the desk clerk called Holmes's name and held up two envelopes which had been delivered overnight. Holmes took them, tore open the first and, after scanning the note within, said, 'Freud will be delighted to meet us at lunchtime. He recommends a café called the Türkischer, of which he speaks highly, and says we will find it facing the Beserlpark Alsergrund.'

'Which is . . . ?'

'A *Beserlpark* is like an oversized traffic island, except that it has grass and trees and benches — in essence, a miniature park set in the heart of the city. And here,' Holmes continued, opening the second envelope, 'are our tickets for Houdini's opening performance this evening.'

Watson beamed. 'That, I suspect, is going to be *quite* an experience.'

They spent the morning exploring the city, known throughout the world as the City of

Music due to the many prestigious composers who had been born there; it was also becoming known as the City of Dreams, in tribute to Freud's groundbreaking work in psychoanalysis.

Shortly before noon they caught a cab to the small park Freud had mentioned in his message and from there quickly crossed the street to the Türkischer Café.

Freud was seated at one of the tables on the pavement outside. The neurologist was younger than Holmes by two years, but looked considerably older. He had removed his black homburg upon his arrival, and they could see that he had a high, domed forehead and thinning, grey-white hair brushed across the pate. His dark, incisive eyes were deep-set, his nose long and slightly hooked, his mouth a wide, sober line that was all but lost in his cropped white goatee beard. At present he was involved in a conversation with a young man who was punctuating every remark with an angry gesture.

'It would appear that Dr Freud is otherwise engaged,' Holmes noted. 'And rather unhappy to be so.'

This was true. Freud, wearing a full-length tweed frock coat buttoned to the throat, sat as if cornered by the young man, his dour expression suggesting he would much rather be drinking his coffee or smoking the cigar smouldering in a nearby ashtray. The young man was standing over him, talking animatedly. In his early twenties, he was small and slightly built. His straight, side-parted black hair was unkempt and his long fringe, which he nervously kept brushing back, constantly fell slantwise across his forehead.

Freud was trying to calm the young man, but he refused to be placated. Freud kept nodding, unable to speak his piece during the tirade.

'I should say the good doctor needs rescuing,' said Holmes, and so saying, broke into a brisk stride.

As they approached Freud's table, Holmes, whose knowledge of Austrian German was as good as his grasp of French and Latin, caught the tail-end of the angry young man's rant.

' . . . you don't understand, Herr Doktor. Our Lord and Saviour should not be remembered only as a sufferer, but as a *fighter!* He recognized the Jews for what they were and summoned men to fight against them!'

'That is your *interpretation*,' Freud said patiently. 'But that's all it is, Kunstmaler.'

It was a curious name — it translated as 'Painter' — but Holmes suspected that it was a pseudonym. He had read that Freud often gave his patients suitable aliases in order to protect their anonymity.

The young man vehemently shook his head. 'No, no! The Bible is perfectly clear about it. It tells us how the Lord at last rose in His might and seized the scourge to drive out of the Temple the brood of vipers and adders. How terrific was His fight against the Jewish poison. And therefore, as a Christian, I have a duty to fight as He fought, for truth and justice. As a Christian I have a duty to protect my people!'

'And your beliefs give you the right to persecute the Jews? Is that it?'

Kunstmaler drew himself up pompously. 'I do not agree with your use of the word *persecute*, Herr Doktor, but if by that you mean to identify and then deal with the enemy, then yes, I believe it does.'

Freud regarded him thoughtfully. 'I am Jewish,' he said. 'Well, Galician Jewish. Why should I be persecuted? What have I ever done to warrant such treatment?'

Kunstmaler offered no reply.

'Your trouble is that you are too easily influenced, Kunstmaler. You have allowed the anti-Semites, who run wild in your Mariahilf District, to cloud your judgement. You must learn to think for yourself.'

'I do!' the young man protested. 'And by

defending myself against the Jews I am fighting for the Lord!'

Holmes cleared his throat, causing the two men to look at him.

'Forgive me for interrupting,' he said to the young man, 'but does not the Bible say, 'You yourselves know how unlawful it is for a Jew to associate with or to visit anyone of another nation, but God has shown me that I should not call any person common or unclean'?'

Kunstmaler glared angrily at him. Then he nodded. 'In Acts ten, verse twenty-eight, yes,' he agreed. 'But John one, verses ten and eleven, also says, 'If anyone comes to you and does not bring this teaching, do not receive him into your house or give him any greeting, for whoever greets him takes part in his wicked works'.'

'Nevertheless,' Holmes said, 'it is not your right to pass judgement upon another race. 'The Lord will fight for you, and you have only to be silent'. Exodus, fourteen-fourteen.'

Kunstmaler replied angrily, ''Blessed shall he be who takes your little ones and dashes them against the rock.' Psalm one-three-nine, verse nine.'

''Judge not, that you be not judged',' Holmes countered. 'Matthew, seven, one.'

Kunstmaler started to reply, realized he had nothing to say, and, frustrated, said threateningly, 'I don't know who you are, but I think you are a trickster, just like all foreigners. One who twists words and meanings to suit his own purpose.'

'Kunstmaler . . . ' Freud began warningly.

'Please, Herr Doktor,' said Holmes. 'Kunstmaler is entitled to his opinion. But I would ask him to consider Colossians, three, thirteen. There can be only one interpretation there, surely?'

Kunstmaler said nothing.

'Coloss — forgive me, gentlemen,' said Freud. 'I am obviously not as familiar with the Bible as you are. What does it say in Colossians, three, thirteen?'

Holmes cocked an eyebrow at Kunstmaler.

Scowling, the young man muttered grudgingly, ''Bear with each other and forgive whatever grievances you have against one another. Forgive as the Lord forgave you.''

'That seems an admirable sentiment,' said Freud, rising. 'Mr Holmes and Dr Watson, I believe. I have, of course, been expecting you.' To Kunstmaler, he said sternly, 'We will finish this conversation at the appropriate time and place. And in future, I will thank you not to attempt to continue your treatment beyond the confines of my office.'

Though still angry, Kunstmaler managed to contain himself. 'I am sorry, Herr Doktor,' he said stiffly. Then, giving Holmes and Watson a disdainful glance, he stormed off.

Freud shook hands with Holmes and Watson. Reverting to English out of deference to his guests he said, 'I must apologize for young Painter's behaviour. He saw me waiting here for you and before I could do anything about it he had invited himself to an impromptu session.'

'He certainly appears to have . . . opinions,' said Watson.

Freud sighed and gestured for them to sit. 'These are worrisome times, gentlemen. You are both men of the world, and as such doubtless keep abreast of current affairs, so you know that. At present Vienna is like a bomb that threatens to go off at any moment — perhaps quite literally.'

'Oh?' said Holmes. 'How so?'

'Our War Ministry has recently confirmed rumours that certain . . . militant factions . . . have been infiltrating our country with orders to assassinate members of the Habsburg Imperial Family, and feelings have been running high. In some quarters the hot-heads have seen this as an opportunity to stir up discontent, claiming that we are being overrun by foreigners.'

'It is clearly having an effect,' said Watson. He watched as Freud's irate patient entered the park, where a surly-looking crowd was gathered around a bearded man in a dark pea jacket who was making an impassioned speech. 'Young Painter there . . . he is a man to watch, I think — and watch carefully.'

Freud smiled sadly and picked up his cigar. 'I'm afraid he is just misguided, as are so many of them. Hopefully, with maturity — and my help — he will see the error of his present beliefs. He has twice been rejected by the Academy of Fine Arts — which is why I refer to him in my notes as 'Painter' — and because of this he feels disaffected. Furthermore, he is an orphan now that he has lost his mother, and lives in a house for poor working men on the Meldemannstrasse. That's where he hears all the foolishness he later espouses, and why I agreed to take him on as one of my 'charity' cases.

'But does he deserve special attention? I think not. I do not believe we need trouble ourselves overmuch with a misguided young man like Herr Hitler.'

8

The Good Samaritan

While Freud ordered fresh coffee and a selection of tortes and strudel for his guests, Watson told him all about their journey, and their chance meeting with Houdini. Freud's English was reasonably good, which was not surprising. Though the language had a somewhat higher profile in neighbouring Germany, it was still seen as valuable in the Austro-Hungarian Empire, where many wealthy Austrians deliberately employed British governesses to ensure that their children became fluent in the language.

'I must say, Herr Doktor, I find your theories on the conscious and unconscious mind fascinating,' Holmes said after a pause.

Freud puffed absently on his cigar. 'You mean, of course, in relation to the criminal mind?'

'Certainly, though by no means exclusively. However, the possibility that our actions can be a consequence not of our conscious desires but rather of our *unconscious* ones could prove revolutionary in the study of criminology.'

'Perhaps so, Herr Holmes. But we are all at

the mercy of our minds. And if you accept that the mind is divided into three distinct divisions — that is, the *id*, the *ego* and the *superego* — then it becomes somewhat easier to see why a seemingly inoffensive man who, in the normal course of events would not even harm a fly, can suddenly become the most heinous of killers.'

'That is the thing I have always had some difficulty with, Herr Doktor,' said Watson, 'these so-called *divisions* you speak of. How do you define them, as such?'

'The *id* is ruled solely by instinct,' replied Freud. 'You feel hunger, so you eat. You feel tired, so you sleep. The *ego*, by contrast, is dictated by order and reality. You feel hunger, but your *ego* tells you that you cannot eat until lunchtime; you feel tired, but it is only one o'clock in the afternoon, and so you accept that sleep must wait until your customary bedtime.

'Sometimes, however, it is not so easy to dismiss the demands of the *id*. If, say, the *id* tells you that your life would be better if only you could murder your harridan of a wife, or your tyrant of an employer, then that prospect may be impossible to resist. That is where the *superego* plays its part. This stronger but oft-times latent version of yourself may be able to stop you from submitting

67

to the will of the *id* when the *ego* itself cannot resist the impulse.

'But if the individual has no *superego*, or a *superego* that is able to be stifled by the *id* . . . well, he may turn out to be the perfect criminal.'

'A man without a conscience,' mused Holmes.

'Or a man *driven* by conscience,' said Freud. 'A man who deliberately allows his conscience to *dictate* his actions, so long as that same conscience also *justifies* them.'

'Is there any way to identify such people?' asked Watson, intrigued despite his original scepticism of Freud's theories. 'I mean, do they exhibit any symptoms that we may come to recognize?'

Freud hesitated, weighing his response. 'The *id* is the dark, inaccessible part of our personality,' he said, blowing cigar smoke into the chilly air. 'We only know that it exists at all thanks to our research into dreams and the identification of specific neuroses. We can say, however, that it is of a negative character. We approach the *id* with analogies: we call it chaotic, a cauldron full of seething excitations . . . It is full of the energy generated by our basest instincts, but it has no organization and produces no collective will. It strives only to bring about the satisfaction of the instinctual needs subject to the observance of what I term 'the pleasure principle'.

'The *id* fails to recognize the difference between good and evil, and often it seeks to express itself as an instrument of destruction directed against the external world. How can one ever identify such deep-rooted emotions with barely a glance? I am afraid that the only way is and always will be with long-term, in-depth psychoanalysis.

'But let us remember,' Freud concluded, 'that the *id* is not always the villain it is made out to be. Sometimes it can be . . . beneficial . . . to dismiss the so-called 'voice of reason' that tells us to ignore it. As an example, take my cigar, here. I began smoking cigarettes thirty-odd years ago, and I cannot tell you how much pleasure I have derived from the practice. I am convinced that smoking has helped me focus upon my work and given me greater energy than I would otherwise have enjoyed. But one day a medical doctor of my acquaintance, a certain Wilhelm Fleiss, told me that it would ruin my health if I continued to smoke.

'As you can imagine, gentlemen, the choice I faced was stark. I could smoke, enjoy the act of smoking, and feel the benefits of it . . . or I could run the risk of encountering all manner of medical problems in the years to come.

The voice of reason told me that I should follow Wilhelm's advice and give it up, but the *id*, that part of me whose actions are based solely upon the gratification of my urges, suggested an alternative . . .

'So I substituted the cigar for the cigarette, and in so doing found a means of smoking that gave me infinitely greater pleasure than it ever did before — without the potential to damage my health.'

Pausing, he studied his cigar as if it were an old and dear friend, then added: 'Think what I would have missed out on, had I listened to my *ego*, or my *superego!* So the *id* can sometimes provide benefits, if one is able to control it and wise enough to heed its less destructive advice. And let us not forget that the act of smoking itself is perhaps the best substitute of all for the one great and harmful habit to which we are all heir.'

'And what might that be, Herr Doktor?' asked Watson.

'Masturbation,' Freud replied matter-of-factly.

Watson almost choked. Holmes, less easily shocked, immediately leaned forward and slapped him on the back. A moment later, eyes watering, Watson managed, 'My . . . apologies. That last . . . mouthful of strudel must have . . . gone down the wrong way.'

He reached for his cup and sipped steaming *Verlängerter* coffee. Then, to change the subject, he said hurriedly, 'I must say, you have a beautiful city, here, Herr Doktor. But I can't say as I care much for the look of that group of rabble-rousers over there.'

Freud followed his gaze toward a gap in the trees, where a crowd had gathered, and his mouth thinned to a disapproving line. Though they couldn't hear what the bearded man was telling the crowd, he was clearly using rhetoric to whip his audience into a belligerent frenzy.

Freud looked grim. 'I fancy that what you are seeing there is a member of a secret society called the Crna Ruka.'

'The Crna Ruka?'

'The Black Hand,' translated Freud. 'Well, that is the name by which it is best known. More correctly it is called Ujedinjenje ili Smrt . . . that is, 'Unity or Death'. Initially its members sought to create a unified Serbia. More recently it has dedicated itself to freeing those millions of Serbs under the rule of my country. And it is this group to which I alluded earlier — one of those 'militant factions' who have been infiltrating our country, our cities and, as you can see, even our very *capital*. They are at work across our empire, practising sabotage and political assassination, propaganda, abduction and, as you see here, rabble-rousing. And yet, though I deplore their methods, I can hardly find it within me to blame them. In our misguided attempts to build an empire, we have mistreated them, seen them and their lands as little more than possessions to be acquired. But I fear that the Black Hand is now attracting the wrong sort to its cause, those disaffected souls — like young Hitler, for example — who join up only for the promise of excitement and violence.'

Watson glanced at Holmes. 'I was right, then. It appears we *have* come at a time of some intrigue.'

'I am afraid so,' Freud sighed. 'But come, gentlemen, let us speak of happier things.'

Before they could follow his advice, however, a dozen burly working men appeared from the direction of the Kolingasse and started across the road toward the park. Many of them carried weapons in the shape of wooden battens or empty beer bottles, lead-lined saps or billy clubs.

Concerned by the probability of violence, Watson said to Freud, 'I must confess, Doctor, I don't care for the looks of *this*, either.'

'You shouldn't, my friend. The police are well aware that the city is riddled with these anarchists, but tell me — do you see any policemen in evidence here today? Of course you don't. That is because the Bundes-gendarmerie use paid thugs like those you see over there to come and break up these gatherings.'

Watson was scandalized. 'Do you know this for a fact, Herr Doktor?'

'Not for a fact, no. But it makes admirable sense. If the very fabric of your country is being undermined by foreigners, it is far more effective to have — or rather, *appear* to have — 'ordinary civilians' defend themselves against such an enemy. These hired thugs can break skulls and arms and legs and then be hailed as patriots. If the police were to do the same thing, Austria would be branded a police state, where so-called freedom of speech could not be practised.'

By now the crowd gathered around the bearded speech-maker was aware that a new faction had entered the park and an ominous quiet descended over them. Then came a few shouted taunts at the newcomers, who aggressively shouted back. Distorted by distance, it was impossible to translate their remarks, but the meaning behind them was clear. The newcomers were issuing a chal-lenge — break up and clear out, or else — and the members of the Black Hand among the bearded speaker's audience, and even some of the ordinary men they were hoping to convert to their cause, were clearly not prepared to do that.

Then one of the newcomers hurled a bottle at the Black Hand speaker. It missed him but hit someone in the crowd. Immediately, both groups suddenly charged at each other, screaming challenges and obscenities at the tops of their lungs.

In seconds the two groups had absorbed each other. Rivals automatically sought each other out and then began exchanging kicks and blows. Billy clubs rose and fell; men collapsed and curled themselves into balls.

More bottles rained down on the Black Hand faction, some finding their targets and sending men to their knees, clutching bloodied faces. Enemies continued to clash, trade blows, then stumble on to find new opponents.

Even as Freud, Holmes and Watson watched, one burly man broke away from the throng. Staggering as far as the park gates he then collapsed, holding the back of his head with bloodstained fingers.

Watson, obeying the dictates of his profession, at once started to go and help him, but Holmes quickly grasped his forearm. 'Best we keep our distance, Watson. This thing is turning uglier by the second.'

It was true. Already the brawlers had broken up into smaller groups, taunting each other, trading punches, and hurling any missiles that came to hand. As the altercation quickly spread beyond the confines of the park, shop windows were smashed and newspaper placards were snatched up and used as makeshift shields or weapons. Worse still, the combatants were slowly coming ever closer to the onlookers outside the cafe.

'I think it would perhaps be prudent if we were to beat a hasty retreat, gentlemen,' suggested Freud.

Watson nodded in agreement. He hated violence and had never quite understood how human beings could treat one another with such cruelty and intolerance. Rising, he had to duck to avoid a brick that was thrown his way. It sailed overhead and crashed through the cafe window, shattering glass with a sound like artillery fire.

'Good grief!'

A third group now came charging around the corner at the other end of the street. Some twenty in number, their military-style uniforms identified them as policemen, finally putting in an appearance now that the dirty work had been done for them. One of the brawlers yelled the alarm and the rival groups quickly scattered in all directions.

Several men came racing toward the cafe, overturning anything in their path in an effort to hamper their pursuers.

One big fellow with a flattened nose and ugly, cauliflowered ears came barrelling out of the melee. Busy keeping an eye on the police, he failed to notice Watson, who was standing directly in his way. Seeing him come, Watson froze, again acutely aware that he was no longer a young man.

Dimly he heard Holmes yell his name, but he still remained rooted to the spot.

Then the onrushing ruffian saw him. He went to push Watson out of his path, but before he could do so, a newcomer came as if out of nowhere, charging in from Watson's right. He caught the bigger man with one hunched shoulder and the impact flung the man aside.

The fellow went sprawling onto the cobbles. Enraged, he scrambled up again and made to attack Watson's saviour. The young man, who was smaller and in his mid-twenties, stood his ground, fists raised in the best Marquess of Queensberry tradition. As the ruffian closed in, the young man hit him with a straight right. His fist struck the big man on the jaw and the fellow went down in a dazed heap, fighting vainly to remain conscious.

Watson sighed with relief and shakily extended his hand to the young man. 'Thank you, sir. Uh . . . *danke schön*. You are quite the Good Samaritan.'

The young man had short, curly black hair, a pleasant face with well-spaced brown eyes, an aquiline nose, wide mouth and a dimpled chin. His black felt derby had fallen off in the initial collision; now, as he bent to retrieve it, he said, '*Bitte erwähnen Sie es nicht.*'

He quickly glanced about him. Chaos reigned as the police sought to detain as many of the fleeing fighters as they could, only to discover that none of them intended to go quietly.

'*Ich glaube, wir sollten besser von hier verschwinden — und zwar so schnell wie möglich,*' said the young man.

Watson frowned, cursing his limited knowledge of German. But the fellow's meaning was clear enough — this area was not the healthiest place to be at the moment.

As if to prove it, another brawler broke away from the group, having seen the unhappy fate of his larger companion. He charged at them like a berserker, yelling obscenities. He was small, dark-skinned and slightly built, and at sixteen years of age seemed shockingly young to be filled with so much hatred.

Seeing him come, Holmes quickly raised his cane and used the handle to hook one of the legs of his chair. He tugged, sending the chair skittering across the cobbles and into the boy's path. The boy collided with it, stumbled, and went sprawling.

The Good Samaritan, meanwhile, hurriedly gathered Holmes, Watson and Freud together and began to shepherd them toward the Kolingasse. But already the dark-skinned boy was back on his feet and snatching up the chair, raised it above his head and hurled it at them.

Fortunately, the chair missed its mark. *Un*fortunately, the boy, consumed by fury, then grabbed a knife from his belt and charged at Holmes.

Holmes turned to meet him. Dropping into a crouch, he hooked his cane around the boy's leading ankle and yanked backward. The boy lost his balance and fell heavily to one knee. Before he could recover, Holmes raised his cane again and struck him a single, punishing blow on the temple.

The boy's dark, malevolent eyes rolled up in his head. Dropping the knife, he collapsed, unconscious.

The young man gestured for Holmes and the others to follow him. He then led them into the Kolingasse, where some semblance of calm remained. As they paused to catch their breath, he said, *'Jetzt müsstet ihr aber in Sicherheit sein.'*

'Thank you,' Holmes replied in English.

Watson frowned disapprovingly. He knew how well Holmes spoke German and thought the least he could do was thank the man in his own language.

'Danke schön,' he said gratefully.

The dark-haired Samaritan smiled and again said, *'Bitte erwähnen Sie es nicht.'*

Then he hurried off.

'Come,' said Freud, patting his pockets in search of a fresh cigar. 'I believe you will find the tranquility of my apartments more conducive to discussion.'

Holmes, who was watching the young man vanish into the distance, nodded. 'Yes,' he replied thoughtfully. 'I rather suspect we shall.'

9

No Laughing Matter

At the Grand that evening they enjoyed an excellent supper of *Eachtlingsuppe*, then followed the thick beef and potato soup with pork pot roast served with grated apple, horseradish and caraway potatoes, and *Salzberger Nockerl* — a sweet soufflé that Watson pronounced as possibly the most delicious thing he had ever eaten.

Holmes, as was his custom, ate sparingly. But he seemed more than happy in their surroundings, for the dining room was as luxuriously appointed as the rest of the hotel, and an excellent string quartet played pieces by Mozart, Beethoven and a relatively new composer by the name of Schoenberg of whom Watson had never heard.

Upon their arrival at Bergstrasse 19, Freud had shown himself to be a most convivial host. Though he approached his work in a studious manner, the neurologist had inherited a charming sense of humour from his father, who had been a textile dealer in Freiberg, Moravia. Watson had begun to see him in a more favourable light. Freud had made a number of interesting observations about humour and its role in society and had even written a book about it.

'Earlier today you asked me if there were any symptoms by which one could identify a criminal, or potential criminal, who is ruled by the *id*,' he said to Watson. 'Though it is not possible to tell at a glance, the use — or indeed the *avoidance* — of humour can reveal much about a man.

'You see, it is the *superego* that allows the *ego* to generate humour. A selfish *superego* will allow nothing more than sarcasm. One that is harsher still will stifle humour entirely. But a kindly *superego* will manifest itself in the use of harmless, almost silly humour. Thus, the wit a man uses has the potential to identify him as one who cannot even countenance the breaking of the law; one who might consider it, if there is no other recourse, and one who will break the law quite willingly, as a shortcut to achieving his desires.'

Impressed, Watson said, 'I have a joke for you, and I do believe it puts me in that first category.'

'Then pray, let us hear it,' said Freud.

Stifling a schoolboy grin, Watson said, 'What is the difference between a tube and a foolish Dutchman?' Chortling, he then said, 'One is a hollow cylinder, and the other is a silly Hollander.'

He finally gave way to a full-throated laugh. Regrettably, neither Holmes nor Freud found the joke anywhere near as amusing.

'I have a favourite joke,' said Freud, after Watson had finally managed to bring himself under control. 'The king meets his absolute double, and asks him, 'Did your mother work in the palace?' The double replies, 'No. But my father did.''

He and Watson laughed as if it were the funniest thing they had ever heard.

Holmes watched them both in bewilderment. 'I am afraid the joke escapes me,' he said dourly.

Freud frowned, surprised. 'You don't understand it?'

'I'm sorry, no. And yet you *do*, Watson.' He seemed mildly peeved by the fact.

'Of course,' said Watson, wiping his eyes. 'The implication in the question is, 'Have we the same father?' The implication of the answer is, 'No, but we have the same mother.''

'So what is the joke?' asked Holmes.

But that only caused Freud and Watson to laugh again, and Holmes could only shake his head in near-complete bafflement.

★ ★ ★

Later, having promised Freud that they would visit him again before the end of their holiday, Holmes and Watson returned to the hotel. Each retired to his room to rest and reflect upon the more tumultuous events of the day.

After an excellent supper, they set out by cab to the Theater an der Burg, and the opening night of Houdini's show.

The Theater was the last in a series of magnificent buildings to be constructed around the Ringstrasse, and came close to dominating them all. As they stepped out of the cab, Watson craned his neck to look up at the magnificent edifice which was guarded by an imposing statue of Apollo. With its white columns and domed roof, the place bore an uncanny resemblance to a cathedral, although Watson suspected that it was considerably larger than most cathedrals.

'My copy of *Bradshaw's* certainly did not mislead me,' he told Holmes. 'This place is absolutely stunning.'

'Quite.'

'Fourteen years in the construction, you know,' Watson continued. 'And it is said to have one of the largest stages of any theatre in the world.'

'Then I fear Mr Houdini will look rather

lost amid so much empty space.'

'On the contrary, I fancy that a man of his stature would be more likely to dwarf any venue at which he appears.'

As they approached the ornate, brightly-lit entrance, they were quickly surrounded by the patrons in evening dress who were filing in.

'Shouldn't we, ah, speak to Houdini first?' asked Watson. 'I mean, we *are* here as his guests, and there is still the better part of half an hour to kill before the curtain goes up. Surely we should wish him luck for tonight's performance?'

Holmes eyed him, amused. 'And perhaps get the opportunity to rub shoulders with some of his more glamorous assistants? Miss Lane, for instance?'

'What? Oh, really, Holmes — '

'Come, now. You've had an eye for the ladies for as long as I have known you.'

'Yes and what has it brought me? Nothing but trouble.'

Realizing that his teasing had been ill-advised in the circumstances, Holmes gave an indulgent smile. 'Nevertheless, old friend, you are right, as ever. We *should* indeed go and wish our benefactor luck — not that I expect such a consummate professional will need it.'

As they went in search of the stage door, tall streetlamps cast a glow over the wide thoroughfare that was filled with a seemingly endless procession of cabs and coaches, while elegantly clad pedestrians crowded the pavements.

They traced the side of the theatre into a quieter crescent, Then continued until they reached a ramshackle stage door beside a loading bay whose doors were now padlocked shut; the area at the back of the theatre appeared as impoverished as its entrance was opulent. They let themselves into a wide hall heated by a single wheezing radiator. A small, open hatch was built into the wall beside a flimsy, glass-panelled door. Further back, the hall led into the usual maze of corridors to be found backstage, complete with a complicated-looking network of copper pipes and cables that were pinned to the dingy ceiling.

There was chaos everywhere, with stage-hands and stage managers, wardrobe staff and even members of a paint crew rushing back and forth to carry out some vital, last-minute chore before the curtain rose — with one exception. Through the hatch an elderly man in a grey woollen jumper was visible leaning against a counter, idly reading a copy of the daily *Reichspost*.

Holmes rapped on the counter to get the stage doorman's attention. The old man peered up myopically, his wispy white hair standing up all over his head. *'Ja?'*

'We would like to see Mr Houdini,' Holmes said in German.

'You would, would you?'

'If you could get someone to announce us . . . ?'

The doorman thumbed at the clock on the wall of his cluttered little office. 'Herr Houdini goes on stage in twenty minutes. I can't disturb him now.'

'We are here as his guests,' said Watson, 'and we want to wish him good luck.'

'Never!' the stage doorman said emphatically. 'I wouldn't allow it! Don't you know that it is bad luck to wish an artiste good luck in our hallowed profession?'

'Well . . . can you at least pass a note along to him?' said Watson in English. 'He invited us to see him after the show, and if the offer still holds we should be delighted to accept.'

Before the stage doorman could respond, a smartly dressed woman came hurrying along the hallway. She brushed past one of the carpenters and a scenic artist whose smock was daubed with a positive kaleidoscope of colour; she called out anxiously, 'Ulrich! Where is Herr Berger?'

She brushed past Holmes and Watson as if they weren't there and peered through the hatch. They were surprised to see that it was

Houdini's assistant, Frances Lane. Watson cleared his throat, hoping to catch her attention, for Holmes had been right: he was delighted to see the tall, Titian-haired beauty again.

'Miss Lane, I believe?' he said, tipping his hat gallantly.

She quickly turned to him and he was disappointed to see that she did not recognize him. Then her curiously slanted green eyes moved to Holmes, and her face lost its blank expression. 'Ah, Mr Holmes, and Dr Watson! I'm sorry. If you were hoping to see Harry, this . . . this isn't the best time.'

'So I observe,' Holmes said.

Her mind elsewhere, she dismissed him with a wave then turned to the stage doorman, demanding, 'Where is Herr Berger, Ulrich?'

'Is he not in his office?'

'No. I've just come from there.'

'Then you will probably find him in the lobby,' Ulrich said. 'He knew the press would be coming and always likes to greet — '

But Frances Lane was already hurrying away, the hem of her gored black skirt swirling around her ankles.

Watson watched her go sadly, muttering, 'Pre-show nerves, I expect.'

'*Ja*,' agreed Ulrich. 'They all suffer from it, you know, from the lowliest ASM to the biggest star. Now, what was it you were saying about leaving a note?'

'Nothing,' said Holmes. 'It looks as if Houdini has more important things on his mind at the moment.'

They retraced their steps to the Ringstrasse and joined the crowd as they descended upon the theatre. The lobby was sumptuous. Cut-glass chandeliers cast a warm glow across a thick red carpet flanked by black and white tiles in a chessboard pattern. Patrons milled around or chatted with friends. There was no place here for the country's many problems; the atmosphere was too light, too cordial, too dedicated to pleasure.

Watson was astounded by the predominantly red, cream and gold decor. The ceiling was lined with frescoes, the walls filled with paintings of some of the greatest actors ever to tread the theatre's boards . . . and here and there were statues and busts of yet more actors and writers.

Holmes, who had little appetite for such splendour, led the way and Watson dutifully followed him up one of two wide staircases — both painted, Watson was thrilled to note, by Gustav and Ernst Klimt and their companion, Franz Matsch.

It quickly became obvious that Houdini, as promised, had treated them to two of the best seats in the house. As an usher showed them into their own box, they got their first good look at the auditorium itself. It was every bit as impressive as the rest of the theatre and able to accommodate more than a thousand patrons. A glance into the hall itself was enough to show Holmes and Watson that Houdini's opening night had been a sell-out.

In the orchestra pit the musicians began to tune up. A sense of expectation filled the auditorium. 'Prepare to be amazed,' Watson said to Holmes. 'I suspect that Houdini has a few tricks up his sleeve that even *you* will be unable to explain.'

Holmes was about to reply when a big, bullish man in his late fifties, with thinning fair hair and a trimmed goatee beard, appeared from stage left. The audience dutifully began to applaud, but the man, whose tuxedo could barely contain his girth, quickly indicated that they should desist.

Holmes leaned forward, studying him keenly.

By the time the newcomer reached centre-stage, the audience began to realize that he was not part of the show. Their applause diminished until it grew very quiet in the auditorium.

'*Meine Damen und Herren,*' he began. 'I am Alfred Freiherr von Berger, the director of the Theater an der Burg. I am pleased to see so many of you here tonight, but I am also sorry to announce that due to unforeseen circumstances, Herr Houdini has been forced to cancel tonight's performance.'

Even as the audience began to react, he raised his voice, adding, 'Please! Please, ladies and gentlemen! I can only apologize and ask your forbearance in this matter. The management will be happy to refund on your tickets or provide replacements as soon as we are able to resume performances.'

'And when will that be?' demanded an angry man sitting in the front row.

'Alas, I cannot say at present,' said von Berger. 'But once again, please accept the apologies of the Theater an der Burg, as well as those of Herr Houdini himself.'

As von Berger walked off stage to boos and catcalls, Watson turned to Holmes and said, 'I wonder what's happened? I do hope Houdini is all right.' And then, 'No wonder Miss Lane was so short with us.'

'Indeed,' said Holmes, rising. 'Well, since unforeseen circumstances have put paid to our night at the theatre — not to mention our supper with Houdini — I suggest we seek our entertainment elsewhere, old friend. And in Vienna, I do not expect that it will be terribly difficult to find.'

10

A Desperate Request . . .

As usual, Holmes slept late the following morning. Watson, rising early, went down to the dining room and ate breakfast alone, then retired to the lobby, there to peruse the day's papers as best he could.

The *Frankfurter Kurier, Berliner Sonntagszeitung* and *Kölner Bote* all mentioned Houdini's opening night cancellation, blaming unspecified personal problems, 'possibly linked to the American entertainer's health'.

This, Watson decided, was entirely possible. If rumour was to be believed, Houdini had spared no effort in his own physical development over the years, working diligently to unhinge and then reseat his joints when required, and increase his lung capacity by deliberately submerging himself underwater for long periods at a time. It was certainly not beyond the realms of possibility that such a gruelling regime might eventually place undue strain upon certain of his vital organs.

Still, the escapologist had appeared in robust health when they met him at the station barely two days earlier, and according to the papers, Houdini's manager — 'the charming Frau Frances Lane,' to quote one beguiled reporter — had refused to issue any statements relating to the showman's health, or the reasons for his opening night cancellation.

In any case, the papers were more concerned with the violent confrontation he, Holmes and Freud had witnessed the day before. The *Kurier* blamed the riot on 'ill-informed hot-heads whose emotions are inflamed by the scaremongering of the enemies of our country'. The *Sonntagszeitung* took the opposite view, its reporter writing that 'the greatest injustice is that the ordinary man and woman on the street are villified, both physically and emotionally, for trying to defend themselves against the enemy within'. It seemed that everyone was keen to blame someone else for the country's problems.

With a pot of coffee and a selection of sugar-dusted pastries at his side, Watson had virtually exhausted his knowledge of German and was idly flicking through his ever-present copy of *Bradshaw's* when Holmes made an appearance.

'Ah, you have finally decided to rise, I see,' Watson remarked, closing the guide.

'I was not aware that we were keeping to a timetable.'

'We aren't, of course. But since we last lodged together, I had forgotten some of your more lamentable habits. The day is almost over, Holmes. It'll be time for lunch shortly!'

Unconcerned, Holmes sat opposite his old friend in a large, button-studded leather armchair. 'Your use of sarcasm,' he said mildly, 'reveals a *superego* of a somewhat harsh nature, Watson.'

'Oh, very droll.'

'But if lunch is so high on your agenda, we shall dine at Karl Gustav's, on the Heldenplatz . . . unless you object?'

'Not at all. Do you know the place? Is it any good?'

'I have no idea. But its proximity to our destination for today is enough to recommend it.'

'Oh? And what *is* our destination for today? Bearing in mind that not two minutes ago you were quick to remind me that we had no particular schedule.'

'The very seat of the Habsburg Empire,' said Holmes. 'The Imperial Palace.'

'I say!' Watson exclaimed. 'That should certainly be something to see.'

Holmes caught the eye of an attentive waiter. 'In that case, my friend, we shall fortify ourselves with fresh coffee — and one of these fine Austrian pastries for which you are developing such a taste — and then we will be on our way.'

★ ★ ★

They began their tour at the Heldenplatz, or Heroes' Square — an enormous plaza, at the far end of which stood the resplendent Imperial Palace. Reading from his guidebook, Watson explained that the square was so-called because of the two enormous statues that dominated it, one depicting Prince Eugene of Savoy, who had defended Austria from an Ottoman invasion in 1683, the other Archduke Karl, who had defeated Napoleon's troops at the Battle of Aspern-Essling in 1809.

Holmes, however, seemed more interested in the palace itself.

It resembled a miniature city more than a royal residence. Originally constructed in the thirteenth century at the behest of Ottakar II of Bohemia, the oldest section now formed a square around the Schweizerhof, the Swiss Court, named after the Swiss Guard, who had been hired in the eighteenth century to protect the monarchy.

Their next stop was the Imperial Stables,

which were separate from the main complex. According to Watson's copy of *Bradshaw's*, this was because the building had originally started life as a residence for Crown Prince Maximilian II, whose father, the Catholic Ferdinand I, did not want to live under the same roof as his Protestant son.

Presently they reached the Burggarten where a beautiful Art Nouveau building towered over the gardens of the Imperial Palace. This, said Watson, was the Palm House. Built some eight years earlier, it now housed a large collection of live tropical butterflies. These permanent residents of the Palm House were allowed to fly unhindered throughout an artful recreation of their original environment which included a waterfall, a pond and a number of ornate bridges. For the further comfort of the *Lepidoptera*, the building was also kept comfortably warm, and on such a chilly day Watson was reluctant to leave its confines when the time came.

Outside, the afternoon had turned distinctly colder and low grey clouds scudded overhead, propelled by a biting wind. Holmes, seemingly unaware of the inclement weather, suggested they walk the circumference of the Palace before calling it a day.

By this time Watson's gammy leg was

starting to play up — as it always did in damp weather — but Holmes seemed so energized by their surroundings that Watson didn't have the heart to destroy the mood, and so agreed without demur.

For all his aches and pains, Watson couldn't deny that it was wonderful to be back in Holmes's company. And, though it had been hard to accept the truth about Irene Hastings, he appreciated that Holmes had not only saved him from being gypped out of his money, but had also managed to lift him out of the dark mood which had threatened to crush him.

'I must confess,' he remarked wearily as they continued their stroll around the palace grounds, 'I never knew you had such an interest in architecture.'

'It is something I have begun to cultivate in my twilight years,' Holmes said, studying his surroundings with such intensity he seemed to be trying to commit them to memory.

As they walked on it began to sleet. Holmes showed no awareness of the foul conditions, or that Watson's limp was increasing. Instead he became more and more withdrawn until Watson finally asked him if anything was wrong.

Holmes shook his head. 'Why do you ask?'

'You seem unusually preoccupied.'

'Not a bit of it.'

'Come now,' Watson said, exasperated. 'You forget — I know you of old. There is something going on in that all-seeing, all-reasoning mind of yours. What is it?'

Holmes started to reply, then stopped as he noticed how difficult Watson was finding the going.

'My dear fellow, forgive me,' he said. 'You are favouring your leg more than usual. And small wonder. It has been a long day and this wet weather certainly cannot do an old war wound much good.'

'That's all right,' Watson said, trying to make light of it. 'I'm fine.'

'No — it was thoughtless of me to drag you along on this interminable circuit — and typical that you should acquiesce without complaint.' Holmes stopped and clapped his companion on the arm. 'Come along — we shall return to our hotel and seek to restore you with a pot of tea, a slice of *Marmor Schnitte* and a short rest.'

'Well . . . if you insist.'

They returned to the Heldenplatz, where Holmes bought an evening newspaper and then flagged down what they still called in England a Forder cab. As they rode back to the Grand, he scanned the paper, found what he was looking for, then folded it and tucked it into his overcoat pocket.

'It appears we shall have to wait another day before we can see Houdini at work,' he announced. 'The show has been cancelled for the second night running, and though the management is hopeful that the curtain will go up tomorrow night, they are by no means sure.'

'What a dashed shame,' said Watson.

Winter darkness stole across the city. By the time they reached their hotel the streetlamps had been lit and Vienna again resembled a scene from a Christmas card of old. As Watson climbed down from the cab, he stifled a yawn and wearily suggested that an early night was in order.

Holmes paid the cab driver and then turned to him. 'I am sorry to hear that, Watson, for I regret to say that an early night will not be possible.'

'No? Why?'

'Because I suspect we are about to receive a visitor. And quite possibly the answer to a mystery.'

Watson stiffened. 'What — ?'

'Have a care, old friend. No need to tip our hand.' Grasping Watson's arm, Holmes guided him toward the hotel's revolving door. 'Let us get in out of the cold.'

As they entered the lobby, Watson demanded

to know what was going on.

'As we alighted from the cab a moment ago,' Holmes explained, 'I spotted a familiar figure across the road attempting, somewhat unsuccessfully, to remain hidden in the shadows of the alleyway there. As soon as this person spotted us, they started forward, then hesitated. I can think of no other reason for such reticence besides a wish to avoid being seen with us on the street. But we shall see soon enough, for here comes our visitor now.'

The revolving doors began to turn. A moment later Frances Lane entered, a check motoring wrap buttoned about her throat and a small handbag clutched in her gloved hand. She hesitated when she noticed Holmes and Watson awaiting her arrival and stared at them.

Watson could not believe his eyes. The woman seemed to have aged noticeably since their last meeting.

'Ah . . . Mr Holmes . . . ' she began.

'You have been awaiting our arrival, I presume?'

She blinked her distinctive green eyes in dismay. She looked so cold and desperate that Watson quickly moved to take her by one arm, saying gently, 'Come, Miss Lane. You are frozen to the bone.'

She started to protest, but Watson would

have none of it. He led her across the lobby toward a corner table that was shielded from the entrance by some artfully arranged potted palms, leaving Holmes to order tea from a passing waiter.

By the time Holmes had rejoined his companion, Watson had seated Miss Lane at a small round table and was studying her with concern. She was close to tears and until this moment had not seemed the crying type. 'There, there,' said Watson, patting one of her hands. 'Don't take on so. You are among friends now.'

'I'm sorry,' she said, drying her eyes. 'I shouldn't — '

'My dear lady,' said Holmes, sitting opposite her, 'if you are, as I suspect, in some sort of difficulty, coming to us is *precisely* what you should have done. Now what, pray, is the nature of your problem?'

'It's not me,' she said softly. 'It's Mr Houdini. But I fear he will be furious when he finds that I've enlisted your aid.'

'And yet you have enlisted it nonetheless.'

She looked absolutely wretched. 'Gentlemen, I can't discuss Mr Houdini's personal business. It's just something I find impossible to do. When he first hired me it was upon the strictest understanding that I employ discretion at all times. I am privy to a great many of his secrets — not personal matters, you understand, but the means by which he is able to perform the feats he does. Many times I've been approached by rival acts, offering large sums of money to make me break that confidence. I would never do that, and Mr Houdini knows it. And that's why I'm so upset to have betrayed him as I've done tonight. But he can't resolve this matter alone, I *know* he can't.'

'Very well,' Holmes said. 'We will come and see him to discuss it, and if he is of a mind to do so, he may give us all the details himself.'

Relief flooded across her tear-stained face. 'Oh, thank you, Mr Holmes — ' She broke off as their tea was delivered and didn't speak again until the waiter had left. 'We had better not go together,' she then added.

'In case we are seen by the press, you mean?' Watson said, pouring tea.

'Not just the press.'

'You believe you are being watched?' asked Holmes.

'I'm convinced of it.'

'And perhaps followed here?'

'Possibly — though I made every effort to evade any follower.'

'Whom do you suspect of following you?'

'I'm not sure. It could as easily have been a reporter after the real reason behind the show's cancellation as . . . as someone else.'

Holmes studied her sharply. 'This . . . difficulty . . . of Mr Houdini's. Is it of a criminal nature?'

'I would rather he explained it to you himself.'

'Very well. Mr Houdini is staying at the Royal, I believe?'

She nodded. 'On the Stephansplatz.' Then, suspiciously, 'How did you know that?'

'It is in the paper,' Holmes replied simply.

Her lashes fluttered. 'Yes . . . yes, of course. Forgive me, gentlemen, my nerves have got the better of me. The Royal. Room 414.'

'Splendid,' Holmes said. 'Now, finish your tea and then make your way back there. Oh, and take this with you,' he said, handing her the newspaper he had bought earlier. 'It may not be the best disguise, but it will suggest to whoever you believe is watching you that you left your hotel in order to do nothing more daring than buy an evening newspaper.'

'Y-Yes, all right.'

'Watson and I will give you fifteen minutes and then set out for the Royal. I should be very surprised if a hotel which has been so recently refurbished has not installed at least one fire exit. When you reach your destination, locate the exit and wait there. When we knock, you may let us in, and in this manner

102

we shall be able to enter the hotel and talk to Mr Houdini unobserved.'

She nodded again, too agitated to calm herself. 'I understand.'

She got to her feet and they rose with her. Impulsively Watson squeezed her hand and said, 'Take heart, Miss Lane. If there is anything Holmes and I can do to help you, rest assured it will be done.'

'Thank you, gentlemen,' she said tremulously. Then, turning, she walked out of the lobby without a backward glance.

Watching her go, Watson felt his pulses begin to race. 'Good Lord,' he breathed. 'This . . . it's just like the old days, Holmes! I wonder what Houdini's problem is?'

Holmes reached for his hat. 'We shall know that soon enough, my friend. That is, if you are up to it?'

'I would not miss this for anything . . . whatever it is.'

'Then let us go.'

'But . . . but you said we would wait fifteen minutes.'

'So I did. But I think it would pay us to keep a close eye on Miss Lane, to make sure that she really *has* eluded her pursuers . . . if indeed they were ever there.'

11

. . . and a Flat Rejection

It was now snowing lightly and the persistent wind was colder than ever. Shunning a cab, for the Royal was only a ten-minute walk from the Grand, Frances Lane hurried through Vienna's wintry streets with her head down, the very picture of torment.

Holmes and Watson kept well back, but made sure to keep the attractive American in sight at all times. However, she appeared not to be being followed by anyone other than themselves.

'Do you imagine she only thinks she was being followed, Holmes?' asked Watson.

'You know that I never guess,' came the crisp reply.

Watson rolled his eyes. 'Of course. Let me see now . . . Ah, yes. 'It is a shocking habit, destructive to the logical faculty.''

'I am glad to see that you have not forgotten *all* my teachings.'

'How could I? It was I who committed most of them to paper.'

Her pace quickening, Frances Lane followed the Burgring past the Academy of Fine Arts.

To her left, the Volksgarten lay in eerie darkness; its world-famous rose beds, monuments and large imitation Theseus temple were quiet and still.

Presently she turned right, onto the Schottenring. The snow began to fall slightly harder, and the cold wind made it spiral and dance. It was now a little after 6.30. The roads were still reasonably busy, but pedestrian traffic was growing noticeably thinner.

As she turned right again onto Franz-Josefs-Kai, Watson could just discern the dark waters of the Danube rising and falling sluggishly on the far side of a small park. A trolley bus clanked past, seeming almost to glide along the tracks in the centre of the wide thoroughfare.

Frances Lane vanished around another corner into the Rotenturmstrasse and it was here that Holmes led Watson across the narrow street, so that they might observe Miss Lane's progress from the opposite pavement.

Another three-minute walk brought her out onto the bustling Stephansplatz. The Royal stood almost directly opposite St Stephan's Cathedral, an impressive brown stone basilica built in the thirteenth century whose architecture still looked remarkable even in these snowy conditions.

As the Royal came into sight, Holmes

quickly sidestepped into the recessed door-way of an otherwise faceless office building, giving Watson no choice but to follow him.

'What is it?'

Craning his neck, Holmes peered cautiously along the street. 'That man there, do you see?' he replied. 'Standing outside that closed cafe on the other side of the road, just a short distance up from the Royal, pretending he is waiting to meet someone.'

Watson squinted through the snow. 'I see only one man foolish enough to be out in this weather — a tall, skinny-looking fellow, just visible under the awning. He's wearing a dark-grey alpaca topcoat and what looks like a linen sporting cap. Got his hands in his pockets.'

'He's the one.'

'What about him?'

'He reacted when Miss Lane came into sight . . . the almost imperceptible stiffening of his shoulders and the involutary twitch of his torso betraying both recognition of who she was and surprise at her return.'

'Perhaps he *is* waiting for someone. Perhaps he thought *she* was the person he was waiting for.'

'Then why seek to disguise his mistake so quickly behind a show of supreme noncha-lance? See — he now appears to be studying the contents of that café window with a level of interest that cannot possibly be warranted. All the time, however, he is really watching Miss Lane's reflection as she enters the hotel.'

Watson felt a sudden chill that had nothing to do with the weather. 'She *was* right, then! She and or Houdini *are* being watched!'

'Perhaps. Almost certainly he is the fellow who attempted to follow her, and whom she subsequently lost before she reached the Grand. But does that make him a villain? He could, as Miss Lane herself suggested, just as easily be a reporter looking for a story that may or may not exist. Still, I think we shall avoid him for the time being, and retrace our steps. We can approach the Royal from the direction of the Hoher Markt — it is only a short distance back the way we have come and from there I expect we will find a way to enter the hotel from the rear.'

The Hoher Markt was a wide, cobbled area given over to shops and offices. It was largely deserted now and as they hurried through the whirling snow the glow from the hissing streetlamps sent their shadows jogging out ahead of them.

At length the rear elevation of the Royal appeared at the end of a darkened alley, looking tall, indistinct and shadowy in the churning blizzard. Holmes at once crossed the deserted, ill-lit street and went in search of a fire exit. It transpired that there were several.

Starting at one corner of the building, they began to work their way along, rapping at each one in turn. At the third fire exit they received a response. The sound of a handle being depressed mingled with the moan of the wind. Then the door opened and Frances Lane, looking thoroughly chilled, allowed them into a dingy stairwell.

There was no need for conversation. With an upward tilt of his head Holmes merely motioned for her to lead the way. A moment later the stairwell was filled with the rustling of her muslin and cotton ankle-length dress, mixed with Watson's laboured breathing as they climbed toward the fourth floor.

At last they reached a door that opened onto a well-lit, carpeted hallway with ornate doors at regular intervals on both left and right. Halfway along the hallway Miss Lane stopped opposite number 414; only then did she hesitate and give Holmes and Watson a fearful look.

'He isn't going to like this,' she whispered. 'But he can't deal with . . . with what has happened by himself.'

Gathering her courage, she knocked on the door and called, 'Harry . . . it's me, Frances.'

The door was wrenched open almost imme-diately. Harry Houdini, in rolled-up shirtsleeves and an unbuttoned waistcoat, with his curly, centre-parted hair thoroughly tousled, said, 'Frankie! For God's sake, where have you — ?'

Then the showman's pleasant blue eyes saw Holmes and Watson, and his whole manner changed. 'What the — ?'

Frances Lane brushed past him, unbuttoning her checkered wrap as she said, 'Gentlemen, come in. Hurry, before anyone sees you.'

The suite itself was luxuriously appointed. The main area was furnished as a combination sitting room and office, with a bedroom and en-suite bathroom located behind a closed door in the left-hand wall. Houdini, however, looked terrible. Dark circles ringed his eyes and his collarless shirt and trousers were rumpled, almost as if slept in.

As Holmes and Watson entered and Houdini closed the door after them, he exclaimed angrily, 'What the devil's going on here, Frankie?' Before his assistant could reply, he added to Holmes and Watson, 'Listen, I don't mean any disrespect, but this isn't a good time for me.'

'So I believe,' said Holmes.

Houdini's frown deepened. 'What's that supposed to mean?'

'I've asked Mr Holmes to lend us a hand,' said Frances.

It went absolutely quiet in the softly lit

room. Then: 'You've *what?* Frankie, how dare you go against my wishes! I told you we were going to — '

'Harry,' she said wretchedly, 'Harry, we've got to do *something.*'

'That's right,' he agreed with an emphatic nod. 'And I *am* doing something. I'm playing this straight down the line!' He turned away from her and, trying to calm himself, said to Holmes, 'Look, whatever Frankie's told you . . . I can only ask you to forget it. All right?'

Before Holmes could reply, Watson stepped forward, determined to defend the young woman. 'Miss Lane has been careful to tell us nothing of your business,' he said sternly. 'Aside from the fact that you are in some sort of trouble and need help, she has been the very soul of discretion.'

'However,' Holmes added, 'we do know *some* things, Mr Houdini. That you are dealing with a number of people who are playing a high-stakes game, for instance. And that in some way it involves your wife.'

Houdini turned on Frances. 'God *dammit,* woman — !'

'I didn't — '

'Mr Houdini,' Holmes said sharply, his tone forcing Houdini to face him again. 'Miss Lane came to us genuinely desiring help. She has told us nothing more than she had to.'

'Then how is it that you know they've taken Bess?'

'That, sir, was deduction at its most elementary. Your close relationship with your wife is well documented . . . and yet she is conspicuous by her absence in what would appear to be your hour of need.' Holmes paused briefly, then said, 'That you have made no attempt to deny my reasoning confirms its veracity.'

'That hardly matters now, does it?' Houdini said. 'The damage has been done — Frankie's brought you here even though these snatchers, or whatever the hell they are, *specifically* demanded that I make no attempt to enlist the authorities or anyone *else*, for that matter!'

'We did not accompany Miss Lane, but came alone and entered by means of the fire stairs,' Holmes said. 'We ourselves were not observed.'

'You *hope*.'

Holmes's mouth thinned. 'I have *said* so,' he answered flatly.

Houdini turned and wandered aimlessly across the floral carpet, using his right hand to massage the nape of his neck. 'OK, so you weren't seen — maybe. But God help us if you *were*.'

Frances Lane shook her head in despair. 'Oh, Harry . . . why are you being so stubborn? Mr Holmes is only trying to help.'

'Help, you say?' Houdini snorted disgustedly. 'You just better pray that your 'help' hasn't harmed Bess or jeopardized my chances of getting her back alive.'

His words had the same effect as a slap. Fresh tears spilled from Frances Lane's green eyes, and she said throatily, 'Oh, Harry . . . Harry, that's the *last* thing I want to do!'

Unable to say more, she turned and walked hurriedly to the door.

Houdini, realizing he had gone too far, called after her. 'Wait! . . . Frankie, I didn't mean to — '

Ignoring him, she let herself out without a backward glance.

Again it grew quiet in the suite. Cursing himself, Houdini went to the sideboard and poured himself a glass of water; he never drank anything stronger.

'The question now,' said Holmes, 'is how we should get your wife back safely.'

Houdini turned on him. '*You*, Holmes, do nothing. Oh, I appreciate your offer, but I'm not about to do anything that'll put Bess at risk. I'm going to play it straight down the line. Still, I'll tell you this much. Once I've got Bess back safe and sound, you see if I don't make those crooks pay!'

'Have they made any demands yet?'

'No, damn them. They're making me sweat.'

'Can you tell us exactly what happened, then, when your wife went missing?'

'What does it matter? She went shopping and never came back. I waited as long as I could, growing frantic all the while, but eventually I had to leave for the theatre. When I got there Ulrich — he's the stage doorman — gave me a sealed note marked urgent. It said that if I wanted to see Bess again I had better do as they said — whoever they are. Their instructions included *not* contacting the police.'

'They must have offered proof of their claim, otherwise you would not have been so ready to accept it.'

Houdini nodded. 'There was a . . . ' He cleared his throat, then continued thickly, 'a lock of Bess's hair in the envelope. I'd have known it anywhere.'

'Did Ulrich see who delivered the note?'

'No. It was chaos backstage. It always is immediately before a performance. He found it on the counter where he couldn't fail to see it.'

'And so you cancelled the show.'

'What did you expect me to do? The key to much of what I do lies in absolute concentration. After I read that note there was no way I could concentrate on anything but Bess.'

'And you have been waiting here ever since, for them to contact you again.'

'Yes. And before you get any ideas to the contrary, I'll go *on* waiting, understand me? I'm not going to do anything to put Bess in jeopardy. Whatever they want, I'll pay it.'

'May I see the note?'

'I told you, I don't want your help.'

'Nevertheless, there may be some clues to be found in their demand.'

Irritably Houdini drew an envelope from his back pocket and thrust it out. Holmes took it by one edge, studied the envelope, sniffed it, then removed the note. He took out a small pocket glass, studied the top edge of the sheet, held it to the light, sniffed that as well, and then read its contents.

'So what does it tell you?' Houdini asked.

'That the kidnapper is an educated man of somewhat more than middle age. He is a man of some standing, but is not in business. He is also . . . ' Holmes hesitated. 'He has made no demand yet for money?'

'No. I told you. Why?'

'Because he is already at least moderately wealthy. This fact casts doubt on the obvious interpretation for his actions.'

Houdini took the note back. 'And you can tell all that from one quick glance?'

Holmes drew a breath and explained

patiently, 'The letters are formed in a bold, masculine hand: we may safely say that our correspondent is male. Although he has tried to disguise his hand by writing his demand in capitals only, he has nevertheless employed a most distinctive curvature every time he uses the letters *a*, *b*, *c* and *h*, among others. This tendency was taught with most prevalency some forty years ago, when he would have been at school and first learning how to write.

'The sheet of paper itself is of a most unusual dimension — I should say approximately eleven inches by eight and a half. I know of no standard paper size that matches it, but the width implies that it is actually a sheet of foolscap which has been cut down. Indeed, if you inspect the top edge closely, you will see that roughly two and a half inches have been neatly removed with a pair of scissors of medium blade — medium because they have spanned the sheet in just two cuts.

'There can be only one logical reason why our correspondent has done this — to remove an address with which the original sheet was embellished. Since the paper is of the type known as *ecru*, and thus of a very pale cream colour, we can assume this is personal stationery. Had he been in business, it would almost certainly have been white. That the address was embossed is confirmed by the very faint odour of resin powder, which has effectively been baked into it during the process known as thermography. It also suggests that he is a man of means, for who else could afford such stationery?'

Houdini snorted. 'All very captivating, I'm sure. But it doesn't do much to get Bess back, does it?'

'Perhaps not. But we begin to build a picture of who has kidnapped her.'

'I don't want a picture of who's kidnapped her,' Houdini snapped. 'I just want her back! And the only way to guarantee that is to do *what* this guy says, *when* he says it. So . . . with respect . . . keep your nose out of my business, Holmes. And keep your mouth shut about what you've learned here tonight.'

'Very well, Mr Houdini, you must do as you will,' Holmes said stiffly. 'However, before we take our leave, I would ask you to show some compassion for Miss Lane. She merely attempted to enlist our help for the best of reasons — a noble gesture, given that she would have much to gain if anything were to happen to your wife.'

'What?'

'Come, now. It's obvious that she is in love with you, as you yourself very well know. But such is the depth, and indeed the *purity*, of her love that she still wants to do whatever she can to reunite you with your wife. I must say, she has made me revise my opinion of the fairer sex.'

'But . . . how do you — ?'

'Even a confirmed bachelor such as I can tell when a woman is hopelessly in love with her employer,' Holmes said. 'And in this case she has my sympathy, for the burden of unrequited love is a heavy one indeed.'

'She's the tops, it's true,' Houdini murmured, hating himself for the way he had behaved to her.

'Then if you are even half as decent and honourable as I believe you to be, she will have your apology and thanks sooner rather than later.'

'She will,' Houdini replied. 'And I'd like to thank you, too. But like I say, I'll handle this business their way: no tricks.'

'I understand,' Holmes said. He removed his glove and they shook hands. 'And now,' he continued as they went to the door, 'we shall leave as discreetly as we arrived, and look forward to a happy resolution to your troubles.'

12

A Change of Heart

When Watson woke the following morning he didn't immediately see the note that had been thrust under his door. He lay there for a while, feeling bleary-eyed and content, vaguely aware by the watery light filtering in through a gap in the closed curtains that it was still early.

He allowed himself a jaw-cracking yawn and then snuggled back down, luxuriating in the warmth and comfort of the bed, and reflecting sleepily upon the events which had brought him to this moment.

It was remarkable how one's fortunes could change so swiftly, he thought. So many highs, so many lows. He had returned to medicine and found great joy in the experience. But then he'd discovered the true nature of a woman he had convinced himself he was coming to love, and the knowledge had threatened to thrust him back into the deep despair he had suffered following the passing of his beloved Grace. And yet here he was now, warm and snug in a soft feather bed in quite probably Vienna's finest hotel, having already met the likes of Sigmund Freud and Harry Houdini.

Abruptly he remembered that not everyone was quite as lucky as he. Poor Houdini: his world, his livelihood and his reputation turned upside-down by kidnappers! And poor Bess . . . being held somewhere by ruthless criminals, unable even to guess at her fate.

He wished that he and Holmes could have helped the escapologist, but Houdini had been determined upon that point. Still, he and Holmes had dealt with abduction before — that business with Melas, the Greek interpreter, for example, and the messy affair of the Priory School — and he considered it among the most heinous of crimes.

But he also found himself wondering what Holmes could have done to help the American. There seemed to be little enough to go on in the way of clues. And even if they did unearth anything of use, they were in a foreign land, dealing with people of a different culture and language.

Of course, Holmes would have seen those as minor inconveniences. Even now he seemed as quick-witted and indefatigable as ever. But like it or not, they must respect Houdini's wishes.

Watson finally threw back the sheets and

got up. The hot-water radiator ticked and gurgled, making the room pleasantly cosy. And that was when he saw the envelope standing out in stark contrast against the wine-red carpet.

With a mystified scowl he bent and picked it up.

He recognized Holmes's handwriting at once; this time his friend had made no attempt to disguise it. He tore open the envelope and read:

I have had to go out. I do not know how long I will be.
Holmes

Watson scowled. Why had Holmes gone out so early? And for what purpose? Had he decided to take a hand in Houdini's problems after all? He didn't really believe Holmes would go against Houdini's wishes, but there had been many times in the past when he had taken matters into his own hands, regardless of the consequences . . .

No. Holmes had always exhibited a flair for the dramatic and, therefore, the truth of the matter was probably far more prosaic. There was in all likelihood some perfectly ordinary reason for his absence.

He refolded the note and slipped it back

into the envelope. He would doubtless receive confirmation of this in good time.

* * *

The Renault cab pulled up outside the Theater an der Burg's stage door. Houdini climbed out and shoved a handful of change at the driver. He was probably handing over far more than was required, but at that point being too free with his money was the least of his concerns. For just when he'd thought his situation couldn't get any worse, it had . . . and that's why he'd decided to telephone Holmes at his hotel.

'Hello, Holmes?'

'Mr Houdini,' Holmes had replied, recognizing his voice at once. Over the wires Holmes had sounded sharp, alert; if Houdini's pre-dawn call had woken him, he showed no sign of it.

'Holmes, I'll come straight to the point. I'm at my wits' end.'

'What is the problem?'

'It's Frankie . . . Miss Lane.'

'What about her?'

'She's vanished!' Houdini said wretchedly. 'I went to see her right after you left last night. You were right, of course, and I wanted to apologize for my behaviour and tell her I

121

knew she was only trying to look out for me. But her room was empty. So I went down to the lobby and asked the desk clerk if he'd seen her. He said she'd gone out.'

'Alone?'

'What? Oh, yeah, yes. Alone.' Houdini sighed. 'It was pretty obvious she was mad at me, and with good reason, so I just sat tight right there in the lobby, waiting till she came back so I could set things right between us, but somewhere along the line . . . '

'Please, Mr Houdini. Slow down, if you will. I have little enough experience with telephones as it is, and even less patience.'

'I'm sorry, but . . . well, I guess this thing's taken more out of me than I realized. I haven't slept a wink since Bess . . . Anyway, the short of it is, I fell asleep, right there in the lobby. Can you believe that?' He sounded furious with himself. 'I woke up in the small hours. The lobby was like a ghost town. I figured Frankie had come back while I was dead to the world and not seeing me there, gone straight to her room. So I went up to my own suite, slept for a couple more hours, then put a call through to her room. There was no answer.'

'Go on.'

Houdini sighed again. 'I freshened up a little, went along and knocked at her door. I still didn't get any response. So I went down to the lobby . . . and learned that her key was still on its hook. She'd stayed out all night! That . . . that's when I started to panic.'

At the other end of the line there was only a crackling, hissing noise.

Houdini continued, 'Well, what with the mood she was in the last time we all saw her, and everything that's happened since we arrived in Vienna . . . I'm worried, Holmes. It's not like Frankie. If anything's happened to her — '

'Let us not jump to any hasty conclusions, Mr Houdini,' Holmes said firmly. 'However, we certainly cannot discount the fact that Miss Lane's disappearance is in some way connected with that of your wife.'

'That's what worries me. I figured I'd just pay their damn ransom and get Bess back . . . '

'You have still not heard anything from them, then?'

'No.'

'Am I to take it that you would now like me to take a hand in the matter?'

'Absolutely. All I ask is that you be discreet.'

'Of course,' Holmes replied a little testily. 'It seems clear that you are indeed being watched by your wife's abductors, and for that reason we cannot afford to be seen together lest we tip our hand. But I will meet you at the Theater an der Burg in forty minutes.'

'I'll be there.'

'Make a point of telling the desk clerk where you are, in case your watchers make enquiries after you leave. Tell the clerk that you are going to check on your props and equipment which, I assume, is presently occupying space in the theatre's basement.'

'Correct.'

'Then that is where I will meet you, and where we may discuss your case in relative secrecy.'

'Sure, but what — '

'Good morning, Mr Houdini,' said Holmes and hung up.

★   ★   ★

The cab turned around and slowly drove away, leaving a trail of exhaust smoke billowing in the chilly air. Houdini surveyed his surroundings. He had the distinct impression that he was being watched, but if he *had* been followed he could find no evidence of it.

He crossed the narrow pavement to the stage door. Even though it was still early, the door was unlocked. In the stage doorman's office, a dark-haired man was rummaging through a stack of old newspapers, his back turned toward the door. Houdini cleared his throat to get the man's attention, and the fellow turned as if startled.

'*Oh, du hast mich erschreckt!*' he said in German. He came closer, walking with something close to a swagger, his shoulders squared and his generous belly pointing ahead of him. He was in his forties, with a full, tanned face and a long nose with flared nostrils. He wore a baggy three-piece suit tailored from sackcloth, the waistcoat buttoned incorrectly so that it hung lopsided on his portly frame, and he had what appeared to be a homburg hat squashed flat and shoved into one jacket pocket. He regarded Houdini through a pair of round spectacles and then, switching to heavily-accented English, said, 'It's Herr Houdini, isn't it? I am sorry, sir. I was just saying, you gave me a fright.'

'I didn't mean to,' Houdini replied, his mind elsewhere. 'Where's, uh, what's his name — Ulrich?'

'He has the afternoon and evening shift,' said the man. 'I am Marius, sir. I watch the place overnight and through the mornings.' He cocked his head at Houdini and scratched idly at his dark, trimmed beard. 'Can I help

125

you, Herr Houdini? There is no one else here at the moment.'

'It's all right. I, uh, I just want to check on my props.'

'Very good,' said Marius. 'I will escort you downstairs.'

'There's no need.'

'There is every need,' the other replied, reaching out toward a jumble of hooks from which hung keys of every size and shape. 'Your props are the tools of your trade, and as such are almost beyond price. We like to ensure that such valuables are safely locked away . . . which means that even *you* cannot get to them until I unlock the door for you.'

Houdini relented, but he was feeling so tense it was difficult. 'Oh . . . OK.'

Marius swaggered out of his little office and led the way deeper into the theatre and then down a flight of narrow stone steps.

'Have you, uh, seen anyone else around here this morning?' Houdini asked, trying to sound casual.

Marius glanced back at him. 'Should I have?'

'Possibly. I'm expecting a . . . colleague to meet me here.'

'I will send him down as soon as he arrives,' the stage doorman assured him.

They reached the heavy double doors and

Houdini's companion sorted laboriously through the keys until he came to the correct one. He unlocked and opened one of the doors and then preceded Houdini into the basement so that he could switch on the incandescent bulbs.

Props and equipment stood everywhere under creased dust sheets; they occupied space beside rows of two-dimensional scenery flats and between shelves stacked with voluminous stage curtains. There were several ladders, stacked cans of paint and all manner of belaying pins, drops, road boxes and wheeled platforms.

The large, high-ceilinged room was cold and the sparse lighting did little to illuminate the shadowed corners. Houdini shivered and said distractedly, 'Thanks. I don't suppose my colleague will be too long now.'

'Indeed not,' said Holmes, as Marius's grey eyes suddenly sharpened behind his small, round spectacles. 'I am already here.'

'What the — ?'

'Forgive what might seem like mere theatricals,' explained Holmes, allowing the squared shoulders of 'Marius' to relax and resuming his usual voice and demeanour. 'However, I did not want to take even the slightest chance that I might be seen and recognized. You yourself, Mr Houdini, easily recognized me a few days ago; I feared it would go badly for you if such a thing came to pass.'

'I've got news for you, Holmes,' Houdini said bleakly. 'It already *has*.'

'I beg your pardon?'

The American sagged. 'As I left the hotel, I did as you said, and deliberately told the desk clerk where I was going. I was about to leave when he gave me this.'

He reached into his pocket and brought out an envelope. Its edge was ragged where Houdini had hurriedly torn it open. Holmes took it, slid a single, folded sheet of paper from within, flicked it open and read:

You will be waiting outside your hotel at ten this evening. You will tell no one of this and make no move to involve the police. If you are not entirely certain that we are deadly serious about the course upon which we have embarked, you soon will be.

'Was the desk clerk able to describe the man who delivered this note?' asked Holmes, adding: 'Before you reply, may I suggest that he was tall, slim, between twenty-five and thirty years of age, clean-shaven and with short, fair hair, wearing a linen cap and a dark-grey alpaca topcoat.'

Houdini gaped. 'How the hell did you know that?'

'Watson and I observed the same man last night, as we approached your hotel. At the time we could not say if he was one of your wife's abductors or a member of the press, hoping to discover the real reason you cancelled your show. The answer now seems obvious.'

'Well, he's the man, right enough. Same description.'

'Yet the note tells a different story,' Holmes mused.

'What do you mean?'

'The handwriting, sir. You will note the neatness of the letters, how round and even they are — small, symmetrical and almost ornate. They have clearly been made by one whose musculature requires more pressure on a downstroke to make a suitable impression, and yet also shows one of great dexterity. To those who study such matters, these are indicators as to the sex of the author . . . this was unmistakably written by a woman.'

'A woman's involved with these bully-boys?'

'You do not recognize the hand?'

'No.'

'Then they did not coerce either your wife or Miss Lane into writing the note for them.'

Houdini paled. 'This really *isn't* a trick, is

it? What would you do?'

'My dear sir,' Holmes replied, 'though it would serve no useful purpose in the circumstances, I could in all probability isolate the area in which the author of this letter received her education, had I sufficient time.' He fell silent a moment, then read the note again.

'They're talking about Frankie, aren't they?' Houdini said desperately. 'When they say how serious they are about this thing?'

'I prefer not to speculate.'

'Come now, Holmes! It's a bit late to spare my feelings!'

Holmes looked grim. 'Very well, yes, I believe we should indeed fear for Miss Lane's safety,' he confessed.

Houdini gave an anguished groan. He turned in a tight, restless circle, his hands repeatedly balling into fists and then flexing. 'Why are they doing this to me, Holmes? I haven't given them any reason to think I'm planning to double-cross them. Hell, they haven't given me the *chance*, yet!'

'Nevertheless, if their demands are sufficiently high, they may wish to impress upon you the folly of not submitting to them.'

Houdini's face tightened. 'But Frankie . . .'

'Take heart, sir. We may be worrying needlessly.'

'But we're not, are we?'

Holmes did not reply. No reply was necessary.

'You were right, Holmes,' the showman said miserably. 'I've known how Frankie feels about me for . . . God, it seems like forever. You'd have to be blind *not* to see it. She's a great girl, and I don't mind admitting, she'd be the girl for me if I wasn't as devoted as I am to Bess. It's made things difficult, Holmes. Just being around her, stifling the feelings *I* have for *her* . . . and out of her great respect for Bess she's been equally strong in keeping our relationship as business-like as she can. Without her, without Bess, without my beloved mother . . . I owe just about everything to those three women.'

'Then you will do precisely as you have been instructed in this note,' Holmes replied. 'Go with them. Offer no resistance whatsoever . . . and place your faith in me.'

Houdini gave a sour, fleeting quirk of a smile. 'It doesn't seem like I have much choice, does it?'

'Perhaps not. But know this, Mr Houdini — whatever happens tonight, I will be with you every step of the way.'

'Thanks, Holmes. But you'll stay out of it, right? I mean, unless there's no help for it. You'll stay out of it and just gather enough evidence to make sure we can find them again once I have Bess and Frankie back . . . and then we can make them pay together.'

Before Holmes could reply there came the sound of footsteps descending to the basement. Houdini turned, startled, but Holmes immediately replaced his glasses and threw back his shoulders.

'I am Ed Martin,' he whispered urgently. 'That is the name I gave to the stage doorman upon my arrival. I am a member of your entourage and arranged to meet you here so that we could inspect your props.'

Houdini gaped. 'I — '

'I then asked the doorman to step out for a moment so that he might fetch us some sandwiches,' Holmes continued. 'I would say that is he now coming to deliver them . . . except that he has two other men with him.'

As he finished speaking, a tall, dark-haired man in a well-cut black suit followed old Ulrich into the basement. Behind them came a police constable, resplendent in a military-cut tunic with two rows of brass buttons and stiff collar.

Holmes, deciding that there could only be one reason for the presence of the police, hissed, 'Hold your nerve, Houdini.'

'Herr Houdini?' called the tall man as Ulrich led them between all the draped

132

props, a sandwich bag in his hand.

The escapologist cleared his throat. 'I . . . I'm Houdini, yes.'

The tall man looked steadily at Ulrich who, taking the hint, nodded respectfully to the policeman, set the bag down on one of the draped props, then turned to go back upstairs.

'Your hotel told me I would find you here,' the tall man continued, reaching into his jacket and bringing out a warrant card. 'I am Kapitan Erwin Janosi of the Bundesgendarmerie. I wonder if I might have a word . . . '

Houdini tried to speak but couldn't. He cleared his throat and managed, 'Of course.'

The kapitan's dark eyes flickered meaningfully toward Holmes. Adopting an American accent, Holmes said, 'My name's Ed Martin. I work with Mr Houdini, here.'

Following his lead, Houdini nodded. 'Y-Yes,' he said. 'Anything you need to say to me can be said in front of . . . of Ed . . . Kapitan.'

Janosi sighed. 'Do you know a Miss Frances Lane?'

Fearing the worst, Houdini swayed slightly. He said, in what seemed like someone else's voice, 'Yes. She works with me. With *us*. She's my personal assistant.'

'Then I must ask you to prepare yourself

for some very bad news, Herr Houdini. Miss Lane is dead, sir. We retrieved her body from the Danube some two hours ago.'

13

Chance Encounter

The news hit Houdini like a slap and Holmes quickly reached out to steady him. 'May we ask what happened?' he enquired softly.

'You may,' Janosi replied. 'The body of the unfortunate woman was seen floating in the water by a resident of Adendorf, who was walking his dogs by the river. The body had been snagged in some reeds at the water's edge. The local Bundesgendarmerie were summoned and brought the body ashore. There were no signs of foul play, which leads us to believe that the woman took her own life.'

'Adendorf?' asked Holmes.

'It is a small market town forty-five kilometres to the north and west of this city.'

'The water carried her quite a distance, then?'

'It would appear so. When was the last time you saw Miss Lane, Herr Houdini?'

Houdini seemed to have retreated into himself. When it became obvious that he hadn't even heard the question Holmes said, truthfully, 'We were together in Mr Houdini's suite last night around seven o'clock.'

'And how did she seem?'

'Distraught,' Houdini croaked, hardly aware that he was speaking aloud.

'We were all pretty distraught,' Holmes added. 'There's a lot hingeing on this tour, and it hasn't got off to a great start. We've had problems with some of our props. You probably heard that we've had to cancel the show until we've had a chance to iron all the problems out.'

'So I understand,' said Janosi.

'Well, as Mr Houdini's personal assistant, it's possible that Miss Lane felt the pressure more than anyone.'

'But is it possible that she would have taken her own life?'

'No . . . ' Houdini muttered.

'Who can say?' Holmes added quickly.

'No,' Houdini repeated, still stunned by the news — or rather, by confirmation of what he had already suspected and dreaded. 'Not Frankie. She was tougher than that.'

'Nevertheless, our preliminary examination suggests that she did indeed take her own life.' Janosi's tone softened as he added, 'I am sorry to bring you this news, Herr Houdini.'

'What? Oh . . . yeah . . . thank you.'

'Someone will have to make a formal identification of the body,' Janosi continued.

'I'll do it,' said Holmes.

'The deceased has been brought to the city and her body is presently being housed at the government mortuary on the Schillerplatz.'

'I'll find it.'

'*Danke*. Once again, Herr Houdini, my condolences.'

They watched as Janosi and the policeman turned and left. Houdini's mouth twitched with emotion, and, obeying the Jewish ritual of mourning, he absently reached up and tore the lapel of his overcoat. 'They killed her, didn't they?' he said brokenly.

Once again Holmes stepped out of his assumed character. 'We will not know that for certain until I have had a chance to examine the body.'

'They did it,' Houdini said with absolute certainty. 'Damn them!'

'If they did,' Holmes said, placing one hand gently on the escapologist's shoulder, 'then rest assured, Mr Houdini, we will indeed make them pay. Upon that, sir, I give you my solemn *oath*.'

★   ★   ★

In Holmes's absence, time weighed heavily upon Watson. He tried to settle in the lobby, there to await the return of his friend, but his

137

thoughts were still dominated by Houdini's misfortunes. Where *was* Holmes, anyway? Not knowing, and not knowing whether or not his disappearance was connected in some way to the events of the previous night, made him feel restless, irritable and, frankly, left out.

Eventually, seeking distraction from his concerns, he decided to go out and explore the city on foot. No longer required to keep up with his energetic friend, he was able to set his own more leisurely pace, and was soon caught up in the elegance and charm by which he found himself surrounded.

The walk was a voyage of discovery. Here was a bank with a glorious marble facade; there a tiny museum dedicated to Richard Wagner. In St Michael's Square he stopped off at a surprisingly grand cafe and enjoyed a pot of tea and a slice of *Dobostorte*: a delicious sponge cake with no less than five separate layers of chocolate butter cream. And then, being mindful of his leg, which had so far behaved itself, he hailed a cab and continued his tour in comfort. He took in the elegant Kursalon, where Johann Strauss had once directed concerts, and then passed the surprisingly small Theater an der Wien, which had been built especially to perform the operas of Mozart.

At length the cab entered a tree-lined boulevard and all at once he realized that they were actually winding their way through an enormous park. On impulse he rapped his cane on the roof of the cab and the cabbie pulled over to the kerb. Watson climbed out, paid his fare and glanced around. Judging that he was not far from the hotel now, he decided to spend a short time in the park, then make the remainder of his journey on foot.

He crossed the road, found a bench and sat down, there to watch several children playing tag on the grass in front of him. As they chased each other around, their laughter was a joy to hear, and he forced himself to banish all further thought from his mind and simply take pleasure from it.

A horse-drawn carriage clattered past. Glancing around, he watched it idly for a moment, until something else caught his attention and his gaze stopped abruptly. He felt something distinctly unpleasant wrench at his stomach as he recognized the woman on the pavement across the street, walking arm-in-arm with her companion whose resplendent uniform identified him as an officer in the Austrian army.

Watson blinked, for a moment quite literally unable to believe his eyes. But a second look confirmed that he had not been in error . . . the woman was definitely Irene Hastings!

Stubbornly, he tried to convince himself that he was mistaken. He *had* to be! Irene was finished; Holmes had said so. And yet he could not convince himself that the woman now laughing and chatting to her officer friend was anyone but she. She had the same tall, willowy build, the same fine, fair hair that was so typical of the Nordic race; pale skin, pink lips, eyes as clear blue as the azure surface of a southern sea.

It *was* her, dammit!

But what was she doing *here?*

The answer, he felt, was all too obvious. She was up to her old tricks again; she had learned nothing from their confrontation at the Shiells Hotel in London!

Feeling his anger growing, he decided to follow her, but first made sure that her brother — or husband — Robert was nowhere in evidence. When he was satisfied as to that fact, he got to his feet and hurriedly left the park.

The traffic was reasonably heavy, for it was the middle of the day, and it took him several moments to cross the street. By then Irene and her companion were a block ahead of him. Heedless of his gammy leg, he pushed

140

himself to walk faster, weaving between the other people walking ahead of him.

He still harboured the belief that he was mistaken. He *must* be. But as he drew closer to the couple, the woman turned to say something to her escort, and Watson had no choice but to admit that she was indeed Irene.

He slowed his pace a little as Irene and the officer entered a restaurant; the man was wearing an immaculate tunic of dark-blue serge and somewhat lighter blue trousers. His epaulettes doubtless denoted his rank, but Watson was unable to work out what it might be. It was only when the restaurant doorman touched the brim of his hat to the man and said, 'Good afternoon, Feldmarschalleutnant,' that Watson realized he was the Austrian army's equivalent to a major general — an ambitious target indeed for Irene.

They entered the building and Watson came to a halt to watch them go. He wondered what he should do next. Did he dare enter the restaurant and risk being spotted by Irene, or should he wait outside until she and her major general came out again, and then follow them wherever they went?

For several moments he was in a quandary. Even if a confrontation with Irene were not to his liking, his conscience dictated that he should not let this man, this innocent victim, have his reputation ruined.

Before he could decide what to do, however, Irene, who was now seated at a table across from the man, happened to glance toward the window. For an instant she, like Watson earlier, doubted her eyes. Then she quickly excused herself, got up and walked swiftly out of sight.

A moment later she appeared in the restaurant entrance. She had removed her coat to reveal a gown of black stripes over ivory satin, and she looked magnificent.

'John,' she said. 'What are *you* doing here?'

Watson glared at her. Even though he was angry with her and wanted nothing more than to see her behind bars, he couldn't deny that just being in her presence, smelling her perfume, was so intoxicating that a tiny part of him still wanted her.

But he quickly stamped out that desire and said bitingly, 'I see you're up to your old tricks again. I should have thought that you would have learned your lesson after what happened in London.'

Irene cast an uneasy glance over one shoulder, then moved aside, where they would not be visible to her major general, who was watching them curiously from the window table. 'John,' she said softly, 'this isn't what it looks like.'

'Of course it isn't,' he agreed sarcastically.

'It *isn't!* I swear it! Things are . . . different now.'

'How?'

She opened her mouth to reply, then seemed to deflate a little. 'I'm sorry, John. I can't discuss it with you.'

'How very convenient.'

His scorn made her wince. 'Bitterness doesn't suit you,' she said.

'I am sure it doesn't,' he replied. 'But how else would you expect me to feel, after the humiliation I suffered at your hands?'

'For that,' she said quietly, 'I am truly sorry. I don't expect you to believe me, but I am.'

He only shook his head at that. 'I had hoped you might have changed after what happened in London.'

'I did,' she said. 'Robert and I both did.'

'And yet I find you here, now, hanging on the arm of yet another conquest — '

'John . . . I don't blame you for being angry. You have every right to be. But I imagine your upbringing was quite different from ours. It was desperation that drove us to larceny — desperation founded upon two childhoods filled with dire poverty. We saw what that poverty did to our parents, how it destroyed their lives, their very *souls*, and we vowed that would never happen to us.'

'Countless people are born into sorry circumstances,' Watson countered. 'Surprisingly few of them become criminals. You are merely seeking to justify your greed.'

'That's easy to say, when you know next to nothing about it.'

Watson reddened indignantly. 'How dare you seek to pass judgement on *me!*'

'Perhaps I do so because I want you to know that it was not an easy decision to make — or a life I have especially enjoyed.'

'You have made money from it,' Watson reminded her. 'If Holmes is to be believed, enough to live quite comfortably.'

'I'll not deny that. Just as I'll not deny that greed played its part, that to one who grew up poor the acquisition of money became addictive. Besides . . . '

'What?' he demanded as she paused.

'Nothing. It doesn't matter.'

He cocked his head at her. 'Perhaps you were going to tell me that your victims deserved the treatment you meted out to them? Because they were just vain enough to fall for the flattery of a beautiful woman?'

'They *did* have it coming, most of them.'

'Did *I?*'

Her expression softened. 'No, John,' she said softly, and he thought he saw the glimmer of a tear in one of her perfectly blue eyes. 'You were different. And taking advantage of a man whose wife had so recently died and whose feelings were so *fragile* . . . that was the worst thing I have ever done. Had it been up to me, I would never have added to your grief in the way I eventually did. But that was only after I began to develop . . . feelings . . . for you. Feelings that I would never dare mention to Robert.'

Against his will, Watson felt another tinge of sympathy rising inside him, and quickly squashed it. 'And the man you are with now . . . does *he* deserve to be hurt in the same way?'

'I told you, John — this is not what it looks like. However, I will tell you that Mr Holmes gave us a second chance — '

'*Holmes!*'

' — and Robert and I took it.'

'I see,' said Watson, though in truth he didn't see at all. Holmes had brought Irene's criminal activities to an end. Why should he then take it upon himself to give her and her husband a second chance? More than that, Watson wondered why Holmes had not seen fit to tell him anything more than that Irene and Robert were finished. He felt a sudden stab of betrayal at the thought.

'Well,' he muttered stiffly, 'I shall leave you to your lunch.'

'John,' she said. '*Please*. I know it's hard, but try not to think ill of me. I know that everything we did was wrong. But we have been given a chance to make amends, and we will not let Mr Holmes down.'

Watson felt his lip curling. 'You'll forgive me if I take that with a grain of salt.'

Before she could reply and possibly melt his anger — anger that was his only defence against the spell she cast over him even now — Watson, ever the gentleman, tipped his hat and walked off.

As he crossed the street, ignoring the angry shouts from the drivers of the various passing vehicles that had to swerve to avoid him, he found it almost impossible to contain his rage. How dare Holmes show mercy to those criminals, when all the time he had assured Watson that they were finished, and would pay for their crimes.

Well, he would certainly have it out with his friend once he got back to the hotel.

14

The Butterfly Bruise

The minute he heard the door of Holmes's suite open and then close again, Watson squared his shoulders and went next door, intending to confront him about Irene and Robert Hastings. He rapped sharply at the door, and a few moments later Holmes answered it.

'Come in, Watson,' Holmes said in a subdued voice.

Watson did so, and closed the door behind him. 'Holmes . . . ' he began, then broke off as he saw his friend unbutton his waistcoat and remove a folded sheet from around his midriff, which had given 'Ed Martin' his additional girth. Holmes had been out in disguise, he realized. But why?

'Have a seat, old friend,' Holmes said.

'I'll stand,' Watson replied. 'There is something about which we need to speak quite urgently.'

'Indeed there is,' Holmes answered. He threw the sheet aside and sat before his dressing-table mirror. There he removed his false beard and returned it to the make-up kit he was seldom without. 'The Houdini business has taken a sinister turn, I am afraid.'

Watson finally realized that the anger he had allowed to build ever since his encounter with Irene Hastings had blinded him to the fact that something was indeed very wrong. 'What is it?' he asked, his voice dropping.

'Miss Lane,' said Holmes, turning in his chair. 'I am sorry, Watson. She is dead.'

Watson blanched. *'What?'*

Holmes turned back to the mirror. Watching his reflection, Watson said in a hushed voice, 'No, Holmes, you must be mistaken.'

'I wish I were.'

'Was it . . . an accident?'

'I do not believe so.'

'The . . . the kidnappers, then?'

'Yes.'

'But . . . what could they possibly hope to gain by . . . ' instinctively he lowered his voice still further, 'by . . . *murder?*'

'I cannot with any certainty say that it *was* murder,' Holmes replied, using a damp cloth to remove 'Ed Martin's' tan in a series of brisk swipes.

'What does that mean?'

'I have just come from the state mortuary, where I identified the body. Poor Houdini was in no fit state to undertake such a task. Though I was not given the opportunity to examine the body as thoroughly as I would have liked, I certainly asked as many questions as I could without arousing suspicion, in order to get a reasonable picture of how Miss Lane came to meet her demise. Fluid was found in her lungs, the lungs themselves were swollen and froth was found around her mouth when she was dragged from the water.'

'Then she died from drowning.'

'That is the view of the authorities, but it is not mine. My expectation is that, should it occur to them to analyze the *algae* found in the water taken from Miss Lane's lungs — which they probably won't — and then compare it to similar single-cell samples from elsewhere on her body, they will find that they do not match.'

'Suggesting that she was dead before she entered the water.'

'Precisely.'

'But if it wasn't murder, and it wasn't suicide, then what the devil was it?'

Holmes turned away from the mirror and faced his companion. 'A *mistake*, Watson. A very unfortunate *mistake*.'

He continued, 'Having formally identified the body, I then asked if I might be permitted

149

a moment alone to pay my respects. More out of deference to Houdini than to the member of his entourage I was pretending to be, the mortuary attendant grudgingly agreed. It was then that I examined Miss Lane's eyes, which were shot through with blood, and found a small, butterfly-shaped bruise upon her right collarbone. I also observed clear signs of *petechiae* in the skin of her face.'

Watson pondered that for a moment. Such distinctive red or purple spots were usually the result of a minor haemorrhage. 'Signs that would indicate raised blood pressure,' he muttered thoughtfully.

'Either that or an indication that a struggle of sorts took place immediately prior to her death.'

'And the, uh, butterfly bruise . . . ?'

'In my experience it is indicative of two thumbprints, coming together at their tips, and exerting great force,' Holmes said. 'The fact that her lingual bone was broken, midway between the chin and the thyroid cartilage, would seem to bear this out.'

'It doesn't sound like much of a mistake to me. It sounds cold, callous and premeditated.'

'Nevertheless, as you have already pointed out, what did the kidnappers have to gain from murder?' Having finished removing his make-up, he entered the bathroom, where he ran hot water into the sink. 'Miss Lane suspected, rightly as it turned out, that she and Houdini were being watched. When she left her hotel last night with the intention of requesting our assistance, she had the feeling that she was being followed and took measures to evade her pursuer. To him — and there is now no doubt that this was the man in the alpaca topcoat — this could only have suggested one thing: that she was going against their demands not to seek outside help. For that alone, the gang we are dealing with may have felt that some sort of response — punishment, if you will — was called for. But murder? I think not. More likely, her death was accidental and the result of a struggle.'

'Which they were ruthless enough to turn to their advantage.'

'Quite.'

'Then I very much look forward to making the acquaintance of the man in the alpaca topcoat again,' Watson said grimly.

Holmes appeared in the bathroom door. 'But there's the rub, Watson, for it was not *he* who killed Miss Lane.'

'No?'

'The butterfly bruise was too small. It indicated to me that the person who killed Frances Lane was a woman.'

'What?'

'In all probability the same woman who penned a second note, telling Houdini to be outside his hotel at ten this evening.'

'Good grief . . . ' Watson was silent for a time before saying: 'This meeting tonight. Do you think Houdini will be up to it?'

'I hope so. As I said, he was a broken man when I left him at the theatre this morning. He considers himself more responsible for Miss Lane's death than the actual perpetrator of the crime. But he is nothing if not a professional. As long as it gives us a chance to discover more about these malefactors and eventually bring them to book, the show *will* go on.'

'And we will be there for the final act,' said Watson.

Holmes nodded. 'You are a man of great and consistent habits, Watson. Even though this trip was meant to be a simple break in the monotony of our lives, I trust you have nevertheless brought your service revolver with you?'

'Of course. It has been our salvation more than once in the past.'

'And it may well be so again,' Holmes answered. 'For all we know, perhaps this very night.'

15

Memories

As winter darkness stole across Vienna, Houdini sat alone in his suite with his head in his hands, his lips moving in prayer.

For the first time that he could remember, he felt that his spirits had hit rock bottom. What had befallen Bess was bad enough, but he consoled himself with the thought that as long as he played fair with the people who had abducted her, they would release her once the ransom was paid.

Then they had murdered Frankie, and now he could only fear the very worst.

He'd never been a man to give in to self-pity. If that had been part of his make-up, he would have abandoned his lofty ambitions to become a stage sensation long ago. He had always held rigidly to self-discipline and determination, self-belief and the unshakeable conviction that whatever he set his mind to do, he could and *would* do.

When his rabbi father lost his tenure at Zion in 1887, the family had moved to New York City, and it was there that Harry had made his stage debut at the age of nine, billing himself in a trapeze act as 'Ehrich, Prince of the Air'.

And that, he reflected, was all he'd ever wanted to do — amaze people, entertain them, show them what he was capable of.

Bess — it choked him just to speak the pet name of his beloved Wilhelmina Beatrice Rahner — had supported him through those early, hungry years of his career. The Brooklyn-born daughter of German immigrants was herself filled with dreams of a career in show business and Bess had been working at West Brighton Beach as one half of a song-and-dance act called The Floral Sisters when she met her first Houdini — Harry's kid brother, Theo. She had liked Theo well enough, but it was Harry she'd fallen in love with. He had fallen for her, too.

Because they'd thought it would garner them a little free publicity, they'd originally put out the story that they'd met in 1894, when Harry, on his way to perform at a birthday party, had accidentally dropped his props, spilt some acid he was carrying and ruined her dress. According to legend, Harry had promptly taken her home to his mother, Cecilia, who made her a replacement.

The truth, of course, was a little more ordinary.

Still, they had married after a whirlwind courtship that lasted just two weeks, despite the fact that Bess's folks, who were Roman Catholic, disapproved of her relationship with the Jewish Harry. Thereafter, touring the country as magician and assistant, the couple had been inseparable.

It was, he thought now, a marriage made in heaven. They had been blissfully happy together. Bess was everything to him. She was a quiet, practical woman who collected dolls and made all of Harry's costumes and never, ever complained when he switched from magician to escapologist and repeatedly put his life on the line. The only thing that ever gave them cause for regret was the fact that they had never managed to have children. Still, until Bess was stolen away from him, at least they had had each other.

The silence seemed unnaturally loud when he finished the prayer.

He'd been thinking about Bess, but praying for Frankie.

Frankie . . .

He still couldn't believe she was gone, any more than he could believe that she'd committed suicide, as the police had said. As he'd told Holmes, he'd known she was in love with him. It would not have been hard to return the emotion, either. But she had worked with him — with him and Bess together — for years now. She knew how devoted he was to his wife.

Now he knew just how devoted Frankie had been to him.

No, he was absolutely convinced that those . . . those animals who had kidnapped Bess had also killed Frankie, because she had dared to try to do something about them while he, the great Houdini, had decided to obey their demands for fear of what they might do to Bess if he didn't.

'Ah, Frankie . . . '

Angrily now, he promised himself that something positive would come of her death. The men responsible would pay. They'd pay for killing Frankie and causing Bess the kind of grief and terror he could only imagine.

The telephone jangled shrilly, making him start.

Almost guiltily, he sprang from the chair and snatched the earpiece from the cradle. 'Yes?'

'Your brother-in-law is here, Mr Houdini,' said the desk clerk in heavily accented English. 'I shall pass him the instrument.'

Houdini frowned, confused. Brother-in-law? What the dickens was John Rahner doing here?

Then, 'Hello . . . Harry?'

Houdini knew instantly it was not John. He knew John's voice as well as his own and he had never heard the accented voice that spoke to him now. Houdini's stomach knotted unpleasantly and, gripping the earpiece a little tighter, he said, 'Who are you?'

'I think we both know the answer to that.'

'You're the man who killed Frances Lane.'

There was a pause, then: 'That is something I regret very much.'

'You *certainly will* regret it,' Houdini promised.

'You'd better get down here quickly . . . Harry. The man I'm taking you to see doesn't like being kept waiting.'

Houdini glanced over his shoulder. According to the wall clock it was a little before seven. 'I thought . . . ' he began.

'Yes?'

'Your note said I should be waiting outside at ten o'clock.'

'We changed our minds.'

Houdini's own mind was racing. Holmes would be expecting the kidnappers to arrive at ten, the same as he. He might show up a little early, just in case, but not three whole hours early.

He was on his own, then.

'Harry?' said the voice.

'I'm here.'

'You'd better get yourself down to the lobby. I'm sure Bess would appreciate it.'

Bess. The name suddenly focussed Houdini's thoughts.

All right, he decided. These people had wrong-footed him, and he was on his own. But even by himself he could be a formidable foe. He was *Houdini*, for God's sake! And he'd damn well do whatever it took to turn the tables on them and rescue his beloved Bess.

Calmly, he said, 'Give me a couple of minutes and I'll be right there.'

Then he set about preparing himself.

16

In Pursuit

'Are you sure that's the same man we saw last night?' Watson asked urgently from the rear seat of their cab. Holmes had requested the driver to park at the far corner of Stephansplatz, within sight of the Royal. 'He went from his cab into the hotel so fast I didn't manage a decent look at him.'

'I am not likely to mistake the man or his attire,' Holmes replied acidly. 'At the moment he is our single link to the woman he has abducted ... and the woman one of his accomplices has killed. As such he is burned into my memory.'

'But if it *is* the same man, then he's early. I mean, the note said — '

'These people, whoever they are, are professionals, Watson. As such, they are unlikely to be so foolish as to provide Houdini with any information he might be able to use against them. They may have *said* they would collect him at ten, but it is far more likely that they intended to collect him earlier than that all along.'

'So that's why we came here early?'

'Of course.'

Flakes of snow feathered down onto the cab's windows. The horse in the traces stamped restively, shook its head and snorted.

They had been waiting patiently now for almost an hour. Watson hadn't seen the point of arriving early, until a Harvey cab had pulled up outside the Royal and its passenger jumped out and hurried inside.

Ten minutes later the man in the alpaca topcoat reappeared on the wet pavement, his collar turned up against the scything wind, his sporting cap tugged low over his brow. This time there could be no doubt as to his identity. Houdini, wearing a slouch hat and his black overcoat, its lapels still ripped in memory of Frances Lane, was at his side.

The man in the alpaca topcoat gestured for Houdini to get into the waiting Harvey first. Then he climbed in after him and moments later, the cab jerked into motion.

Holmes waited a few seconds then tapped his cane twice against the roof of their own cab. The heavily muffled driver, exposed to the elements on a high seat set above and behind the cab, immediately snapped his reins and the horse broke into a trot.

Holmes had told the fellow they would be following someone that evening, and if he wanted to collect a handsome bonus for his efforts, he would ask no questions but instead take pains to keep a discreet distance behind their quarry. Should their quarry suspect they were being followed, the promised bonus would be forfeit.

Holmes and Watson's cab followed the vehicle ahead as it turned left and passed between the palatial apartments of the Brandstätte. Another left took them onto the equally grand Vorlaufstrasse. In the darkness of the cab, Watson reached into his pocket and felt the grips of his Webley Mk II. Its touch alone was comforting.

The cab in front turned left again and the horses trotted along the snowy cobbles of the Salztorg.

'Where in heaven's name are they going?'

Holmes leaned forward to study their present location. 'This much I can tell you. We are about to leave the First District behind us.'

A chain suspension bridge loomed out of the snow-speckled darkness ahead. They clattered across it. The waters of the Danube seemed to dip and sway thick and heavy below them, sending reflections of the streetlamps skittering across its waves like spilled gold.

They left the bridge behind them. They

followed the Praterstrasse into an increasingly suburban environment. Watson took out his pocket watch and held it to the poor light. They had now been following the cab carrying Houdini for ten minutes.

The Praterstrasse yielded to the Lassallestrasse and they turned left onto Handelskai. Watson recognized the name from his reading of Bradshaw's. It was, claimed the guide, one of the longest streets in Vienna.

It ran along the right bank of the Danube until the Brigittenauer Brücke took them across the Old Danube, an oxbow lake separated from the river itself by a dam.

The streets around them changed abruptly showing a profile reminiscent of the late Middle Ages: the roads narrowed to cobbled alleys; the pavements shrunk to little more than uneven ribbons of stone. The buildings they passed were ornate and beautiful, as were the signs that hung outside each one, but they were also unmistakably relics of an earlier time.

Houdini's cab turned left into a narrow alley between two vast warehouses and pulled up. Watson caught sight of the street name and scowled uneasily.

Blutstrasse.

Blood Street, indeed!

Holmes used his cane to push open the

little trap through which the passenger could communicate with the driver and hissed in German, 'Go on for another twenty yards, then stop!'

The driver's voice came down to them on the biting wind. *'Ja.'*

Once the cab came to a halt, Holmes opened the bow door and leapt out into the street like a man half his age. 'What is down there, in Blood Street?' he called up.

The cabbie, mystified by the actions of his two English passengers, shrugged. 'It is just a thoroughfare like any other. No one uses it much any more. There's nothing down there, just the church.'

'The church?'

'St Romedius, *mein Herr*. Well, what's left of it. It burned down about seven or eight years ago. All that remains now is a charred shell.'

Even as he digested that, Holmes heard the renewed clopping of hooves. He looked toward Blood Street just as the Harvey cab reappeared, then turned back the way it had come. Though Holmes only caught a glimpse of it, he saw that it was empty.

'Wait here,' he told Watson.

Before Watson could respond, Holmes disappeared into the swirling blizzard.

17

What Happened in Blood Street

Holmes hurried back toward Blood Street. The area seemed to be devoid of life, the tall warehouses all locked up for the night.

At the corner, he slowed and peered cautiously into the narrow thoroughfare, his astute grey eyes squinting against the sleet. There were no gas lamps here, but the watery moonlight was sufficient to show him the ghostly outline of what had once been a church standing some thirty yards further down the street on the left.

He could see Houdini and the man in the alpaca topcoat standing outside the buckled iron railings that separated the church and its weed-strewn, headstone-littered grounds from the pavement. As he watched, Houdini's companion pushed him through the drooping gates and on toward the twisted, blackened ruins of the church.

Holmes continued to watch until they had entered the ruins. Then he hurried silently down the alley in pursuit.

The cabbie had been right. All that

remained of the church was a shell; four tall, crumbling walls partially covered in thick spills of ivy that looked more black than green. There was no roof and the tall, arched windows had been shattered, so that all that remained were just ominous, inky gaps.

Holmes stood a moment longer, watching, listening and waiting. Only when he was sure that there was no one in the darkness to observe him did he enter the once-hallowed grounds and follow the faint memory of a path to the remains of the vaulted entrance.

Reaching his destination, he pressed himself to the wall. Behind him the alley was silent. The traffic of the main thoroughfare was faintly audible in the distance, but he could not hear anything from within the church and chanced a look inside.

There was nothing much left of the interior save the vaguest impression of where the aisle had led to the altar. Both sides were flanked by the blackened remains of the pews that had once stretched from nave to chancel. Long grass, uncut weeds and the occasional pile of rubbish or rubble had replaced the original grandeur of a decade earlier.

Holmes entered the building. Sleet pattered gently against his hat and shoulders. He went about a dozen feet, thought he heard the softest sound ahead of him and quickly ducked down behind a stack of rotted wood.

He heard no further sound.

Shortly, he stood up and moved on. Despite a lengthy search, however, he could find no sign of the men he was pursuing. Puzzled, he wondered what had become of them. He refused to believe that they had vanished without trace. No, there was obviously some logical explanation for their apparent disappearance.

Again he paused, this time to review his knowledge of church architecture, and then he made for the spot where the altar had stood, its cement base still roughly visible among all the tangled, snowy weeds.

A grim smile tightened his thin lips when he discovered a place where the rubble had been swept aside exposing a trapdoor.

It was just as he had suspected. Houdini and his companion had quite literally gone to ground — or more accurately, into the very earth itself, by way of the crypt. Having reached that conclusion, there was no mystery as to where he would locate the crypt entrance, for tradition dictated that it was never far from the altar.

Holmes reached down and cautiously raised the trap. Slowly, a narrow flight of worn wooden steps came into view. One look verified that they led down to a dusty, stone-flagged floor twenty feet below. As best he could see, the crypt — where the wealthy dead could await Judgement Day in comfort and assurance — had been untouched by fire. But the air was permeated by a stale mustiness that even the biting cold could not disguise.

Lamplight glowed dully from somewhere below. It threw the shadows of long, neoclassical Doric pillars across the wall attached to the steps. Holmes listened intently. At first, he couldn't hear anything. Then, as if from far off, he heard someone below speaking in very precise English, his words distorted by echoes so that it was little more than a murmur.

Holmes removed his hat, dropped to his knees and leaned forward. Gradually more of the crypt came into sight, albeit upside-down. A series of pillars rose to support the shadowed ceiling. At their bases lay scattered headstones, many of them broken, and dusty equipment — shovels, brooms and such like.

Holmes regained his feet, then began to descend, a step at a time, keeping his weight on the outside of every step so as to make as little noise as he could.

At the bottom of the steps, he paused again. The air was colder here even than outside. Ahead, the rough-hewn walls were pitted and crumbling. Dust tickled his nostrils.

He made his way along the narrow passage until he reached a corner some ten feet away. With every cautious step, the muted voices grew more distinct.

Reaching the corner, Holmes removed his hat and cautiously poked his head around the screening wall.

The passage opened out into a large stone burial vault. At the far end of the crypt, Houdini, accompanied by the man in the alpaca topcoat, stood facing two other people. One was short and portly, dressed in a dark suit and bald but for a fringe of oiled black hair around the pate. Light from a brass carbide lamp balanced on one of the ornate stone shelves showed Holmes a man of perhaps fifty, with a round, jowly, sickly-pale face; the lamplight glinted on his tortoiseshell glasses.

The other figure was that of a girl of twenty-five. Beneath her dark teardrop hat, she wore her raven-black hair pinned up in a glossy spill of ringlets and curls. Her face was oval, pale like that of the portly man, and almost ethereal in the harsh light. Her unblinking eyes glittered like chips of obsidian; her long, narrow nose swooped to a full red mouth that was set in a cool, disdainful pout. She stood beside the portly man, with her hands stuffed into the pockets of an overcoat, and even from this distance Holmes could see the hatred she harboured for their captive.

Holmes studied her with especially close interest for here, almost certainly, was the girl who had killed Frances Lane.

'. . . patience, Mr Houdini,' the portly man had just finished saying.

'To hell with that!' replied Houdini, his voice echoing around the vault. 'I've come for my wife, dammit, and I'm not leaving without her!'

The portly man stepped forward and slapped Houdini across the face. The blow rocked the escapologist back on his heels. Before he could react, however, the man in the alpaca topcoat — Holmes saw now that he was perhaps a year or so older than the girl, with a long, melancholy face, blue eyes and short fair hair — drew a pistol from his pocket. A Webley Mk IV, Holmes noted clinically. Seeing the gun, Houdini had no choice but to control his urge to strike back.

'I have waited quite a considerable time for this moment, Houdini,' the portly man continued. English was clearly his second language. He spoke it too precisely, as if rehearsed, every word accompanied by a cloud of vapour, for the vault was cold enough to serve as an icehouse. 'And now that it has arrived, I intend to enjoy it.' He glanced around their Spartan environment. 'The location of our meeting, for example, is no mere chance. Are you familiar at all with the legend of St Romedius, in whose hallowed surroundings we find ourselves this night? No? Then please, allow me to enlighten you.

'St Romedius was a young nobleman from Thaur, near Innsbruck. Though he had all the wealth and privilege he could ever want, he one day decided to closet himself away in a secluded cave and meditate upon life and its possible meanings. He was quite a remarkable man, possessed of every saving grace, qualities in which I myself am sadly lacking.

'In later years, following the death of his parents, he gave away all his possessions and set out on horseback to visit a childhood friend, St Vigilus, in Trento. On his way there a wild bear attacked him. The bear killed his horse, and it seemed certain that it would also kill St Romedius. But to the amazement of his companion, a disciple named David, St Romedius tamed the bear with but one look. Indeed, the bear grew so tame that David was able to bridle him. And that was how St Romedius made the remainder of his long trek to Trento . . . upon the back of the bear.'

He paused to let his words sink in before adding: 'Do you follow my meaning, Houdini?'

'I can't say that I do.'

The portly man smiled coolly. 'The bear was wild and untamed, used to getting its own way and doing whatever it wanted, *when* it wanted. Then it came upon St Romedius, who broke the bear's spirit and used the creature to carry him to his destination. That bear is *you*, Houdini, and I am going to be *your* St Romedius. I'm going to break you, and then allow you to carry *me* where *I* want to go.'

'Quit talking in riddles,' said Houdini, flaring. 'Just tell me how much money you want and I'll do everything in my power to get it to you, as fast as possible.'

'You're not *listening*, Houdini,' the portly man said disapprovingly. 'This isn't about money. Or rather, I should say that this is not *directly* about money. This is about *your* carrying *me* to where I want to *go*.'

Houdini sighed and shifted his weight. 'All right, have it your way. Tell me what it is you want and I'll do it. All I ask is that you let my wife go.'

'She will be released when the job is done. You both will. You have my word upon it.'

'I hope you mean that, mister.'

The portly man turned his glittering, chocolate-coloured eyes on the man in the alpaca topcoat. 'Did he do as I ordered, Wolf? Tell the desk clerk at the Royal that he would be out of town for a few days?'

'Ja.'

'Then we are all ready to go.'

'Not so fast, Buster,' broke in Houdini. 'What's this all about?'

'It's really quite simple, Herr Houdini. Supposedly, you are the world's greatest escapologist. A celebrity who has travelled across Europe, always demanding to be locked up in the strongest and most impregnable of prisons, yet always somehow managing to escape. Now, correct me if I am wrong . . . but does it not follow that a man who is so successful at escaping from buildings should also be able to work out a way to break *into* one?'

He fell silent and waited for Houdini's response.

Houdini said only, 'You've lost me.'

'Then I shall make it clearer. Wolf, here, needs to enter and leave a certain . . . building . . . unobserved. I have the plans of this building, but so far I have not been able to work out exactly how our aims might be achieved. Neither do I have time on my side.

172

The sooner Wolf is able to complete our mission, the sooner we receive a quite exceptional payment from our employer. And so I have decided to enlist your brain, Herr Houdini. And in return for finding a safe way into and out of this building, you and your precious wife will be released.'

'You're crazy.'

'I think not. And I would counsel you not to put such a ridiculous theory to the test. Now you are coming with *us*, Houdini. And if you know what is good for you — and your wife, of course — you will give us no trouble.'

Houdini shrugged. 'All right,' he said in defeat. 'Whether I like it or not, there's one thing I'll grant you. Right now, you hold all the aces.'

'Then we shall get along,' decided the portly man. Without warning, his smile suddenly vanished. 'We shall just search you first.'

'What?'

'I am not in the habit of repeating myself. Now, empty your pockets.'

'But — '

'Believe it or not, I know something about your trade, *Amerikaner*, about all its little *tricks*. First you will empty your pockets, and then we will search your scalp and the soles of your feet — areas in which you have often

173

secreted needles before now, because they are the two places no one ever thinks to check. Your mouth, too.' Without warning, he clapped his hands together, awakening fresh echoes in the vault. 'Open wide!'

The man in the alpaca topcoat, Wolf, made another gesture with the revolver. Grudgingly Houdini opened his mouth, using his fingers to pull his cheeks outward, but the portly man only chuckled.

'I told you, Houdini, I know all the tricks.' Then he went closer, and hissed, 'Pull your lower lip down.'

Slowly Houdini obeyed. The portly man said, 'Ah,' and then plucked a packet of razor blades from where they had been tucked between gum and lip. '*Sehr gut*. Now take your shoes off.'

Grimly Houdini raised one foot and quickly untied his shoe, slipping it off from the heel and allowing it to fall with an echoing thump to the crypt floor. The sock came next and he then repeated the procedure with his other foot. When he had finished, the portly man stepped back and snapped the fingers of his right hand.

'Annalise,' he said.

The girl came forward. Houdini turned around and lifted each foot in turn. She examined the soles of his feet much as a

174

farrier might examine the feet of a horse he was about to shoe. Eventually she removed some pins from where Houdini had threaded them beneath the calloused skin. She then took more pins from where he'd hidden them in his thick, curly hair.

Then they confiscated everything Houdini took from his pockets.

'So now,' the portly man said, when they had finished, 'we have drawn your teeth. But I know you are still a dangerous man, Houdini. Your knowledge of the intricacies of locks and the locksmith's art are legendary. And for that reason we intend to take no chances with you. At all times until you complete your task, you will be *bolted* safely into your — '

He stopped abruptly, for just then there was the last thing anyone expected to hear — the scream of a woman in apparent agony.

18

A Helping Hand

The portly man whirled around and faced the entrance to the passage, his pasty face going slack. '*Was ist — ?*'

No one seemed to know what it was. The cry had frozen them all.

Wolf, recovering first, said, 'I'll go and find out.'

Holmes, though thoroughly absorbed by what he had been witnessing, had straightened up at the scream and was already retracing his steps along the narrow passage to the staircase. It was only imagination, he knew, and yet he felt sure he could hear the sound of Wolf's footsteps right upon his own. Ignoring the warning, he hurried on, reaching the staircase and bounding up the wet steps as soundlessly as he could, two at a time.

Seconds later, he was back outside in the swirling snow. He turned, closed the trapdoor and searched around for a place to hide. Knowing that if he were caught things would go badly for Houdini and his wife, he ran through the empty shell of the church. Every step he took he seemed to encounter weeds or drifts of snow and slippery ice that threatened to trip him up.

The scream came again — this time accompanied by a darting, amber flash of movement to his right. He realized that the blood-curdling scream had come from a prowling fox.

In the next moment Holmes *did* slip, falling to his knees in a spray of snow. He quickly jumped up and hurried on, knowing he could not now possibly leave the abandoned church before someone came up from the crypt to see what was happening above ground.

Even as the thought struck him, he heard the trapdoor squeak. He threw himself behind a small, snowy mountain of dirt, rubble and refuse, heedless of the possible injury his fall might cause.

He hugged the mound of earth, well aware that his very life — and that of Houdini — depended upon it and waited, straining his ears to pick up every new sound.

Moments later Wolf climbed the last few steps out of the crypt. Holmes risked a quick glance around the side of the mound and, squinting to see in the darkness, watched Wolf, hoping that he had been in too much of a hurry to notice the telltale covering of snow on the steps. Silence followed as the young German looked around, searching for the source of the scream. His puzzled expression suggested his bemusement to Holmes: how could he and his companions have heard the cry so clearly below ground if the trapdoor had been closed?

The moon now slid behind the clouds, deepening the shadows while the falling sleet reduced visibility even further. Holmes felt this to be to his advantage, for it would hide his tracks in the snow, tracks that could lead Wolf directly to him.

Hardly daring to breathe, Holmes chanced another peek past the mound and this time pulled his head back immediately. Wolf was inspecting the ground by his feet, trying to decide whether the imprints in the snow — imprints that the sleet was already covering — could possibly be footprints.

Moments later the wind dropped slightly . . . and Holmes heard the young German shushing toward him through the darkness.

He stiffened. Wolf was approaching him, no doubt with revolver still in hand, trying to pick up any small sound that might betray his quarry.

The only weapon Holmes had was his cane — that, and his knowledge of *baritsu*. Under the circumstances, he could only hope they would be enough.

More *shushing*. Wolf was still approaching,

coming steadily, remorselessly closer.

Hardly daring to breathe, Holmes told himself he must time his move to perfection and exploit what little element of surprise he might still possess. Even so, he knew the damage had been done. The kidnappers would know that Houdini had been followed, that, despite their orders to the contrary, he had involved someone else in this business. That they would seek to punish the indiscretion, Holmes had little doubt.

Shush . . . shush . . . shush . . .

Holmes tightened his grip on the cane even as the moon reappeared suddenly through a break in the clouds. Its light cast Wolf's pale shadow across the ground, its very tip just beginning to slip into view . . .

The shattering of a bottle about midway along the boundary of the church grounds provided a much-needed distraction. Wolf's shadow turned away from his previous destination, and an instant later there came another scream — the prowling fox again.

Holmes froze. His back and calves were aching, crying out for release. A few seconds passed. Then he heard Wolf moving away from him, heading back toward the crypt. Holmes sagged, softly exhaled and thanked his good fortune.

The trapdoor gave another creak and Wolf

called down quietly. '*Da war nichts. Nur ein Fuchs. Wir sollten jetzt trotzdem gehen.*'

Holmes swallowed, relieved by Wolf's injunction to his companions not to worry. It seemed that the fox which had very nearly betrayed him had now come to his rescue.

Again, Holmes glanced around the side of the mound. Wolf was helping Annalise out of the crypt. As she stepped aside and smoothed the creases from her coat, Houdini appeared behind her. Holmes's mouth tightened when he saw that the escapologist was still barefoot and that his hands were now cuffed behind his back.

Finally, the portly man emerged from the crypt with the carbide lamp in one hand, Houdini's sock-stuffed shoes in the other.

With Wolf's gun pressed into his back, Houdini made his way over the snow and rubble toward a narrow gap in the rear wall that Holmes had missed during his initial search due to a dense covering of ivy. Walking erectly, Houdini gave no indication of the discomfort or humiliation he must be feeling as he and his abductors vanished into the darkness beyond the break in the wall.

Holmes waited as long as he dared, then stood up stiffly and went after them. He moved quickly, his breath misting before his hawkish face. Cautiously he pushed through the leafy gap. On the other side was a narrow alley that, after a hundred yards or so, ended at the main road.

There was no sign of Houdini or his captors. Holmes wondered where they were. The cobbled alley ran string-straight, flanked on both sides by the blank walls of more warehouses. There were no other exits that Houdini's abductors might have taken between there and the end of the alley and, if they had elected to walk to the main road, he knew they would still be in sight.

Even as he pondered the mystery, he thought of another possibility and quickly retraced his steps until he heard the crunch of broken glass beneath his shoes. Here he stopped and examined his surroundings with great care. Finally, satisfied, he pushed on.

He halted again when he reached a shadowed area just inside the entrance where the remains of two pillars had once formed a bay. He knelt down, thrust his cane under one arm and turned his back to the wind. After several attempts he finally managed to light a phosphor match. Cupping the flame, he did his best to examine the ground by its poor, erratic light.

Even before the match failed, though, Holmes believed he had already solved one particular mystery.

Watson found himself becoming increasingly edgy as time hung heavy. At last he could stand it no longer, and was about to go in search of his friend when Holmes suddenly strode into sight and climbed back into the cab.

'Holmes! What the devil — !'

Holmes tapped his cane against the roof and called in German, 'The Grand, if you please.'

As the cab began its long journey back toward the heart of the city, Holmes briefly recounted the events in Blood Street. At the end Watson exclaimed, 'Good Lord! Then if we have no idea where they've taken Houdini, all is lost — '

'We have no idea *yet*,' Holmes interrupted. 'But we have more information than you might imagine. Indeed, I have been a fool not to have seen it before.'

'Seen what, Holmes?'

'A few things — including the fact that we have been followed ever since we arrived in Austria.'

'What?'

'Patience, Watson. I suspect that we shall have *some* answers, at least, before the evening is out.'

To Watson's complete surprise, Holmes then peered out into the passing darkness and began to mutter softly under his breath.

'What was that you said?'

'Nothing.'

'It sounded like *poetry*.'

'I was merely quoting the opening lines of O'Shaughnessy's *Ode*.'

Watson tried to place the poem, but quickly gave up. 'You'll have to help me, I'm afraid.'

' "We are the music makers, And we are the dreamers of dreams, Wandering by lone sea-breakers, And sitting by desolate streams',' Holmes quoted, ' "World-losers and world-forsakers, On whom the pale moon gleams: Yet we are the movers and shakers, Of the world for ever, it seems." '

'Very profound, I must say,' Watson muttered. 'I take it that this verse is supposed to mean something?'

'Oh, yes.'

'But you're not going to enlighten me?'

Holmes smiled. 'It will come to you in the fullness of time, I am sure.'

He said no more until the cab had dropped them outside the hotel twenty minutes later. He climbed out and paid the cabbie, adding a generous tip as he had promised. He then turned to Watson saying, 'Wait here.'

What he did next left Watson speechless. With scant regard for his age or safety, he walked straight out into the street. There he raised his arms to stop a Unic cab that was heading directly towards him, and which he had noticed following them at a discreet distance ever since they had left Blood Street.

'*Holmes!*'

The driver stamped on the brake and honked the horn energetically. Paying the irate cabbie no mind, Holmes walked around the vehicle and opened the passenger door.

'It has been a rather eventful evening,' Watson heard him say amiably, 'and I should very much like the opportunity to thank you for the assistance you gave me not half an hour since.'

Watching from the pavement Watson tried his best to see inside the cab, but all he could make out was an indistinct silhouette. The passenger appeared to say something — perhaps to tell Holmes he had no idea what he was talking about — but Holmes would have none of it.

'Come now,' he said, 'there is no further need for secrecy. I am onto you, albeit somewhat belatedly, and since we are both working toward the same end, I suggest we pool our knowledge, preferably over a warming glass of brandy.'

This argument seemed to win the day. The passenger grudgingly leaned forward and paid his fare, then climbed from the cab.

As Holmes stood back, Watson was astounded to see a man of about average height and athletic proportions whom he recognized at once. It was the Good Samaritan who had come to his aid during their meeting with Freud, the German fellow who —

Except that the man was *not* German.

For speaking crisply and in a cultured British voice, he said, 'Very well, Mr Holmes. But I would much sooner have remained in the background until this business is settled. I have a feeling I would have been more use that way.'

'Nonsense,' said Holmes, grasping the man's arm. 'Come . . . let us get out of this foul weather. We have much to discuss, you and I. Much indeed, I believe.'

19

Two Birds, One Stone

Up in Holmes's room, the Good Samaritan took off his hat, self-consciously ran his hand up through his curly black hair then took a small warrant card from his pocket and passed it over. Holmes scanned it briefly and then handed it to Watson.

'So,' said Holmes as Watson inspected it, 'you are Mr Roger Purslane. And, as I suspected, you are connected in some unspecified but doubtless important capacity with His Majesty's Government. It therefore follows, does it not, that you were dispatched to keep an eye upon me and my colleague here by my brother, Mycroft?'

Watson looked up, surprised. 'Mycroft?' he repeated. 'What the devil has Mycroft got to do with this business?'

Mycroft was seven years older than Holmes, as fat as Holmes was lean, and as seemingly indolent as Holmes was industrious. Over the years, Watson had come to learn that there was more to him than met the eye. Mycroft held some vaguely defined but vital position within the government. Not for one moment did Watson believe Mycroft's claim that he carried out the audits for various government departments. He was more inclined to believe Holmes's contention that, when the occasion demanded it, Mycroft himself *was* the British government and that his usual haunt, the Diogenes Club, was little more than a front behind which Mycroft's shadowy department operated undetected.

As the thought occurred to him, he realized the significance of Holmes's earlier quotation, just as Holmes had said he would. For if ever there was an example of O'Shaughnessy's 'movers and shakers', it was indeed Mycroft.

Mycroft shared his younger brother's eye for detail and observation; he was possibly even more skilled in the art of deduction. But, despite his brilliance, his extreme indolence meant that he seldom used his abilities to their full advantage, allowing others to do the work on his behalf.

Watson had not seen Mycroft for years, not since the affair of the Bruce-Partington Plans, in '95. It seemed impossible that Mycroft should still occupy such a lofty position within the government almost two decades later. More puzzling still was why he should interest himself in Houdini's present difficulties.

Purslane broke into Watson's thoughts by saying: 'Mycroft Holmes? I'm sorry, gentlemen, the name means nothing to me.'

'Come, Mr Purslane,' said Holmes impatiently. 'It was no mere chance that brought you to Vienna at this time, no mere coincidence that you were on hand to help us escape the mob in the Beserlpark Alsergrund. And certainly it was no mere happenstance that you were on hand this very evening to throw a discarded milk bottle at a prowling fox, thereby saving me from discovery by a man who would most certainly have done me harm had he caught me.'

'I'm sorry, Mr Holmes. I have no idea — '

'You have uncommonly small feet, I observe,' Holmes interrupted. 'I should say they are not larger than a size six — small indeed for a man of your height and build. And yet I found prints of a similar — I am tempted to say *identical* — size at the very spot from which I calculate that the bottle was thrown. That, plus the unmistakable aroma of Penhaligon's Blenheim Bouquet — an aftershave I detected upon you during our first encounter, and of which you smell even now — makes denial a rather futile business. Incidentally,' he added, 'your German is very good, Mr Purslane. I could almost believe you were German or Austrian,

188

but when we thanked you for your assistance the other day, you responded twice with the curiously formal '*Bitte erwähnen Sie es nicht.*' I rather fancy that a native would have replied with the more casual *Bitte*, or perhaps *Bitte sehr.*'

Purslane sighed in defeat. 'Mr Holmes, you are clearly everything your brother says you are.'

'Then Mycroft *did* send you.'

Purslane shifted uncomfortably in his chair. 'I will put the matter delicately, sir. None of us is getting any younger. And in sending you here upon a mission of what we believe to be some gravity, your brother also dispatched me with orders to keep an eye on you and ensure that neither you nor Dr Watson, here, came to any harm.'

Growing more confused by the minute, Watson said, 'What does he mean, Holmes, that Mycroft sent you here? I thought this was supposed to be a simple holiday.' Before Holmes could reply he added somewhat testily, 'And didn't you say something earlier on about a glass of brandy?'

Holmes turned to the drinks cabinet and filled three glasses with Denis Mounie Grande Reserve. 'All,' he said as he turned back to his companions, 'is not entirely as it seems.'

'So I am beginning to realize,' Watson murmured darkly.

'Have a care, Mr Holmes,' warned Purslane, taking his glass. 'This business is about as secret as it can possibly be.'

'There is nothing I cannot say in front of Dr Watson,' Holmes informed him. 'I trust him with my life. Indeed, I have done just that, and more than once, in the past and he is equally well trusted by my brother.'

'Even so — '

But Holmes had already turned his attention back to Watson. 'My apologies, old friend, but perhaps when you hear the story, you will understand why I did not involve you sooner. It might just as easily have been something as nothing. As it is, I now believe that it is something very dark indeed.'

Somewhat mollified, Watson wandered to one of the radiators and, setting his glass down on the windowsill, warmed his hands. 'I'm listening,' he said.

'For some time now Mycroft has become increasingly concerned about the precedent set by Emperor Franz Joseph's annexation of Bosnia and Herzegovina and the ill-feeling that has engendered among the Serbs. He fears that Franz Joseph's continued attempts at empire-building will foment discord across Europe and provide the catalyst for the world war he is sure is coming. His misgivings only increased when he read about the robbery that occurred at Christie's a little under two weeks ago.'

'I remember that business,' said Watson. 'The robbers stole some antiquities and took a hostage to ensure there was no pursuit after they made their escape. The hostage, an unnamed spinster, as I recall, was never seen again.'

Holmes nodded. 'It was the object of the robbery which first drew Mycroft's attention — not antiquities, Watson, but rather part of a collection of papers and cyanotypes, blueprints in other words, relating to the architecture of the Habsburg Empire.'

'That's it! I remember wondering at the time what possible value such papers could have had to anyone but a collector.'

'In that you were correct. To you and me they are merely curiosities, but to a collector or historian they would be worth a small fortune. Far more money than the thieves could have raised to buy them legitimately.'

'And so they chose to steal them in such a public manner because . . . ?'

'Because Christie's has excellent security, my dear fellow. And the gang had no way of breaching it. Had they been able to break in, locate and then break into the strongroom, I have no doubt they would have done so. That proved to be beyond them. So they elected to wait until they could simply enter the building as prospective bidders, and then snatch what they wanted once it had been removed from the vault.'

'I still don't understand. What makes these papers so valuable?'

'Mycroft grasped their potential significance at once,' Holmes said. 'You see, suggestively the plans and papers that were stolen contained a preponderance of work by architects — Lukas von Hildebrandt, Emmanuel Fischer von Erlach and the like. Men who had all, at one time or another, worked upon the same project.'

'Which was . . . ?'

'The Imperial Palace.'

'The very place we visited yesterday.'

'Indeed. You see the significance, of course?'

'Not really.'

'Think, man. Why would anyone want the plans to such a building?'

Watson weighed his answer. 'Because it is a target of some kind? That anarchists would wish to somehow destroy it and — ' He broke off suddenly. 'Good grief! Are you saying there are plans afoot to assassinate the Austrian Royal Family?'

'Not at all. Rather, there was something

else about these cyanotypes that could potentially provide the thieves with what they really wanted — a means of entering and then leaving the palace undiscovered.'

'Why would they want to do that?'

'That is what Mycroft asked himself. The crime itself was an uncommon one. Therefore, it followed that the motive must be similarly uncommon. To steal some of the valuables contained in the Palace? Possible, but unlikely. To assassinate the Royals? They might just as easily kill them during any one of their many public engagements. So what was the true motive? When even Mycroft's vast intellect failed to provide a plausible answer, he asked me to come here on his behalf and see if I might have better luck.'

'So that's why you were so preoccupied as we traipsed around the Palace!'

'I am afraid so.'

'Then young Purslane here ... his presence has nothing to do with Houdini?'

'That's a point,' Purslane interrupted. 'Perhaps you can clear up that particular mystery for me, Mr Holmes. I've been somewhat curious as to your comings and goings where Mr Houdini ... is concerned.'

'Houdini's wife has been abducted and is being held to ransom,' Holmes replied laconically. 'That her abductors are indeed serious about this business is illustrated by their killing Houdini's personal assistant yesterday evening, though whether by accident or design remains to be seen.'

'And tonight . . . ?'

'Tonight they revealed to Houdini exactly what they want in return for his wife's safe return.'

'Which is . . . ?'

Holmes looked bleak as he remembered something the portly man had said earlier. '"I am going to break you, and then allow you to carry *me* where *I* want to go,"' he muttered.

Watson chuffed irritably. 'Just for tonight, Holmes, can you please spare us your riddles?'

Holmes's grey eyes sharpened. 'This evening, the price the kidnappers are demanding for the safe return of Bess Houdini was spelled out quite clearly. For reasons as yet unknown, they need to enter and leave a certain building unobserved. They have the plans to this building, but so far they haven't been able to work out how they can get in and out again without being detected. It is hardly a stretch of one's imagination to identify the building as the Imperial Palace.'

'Then these people were also the Christie's robbers?'

'Correct.'

'And I fear we must take Frances Lane's fate as some indication as to what befell the spinster they took hostage during the robbery.'

'There,' said Holmes, 'you are mistaken, Watson.'

'Eh?'

'There never *was* a spinster,' said Holmes. 'She was one of the gang all along, and only acting the part. I saw her tonight, out of the disguise she wore on that fateful day. And I believe she is the most dangerous one of them all, for I'm certain it was she who killed Frances Lane.'

'You have proof that she was there on the day of the robbery at Christie's?' asked Purslane.

'No. But no one had ever seen the spinster at Christie's before. No one knew her name, no one came forward subsequently to report a missing person, and no one responded to the description of the unfortunate hostage which was quite fully reported in all the newspapers at the time. All of which leads to one inescapable conclusion.'

'That the spinster never existed,' breathed Watson.

'Precisely.'

'The cunning beggars!'

'Yes. But one thing is crystal clear: if we

apply ourselves diligently to the task before us, we will save Bess Houdini and prevent whatever these people have planned for the Imperial Palace.'

'In other words,' Watson said, 'we kill two birds with one stone.'

Purslane said, 'I am completely at your disposal, Mr Holmes. What do you want me to do? Shall I arrange for our embassy here to issue a discreet warning to the Palace staff that an attack of some sort is imminent?'

'No,' replied Holmes. 'In the first place, we don't yet know the true purpose of this business. Is it an attack of some sort? Burglary? Assassination? Who can say, based upon the data we presently have before us? Secondly, we do not want to do anything to scare these criminals off, or force them into the murder of Houdini and his wife. For the moment, they do not suspect that anyone is on to them. Let us keep it that way.'

'I will, of course, have to inform your brother.'

'By all means do so, and as discreetly as you can. Tell Mycroft to put his trust in me, that I will manage this business and if at all possible bring about a satisfactory conclusion.'

'Yes, sir.'

'Our priority for now must be to ascertain

the motive for this affair, which in turn may lead us to the identities of its perpetrators.' He gave Purslane an incisive look. 'Did you see our quarry leave the church grounds earlier?'

'No, sir. I did what I could to draw that fellow with the pistol away from where I'd seen you take cover, and then made myself scarce.'

'Well, it is certain that they did not vanish into thin air, though that is the way it seemed. Tomorrow we will return to St Romedius's and see what clues we may find in daylight. In the meantime, you may request that Mycroft open some diplomatic channels for us. I believe we will need cooperation from the Austrian government to get what we require.'

'And that is?'

'The approximate time of Miss Lane's death, according to the coroner, and the exact spot where her body was discovered. We also need to identify the enemies of the emperor and his family, and for that we will need someone who understands the political and social situation here far better than we.'

'If anyone can point us in the right direction,' said Purslane, 'it is your brother.'

'Then contact him as soon as possible and tomorrow we will begin our investigations in earnest.'

'Very good, sir.'

Purslane rose, collected his hat and bade them both goodnight.

After he had gone, Watson finished his drink and set the empty glass back on the tray. The room was quiet but for the faint tapping of sleet at the window. 'I think I'll call it a night, too,' he said. Gathering up his overcoat, he started toward the door.

'I am sorry if I seemed to have misled you, old friend,' Holmes said quietly.

Watson turned, said shortly, 'That's all right.'

'By your tone of voice, I would say it is anything *but* all right.'

For a moment Watson hesitated. Then he said, 'I'm sorry, Holmes, but . . . well, I should think that after all our years together you would have trusted me with the true purpose of this so-called 'holiday'. But then,' he added before Holmes could reply, 'you seem to have made quite a habit of keeping secrets lately.'

'I beg your pardon?'

'I believe you know what I mean.'

'I can assure you that I do *not*.'

'Irene,' said Watson. 'Mrs Hastings, or Channing, or whatever she calls herself.'

'What about her?'

'Don't pretend, Holmes! I happened to see

her this morning. Here — in Vienna — as free as a bird and up to her usual tricks.'

Holmes studied him intently, then said, 'Ah.'

'*Ah*, indeed,' Watson replied. 'Good Lord, man, why did you tell me she and her husband were finished, when all the time you had decided to give them a second chance? Surely I deserved better from you than that?'

'Is that what she told you?' asked Holmes.

'Yes.'

'Those were her *exact* words?'

'More or less.' Watson thought a moment. 'She said you had given her a second chance, and that she would not let you down.'

'She mentioned me by name?'

''Mr Holmes', she said. Twice, as I recall.'

'And you naturally assumed she meant me.'

'Of course. Why would I do any . . . ?' Watson broke off as it dawned on him; then somewhat sheepishly he said, 'Mycroft again?'

Holmes nodded. 'For what it is worth, I was no happier about the Channings' fate than you, my friend. But there is very little that Mycroft does not know. When he discovered that I was investigating them, he at once saw that he could harness their particular talents in the interest of the Crown.'

'Turn them into *spies*, you mean?'

'Yes.'

'But they're *criminals!*'

'That is certainly true. But Mycroft is in the business of information, Watson. He will gather that information in any and every way possible, no matter how distasteful it may be to the likes of you and me. If Mrs Channing can beguile someone of high political or military standing, and by doing so discover something that may be of interest to His Majesty's Government, then as far as Mycroft is concerned it matters not one whit where the information comes from or how it was obtained.'

'Or how it affects anyone connected to it?'

'Or anyone connected to it.'

'By God, it is a foul business.'

'Of course. But like many other evils, it is also a necessary one. Whether we care for it or not, it is a business in which one bites, or is bitten.'

'I suppose so,' conceded Watson.

'Of course it is!' Holmes said with feeling. 'Do you think the other nations of the world baulk at using similar methods whenever they spy upon their neighbours and rivals? Of course they don't. And that is why Mycroft saw an opportunity to enlist a spy who might conceivably be more successful than most and, as you say, gave her a second chance.'

'How noble of him.'

'Who knows? Perhaps it *was*. Perhaps he saw something in the Channings that we missed, something that told him they would take that second chance and become better, more useful members of society because of it.'

Seeing that Watson still wasn't convinced, he shook his head. 'I do not expect or even ask you to understand it,' he continued. 'But it is the way of this modern world of ours, and it will in all likelihood only get worse. In any case, we have our own matters with which to contend. Let us be satisfied with that challenge.'

Watson allowed himself a brief smile. 'You *do* know, of course, we are far too old to go gallivanting around as we once did.'

'Nonsense,' Holmes said, brightening suddenly. 'I promised you one last great adventure, Watson. Well, now that we have it, let us play it to the hilt.'

20

As Silent as Sleep or Shadow

They were breakfasting in the hotel dining room the following morning when the *maître d'* came to their corner table and, clearing his throat discreetly, said, 'Excuse me, Herr Holmes. There is a man here to see you. He gave his name as Purslane.'

'Ask him to join us, if you will,' Holmes replied, dabbing at his mouth with a napkin.

A few moments later Purslane followed the *maître d'* up to their table, where Holmes bade him sit down and requested an extra coffee cup.

'What do you have for us?' he asked eagerly.

Purslane said quietly, 'Your brother has given me the name of a journalist who might be able to clarify the political situation here in Vienna.'

'Splendid. What is his name?'

'Walter Lenhard. He lives in the Wieden district of the city and works for various free-press newspapers. He is sympathetic to Britain through his marriage to a British woman. He can be trusted.'

'Then we shall pay him a visit directly,' Holmes decided. 'What did you find out about Miss Lane?'

'She was found outside a place called Adendorf, as I believe you know. Apparently, the poor woman's body, while afloat, became entangled in the reeds growing alongside the river. Had it not been for that, there is no telling how far the river would have carried her. Anyway, before being transferred to the city morgue here, she was taken to a local hospital in Adendorf, where the police surgeon performed a preliminary post-mortem and calculated the approximate time of death as ten hours before the body was discovered.'

With a sudden nod, Holmes abruptly rose to his feet. 'Excellent work, Purslane. I can see why you were Mycroft's first choice for this business.'

'I beg your pardon, sir?'

'But that, of course, is obvious,' Holmes continued as if Purslane hadn't spoken. 'In every aspect of his life Mycroft only makes one choice, and that only after considerable deliberation. Now, enjoy your coffee while I go back to my suite and consult my map.'

Without another word he strode purpose-fully away.

Purslane watched him go, then turned to Watson and asked, 'Is he always like this, Doctor?'

'By no means,' replied Watson. 'Sometimes he is much, much worse.'

They drank coffee for a moment, and then Watson said carefully, 'Would you mind very much if I . . . asked you a personal question, Purslane?'

Purslane gave him a curious look, then said, 'Not at all, sir.'

Watson hesitated, still not sure if he should share his thoughts with the younger man. Then he said, 'This wretched cloak-and-dagger business you're in . . . does it ever trouble you?'

'Trouble me, sir? I'm not quite sure what you mean.'

Watson looked around uneasily and then lowered his voice still further. 'Espionage. It is a dirty business, as far as I can see, and one that raises all kinds of ethical questions. I do not think I could stomach it, myself.'

Purslane considered that for a few moments, then said, 'Nevertheless, Doctor, *someone* has to do it.'

'Yes, of course. A necessary evil, Holmes calls it.'

'Quite so. And generally, the ends justify the means, in all sorts of ways that the man on the street is rarely if ever aware of. If we are able to gather as much information upon our enemies as possible and act accordingly to keep our country safe, then we have done our job to ensure the continuation of our peaceful way of life.'

'The end justifies the means,' Watson mused.

'Indeed, sir.' Purslane fell silent again, then leaned forward and said earnestly, 'It is an irony that so many of my colleagues have risked all in the protection of our country, paid the ultimate price for it, and yet they remain anonymous, unsung heroes. And make no mistake about it, Doctor, it can be a dangerous business, *highly* dangerous — even fatal, if one's identity is exposed to the enemy.'

'I am well aware of that,' Watson said soberly.

'Perhaps you are, sir. But *knowing* that, and still having the courage to take the job regardless . . . well, those individuals are truly the bravest of the brave.'

'Indeed.'

Watson allowed his mind to wander briefly. *The bravest of the brave*, he thought. It seemed difficult to imagine Irene . . . Violet . . . as a brave woman. And yet in accepting her role of spy, with all its attendant risks, was

205

she not showing more courage than he would have given her credit for?

He remembered what she had told him yesterday, about making amends. He had found that impossible to believe at the time. But now he was prepared to accept that perhaps she really meant it.

Fifteen minutes later Holmes returned to the table, dressed for travel and seemingly invigorated. 'Watson, get your hat and coat. Purslane, summon a cab, if you will. We are going to Enghilstrasse.'

Watson and Purslane exchanged puzzled glances.

'May we know *why* we are to go to Enghilstrasse, wherever it is?' Watson asked.

'Because it was there that Miss Lane met her death,' Holmes replied, as if the answer were obvious.

'How can you possibly know that?'

'Elementary, dear fellow.' But Holmes said no more until they had signed for their breakfast and tipped the waiter; then as they left the dining room, he explained, 'The Danube is divided into three sections, based upon the gradients through which it has to flow. They are as one might expect, known as the upper, middle and lower basins. The middle basin flows through Vienna at a rate of approximately four and a half kilometres an hour — roughly half the speed at which it flows through the upper basin, and about twice as fast as it flows through the lower basin. If we assume that the police surgeon's estimate as to Miss Lane's time of death is approximately correct and that she became 'entangled in the reeds' where she was found for, say, twenty minutes to half an hour, we can, therefore, identify the scene of the crime as Enghilstrasse.'

'Because it is forty-five kilometres upriver from where the body was found,' said Purslane, suddenly understanding. 'Forty-five kilometres being the distance the body was carried by the current.'

'Precisely.'

'What do you hope to discover there, sir?'

'That I cannot say,' Holmes said. 'But even the smallest, seemingly insignificant fact may act as a signpost.'

A few minutes later, they were in a cab and passing through the misty streets of Vienna, bound for Enghilstrasse. They soon found themselves dropped at one end of a long row of large, bow-fronted residential houses that faced the Danube. The day was grey but dry, and what little snow had fallen the night before had nearly melted. The river looked especially cheerless, its waters a sluggish and uninviting olive green.

Holmes paid the driver then turned to his companions. 'Knock at each door in turn, if you will, and enquire as to whether or not the occupant noticed anything unusual the night before last,' he instructed. 'Anything at all, no matter how seemingly trivial. Meanwhile, I shall examine the pavement that runs along the river.'

He crossed the road at his usual brisk pace, already fully intent upon his task. Shaking his head, Purslane then turned his attention to the row of houses before them. 'How is your German, Doctor?'

'Nowhere near good enough for the kind of questioning Holmes has in mind.'

'Then we'll work together.'

While Holmes paused every so often, occasionally kneeling in order to examine the kerb or the low brick wall beyond which a chill wind rippled the surface of the Danube, Watson and Purslane walked up the path of the first house. Climbing the steps to reach the front door, Purslane rang the bell.

Their investigation quickly proved to be fruitless; they got no response at most of the houses. At others, the residents eyed them with understandable suspicion and said they had seen nothing at all.

Disappointed but persistent, they kept at it, until, near the end of the street, they came to a property that seemed to be in such poor condition that Watson assumed it must be empty. He was wrong, for when Purslane knocked at the flaking door panels the door was opened almost at once by a tall, thin woman in her seventies, whose long, wrinkled face was crowned by a wild mane of frizzy, near-white hair.

She looked from Purslane to Watson with open distrust, and said, '*Ja?*'

Purslane tipped his hat and spoke in rapid German. 'We're sorry to disturb you, madam, but we believe there may have been some sort of disturbance in the street here two nights ago and we are looking for information that might corroborate this.'

The old woman's watery blue eyes shuttled from one face to the other. Watson smiled somewhat hesitantly in an effort to assure her of their honest intentions.

'Are you the police?' she demanded finally.

'We are on official business, yes,' Purslane replied, deciding that since he was working for the British government, he was bending the truth only slightly. 'Have you seen or heard anything unusual?'

'I have indeed. And a more shameful sight I have never beheld in all my life. Two women fighting like common trollops!'

Watson and Purslane exchanged a quick

look. 'What time was this, Frau . . . ?'

'Seidl.'

'What time was this, Frau Seidl? And what happened, exactly?'

'Well, I don't know the exact time. Sometime between seven and eight o'clock, certainly,' said the old woman. 'I was just resting my eyes, you see. I don't sleep well at night, I never have. I prefer to nap during the day and spend my nights reading. So there I was, just resting my eyes, when suddenly I heard a scream outside. I looked out of my window' — she gestured vaguely towards a window on the first floor, directly above the door — 'and there they were, two women, fighting with each other, as if they hadn't got the shame they were born with.'

'What happened?' Purslane prodded.

'They were struggling with each other — drunk, I daresay! Then one of them hit the other one on the head and her hat fell off. Well, I knew then that if they were going to carry on like that, one of them was going to injure the other or worse, so I decided to come down and tell them to take their differences else-where. I mean, the man with them wasn't doing anything more than just standing there, watching them — useless, like all men!'

'So you decided to break it up yourself?'

'Yes. And I would have, too! They didn't

frighten *me!* But as I was putting on my dressing gown the girl who was doing all the screaming suddenly stopped. I went back to my window and saw that she'd passed out, and the other girl and the man were now standing over her. Dead to the world, she was!'

'What happened then?'

'They all got back in their car and drove away.'

Speaking slowly to allow for his less-than-fluent German, Watson said, 'They had a car then?'

'Oh yes,' Frau Seidl replied. 'Most definitely. Saw it with my own eyes, I did. They'd stopped it in the middle of the road, right where that man is . . . what *is* he doing, anyway?'

Watson glanced over his shoulder. There, in the middle of the street, Holmes was crouched down using his pocket glass to study some barely discernible marks in the road. 'I think he is a surveyor of some sort,' he said, using the first thought that came to mind. 'Now, if you could tell me more about this car — ?'

'Nothing to tell. It just drove right off and that was that,' the old woman replied.

'You mean that was the last you saw of them?'

The woman nodded.

'So you actually saw them drive away?'

'Yes.'

'All of them?'

'What kind of a question is that? Of course, all of them!'

'You're sure?'

'Well, obviously I can't be *completely* sure. It was dark, for goodness' sake, and the weather was wretched. But they didn't leave anyone behind, I can promise you that!'

'Could you see what colour the car was?' asked Purslane.

'I didn't notice.'

'Was it large? Small?'

'I know little about such contraptions,' said Frau Steidl.

'But surely you could tell, at least within a little, how big or small it was?'

'Small.'

'Are you certain?'

'I told you so, didn't I?'

'Yes, of course. Can you describe the two women for us? And the man with them?'

Frau Steidl considered briefly. 'Youngish. The man was very tall. I didn't see much of the woman who hit her friend. She had black hair, I think. The woman who passed out, when her hat came off, I saw that she had fair hair.'

'Blonde, you mean?'

She frowned in thought. 'No. Light, but not blonde. Sandy or perhaps red. It was snowing, so it was difficult to see anything properly.'

'So you didn't see their faces?'

'No.'

'Very well. You have been most helpful, Frau Steidl. *Danke schön.*'

They turned and started down the steps.

The woman called after them. 'There was one thing,' she said.

They turned back. 'Yes?' Purslane asked.

'Well, I know I'm deaf,' the old woman said. 'Who wouldn't be, at my age? But I'm not *that* deaf.'

Purslane narrowed his eyes. 'I'm sorry, I don't understand.'

'The *car*,' Frau Steidl said irritably. 'It passed right by me. I stood here and watched it go. But it didn't make a sound.'

'You mean the motor was turned off?' asked Watson.

'No, no. It couldn't run if the motor was off, now could it?' she replied. 'It was silent!'

'It made no sound whatsoever?'

'It was as silent as sleep or shadow,' she confirmed.

'And it *drove* off? You didn't see anyone pushing it?'

'Sir, I am not blind,' she said petulantly.

Purslane tipped his hat. 'Thank you again, Frau Steidl. You have been a great help.'

They crossed the road toward Holmes, who had just finished his examination of the road and was waiting for them. 'What did you discover?' he asked.

Watson gave him a brief report of the exchange. When he'd finished, Holmes said, 'So my hypothesis was correct. It was the girl who killed Frances Lane.' He turned and peered out across the river above the rippling surface.

'The Steidl woman's testimony would seem to confirm my own suspicions,' he continued. 'When she left the Royal during our meeting with Houdini, Miss Lane was somehow captured by the gang for purposes as yet unknown. I believe it is most likely that they wanted to find out where she had been that evening, since it is doubtful they would feel the need to apply any more pressure on Houdini than he was already under. In any event, she was bundled into their car and, as they were taking her to their base of operations or some secluded spot where they could question her without fear of interruption, she tried to escape.

'The car came to a halt approximately where the Steidl woman indicated. On the

214

road surface there,' he pointed, 'I detected minute traces of what appear to be carbon-enriched rubber, suggestive of automobile tyres coming to an abrupt halt.

'So — Frances Lane makes a dash for freedom, the second woman goes in pursuit and there is a struggle. The blow intended to quieten Miss Lane only serves instead to make her more desperate to escape. Her captor panics; he grabs her around the throat, perhaps to silence her screams, and caught up in the heat of the moment, applies sufficient force to choke her to death instead.

'There follows a moment of shock. Then, thinking quickly, one or other of the kidnappers drags the body to the retaining wall there and drops it into the river before deciding to turn the event to their advantage.'

'How much of this is just speculation?' asked Purslane.

Holmes gave him a withering glance. 'Hardly any of it,' he replied, making a careless gesture back toward the pavement. 'The last time we saw her, Miss Lane was wearing a sage-green pair of what are popularly known as Astoria shoes. That particular style of shoe has very smooth leather soles, which make them ideal for dancing in. The scuffed heels I noticed when I examined Miss Lane's body at the morgue told me she had certainly been dragged *somewhere* post-mortem. Had both her companions been involved in the disposal of the body, they would have *carried* her to the retaining wall. And caught in the uneven surface of the bricks which form the wall nearby I have found two strands of some distinctive chequered cotton fibre which would seem to match those of the wrap she was wearing at the time of her death. I imagine these marks indicate the spot where the body was pushed over into the river.'

'So it wasn't murder, as such,' breathed Watson.

'No. But once it happened, the malefactors were certainly not burdened by conscience.' He tapped his lip with the edge of the pocket glass. 'A car that makes no sound . . . ' he murmured. 'That would certainly explain how they could have left St Romedius's so quietly and without alerting me to the fact that they had a car waiting for them in the back alley. But is there such a thing, Purslane? A car that makes no sound?'

'If there is,' replied Purslane, 'I have yet to hear about it. But that's not to say it doesn't exist.'

'Well, if it exists and we haven't heard about it, there cannot be too many of them. If we find the car, it follows that we may well find our quarry.'

'I'll see to it immediately,' Purslane promised.

'Good man,' said Holmes briskly. 'And while you are thus occupied, Watson and I will go and see this reporter Mycroft has recommended — Herr Lenhard.'

21

The Fourth Threat

Walter Lenhard's apartment was located in a small, densely packed region near the city centre. Lenhard, a freelance journalist whose work appeared mostly in such papers as the *Czernowitz Allgemeine Zeitung* and *Czernowitzer Tagblatt*, occupied a small flat within the Freihaus, a sprawling tenement complex that had been built two centuries earlier and was now completely at odds with the district's more opulent palaces.

As Holmes and Watson climbed the echoing stone staircase to the fourth floor, where Lenhard lived, it was hard to imagine that this area, now almost a slum, had once sheltered the likes of Brahms and Strauss the Younger. The block itself was drab, its square, unimaginative lines constructed from cheap, pitted bricks now stained black by decades' worth of accumulated grime. Orderly rows of small, dark windows had overlooked their arrival in a narrow street where the sun never quite managed to penetrate and here and there on the few small balconies, the

218

occupants had tried to cultivate window boxes in an attempt to soften the harsh reality of their mean existence.

It was difficult to imagine a journalist with such prestigious credentials living in such squalor, but when they introduced themselves to Frau Lenhard, and she led them into a small, chilly living-room, the answer became all too obvious.

Lenhard sat in a wheelchair by the room's only window, his withered legs covered by a threadbare blanket. He was in his early forties, but his illness had taken a shocking toll. To Watson, Lenhard's laboured wheezing as he took each breath, the high colour in his cheeks and the apparently complete paralysis of his left arm all suggested paralytic poliomyelitis. He was badly emaciated, his chin covered in stubble, and his dark eyes — the single most alert thing about him — were couched in fleshy pouches. His hair was fine, brown, uncombed and untrimmed.

His wife looked little better. She was almost as gaunt as her husband. Her face was long and hollow-cheeked, almost bloodless, her deep-set eyes were of the palest blue, her hair wispy and fair. 'Walter,' she called ahead as she showed them in, 'you have visitors. This is Mr Sherlock Holmes and Dr Watson.'

Lenhard had been staring out the window,

tapping his right hand impatiently upon the arm of his chair. Now he turned around, as if disturbed from deep thought, and looked happily surprised to see the newcomers. He nodded, as if comparing them to the images he had seen in *The Strand*, then wheeled himself forward to greet them.

'Well, we certainly do not get many visitors here, Mr Holmes, and certainly not of *your* calibre.' He shook hands with them, his grip showing surprising strength. 'If you have come to see me, it is because your brother has sent you. And if Mycroft has sent you, it is because you need information. Am I correct?'

'I cannot fault your reasoning,' Holmes replied. 'Is this a convenient time for you?'

'Any time is convenient for me,' Lenhard said wearily. His English was good, but his voice was just a low, papery memory of what it had once been. 'As you can see, I seldom leave this apartment, which means that my stories — they are little more than fillers these days — have to find *me*.'

'And yet,' said Holmes, indicating a writing table in the corner that was covered in papers and open reference books, many of which had slips of paper marking relevant pages, 'according to my brother, you are the man to seek out if one wishes to know the political landscape of Austria.'

'Your brother . . . ' Lenhard smiled. 'How is Mycroft these days? I have not seen him since . . . ah, but that would be telling, and he is a great one for secrets.'

'He is well,' Holmes said. 'And still has an interest in international politics.'

'More than an interest, I would say,' Lenhard said with a knowing smile. 'But you are correct in what you say, Mr Holmes. Before I was struck down by this miserable disease I built an impressive network of, ah . . . shall we call them 'sources'? The word is infinitely preferable to 'informants', which carries all manner of distasteful, even criminal, connotations. And even though I am now but a shade of my former self, I am still reasonably well informed. Furthermore, I owe your brother much. Though he would probably have me killed for saying it — and he *could* do, quite easily, I suspect — he is a kind man with a big heart.'

He gestured with his good hand. 'Please, gentlemen, be seated. While you tell me what it is that Mycroft — you — wish to know, Margaret here will be pleased to prepare tea and scones — her one concession to the land of her birth.'

'We have already eaten,' Watson said quickly. That this couple was already living a hand-to-mouth existence was all too obvious.

The last thing he wanted to do was deprive them of the few luxuries they still possessed.

'Then please, ask away,' said Lenhard. 'You may speak freely before Margaret.'

As they made themselves comfortable, Holmes said, 'We have reason to believe that someone is planning to break into the Imperial Palace. What we should like to know is *why*.'

Lenhard absorbed Holmes's words. Then remarked, 'Is it an assassination plot, do you think? Aimed at our emperor?'

'I do not believe so, but neither can I rule it out completely. What we *do* know, however, is that we are dealing with an enemy who has already shown themselves to be quite capable of abduction and murder.'

'So you are trying to piece together a list of suspects,' mused Lenhard. 'Who would wish to enter the Palace, what they plan to do when they gain that entrance, and how they stand to benefit from it.'

'Precisely.'

'Then I do not envy you your task, Mr Holmes. For if it is suspects you're after, I can provide you with four distinct threats straight away.'

'Then let us begin with the most likely one.'

Lenhard considered the matter for a few

moments. His breathing was a painful, liquidy rasp in the cold silence of the cluttered room. 'Archduke Franz Ferdinand,' he said softly.

'Franz Joseph's son?'

'His nephew,' corrected Lenhard. 'Franz Joseph's only son, Archduke Rudolph, committed suicide over twenty years ago. And the emperor's brother, Karl Ludwig, died whilst on a pilgrimage to the Holy Lands.'

'Was there any suspicion of foul play?' asked Watson.

Lenhard allowed himself an ironic smile. 'None, I'm afraid. The poor man drank some infected water; it was as simple as that. As for Franz Joseph's wife . . . well, she was assassinated by an Italian anarchist in 1898 . . . all of which means that Franz Ferdinand is next in line.'

'Interesting.'

'Perhaps more interesting than you think, Mr Holmes. You see, there is no love lost between Franz Joseph and his nephew. Indeed, I have it on the highest authority that Franz Joseph will only allow Franz Ferdinand to succeed him at all on condition that his children — that is, the children Franz Ferdinand has had with a woman called Sophie Chotek von Chotkova, of whom Franz Joseph heartily disapproves — will not be allowed to succeed him to the throne.'

'Could that change if Franz Joseph was somehow . . . removed from power?'

'Not easily, and I suspect, certainly not in Franz Ferdinand's lifetime. He has made too many enemies in the past, powerful ones who would I am sure do everything they could to delay or otherwise obstruct any attempt he made to change the line of succession.'

'Nevertheless, we cannot afford to discount him,' Holmes decided. 'Please, continue.'

But Lenhard began tapping at the arm of his wheelchair again, his mind wandering as he gazed aimlessly about the room.

'Herr Lenhard?' Holmes prompted.

'Uh, my apologies. My mind was elsewhere.' He took another bubbling breath and said, 'Well, you could do worse than consider Count Franz Conrad as another suspect. Conrad controls the army and is known to favour an aggressive foreign policy enforced by military action. At the moment the only thing stopping him from plunging Austria into another crisis is Franz Joseph, who has, in light of our recent troubles, become rather more . . . diplomatically minded.'

'I can see that he might be a possibility,' Holmes agreed. 'But surely he may come and go as he pleases at the Palace, and therefore has little if any need to find an alternative means of entry. Besides, I feel that there is something else at stake here, something less . . . obvious.'

'There is always the Black Hand.'

'The Black Hand,' said Watson. 'We have already had a run-in with those devils.'

'Then you would do well not to under-estimate them. It is known that they have infiltrated Austria. It is known that they are right here, in the capital, and are plotting some sort of terrorist act to destabilize our government.'

'It seems then that we are spoilt for choice,' Watson said. 'But forgive me, Herr Lenhard. You mentioned *four* potential threats. What is the fourth?'

'The most dangerous threat of all, I am afraid. The threat we simply are not yet *aware* of. We know the Russians are fomenting discord throughout the Balkan States. The French? They have no love for our emperor, certainly not since we allied ourselves with Germany in order to limit French interests throughout Europe. And what of Italy? They are already threatening military action, should we send troops into Serbia to quell the growing unrest there. Who can say?'

Holmes nodded. 'Well, you have been most helpful, Herr Lenhard, and you have certainly given us much food for thought.' He stood, and drew on his gloves. 'Incidentally, I believe you are missing your favourite pipe. A cherry and birchwood Ropp?'

Puzzled, Lenhard glanced at his wife then back at Holmes. 'How on earth did you know that?'

'Herr Lenhard, when I enter a room and smell the unmistakable aroma of Afrikander Colonial Flake, when I see a pipe-rack with one missing pipe and I see its owner displaying all the classic signs of the habitual pipe-smoker who is not able to indulge his craving, all that leads me to suspect that he has mislaid his favourite pipe. If it were *not* his favourite, he would simply take another from his otherwise well-stocked pipe-rack. Besides, sir, the mouthpiece of your favourite pipe shows ample evidence of its near-constant use.'

'Remarkable!' breathed Lenhard. 'Yes . . . yes, I have indeed mislaid my favourite pipe. I cannot for the life of me remember where I put it. But how could you describe it so perfectly to me?'

'It is within my line of sight at this very moment,' Holmes said. Crossing the room, he picked up the pipe from the carpet behind the journalist's desk. 'It must have fallen here without your realizing it.'

'Sir, you are a life-saver,' Lenhard said as he eagerly accepted the pipe.

'Let us hope so,' Holmes said soberly, 'for the sake of the people whose lives I am indeed trying to save.'

22

An Uncommon Anarchist

As they left the overcrowded tenement behind and made their way back to the main thoroughfare, Holmes said, 'I shall, of course, wire Mycroft later today and tell him that Herr Lenhard was of great help to us. Within a very short time thereafter I imagine Lenhard will receive some small and secret remuneration from His Majesty's Government.'

'Well, tell Mycroft not to make it *too* small,' Watson said. 'The poor fellow could certainly use it.'

'Well said. Now, are you fit enough for the next stage of today's itinerary, or would you prefer to stop and feed the inner man first?'

'I need no break, thank you. That's something else about growing old. The appetite — once such a source of pleasure — tends to desert one.'

'Then we shall hail a cab and make directly for the church of St Romedius. It is my hope that in daylight I may discover something I overlooked last night — something that may enable us to find our quarry.'

They caught a cab and once again followed the winding route out to Vienna's Second District and the isolated Blutstrasse with its jagged remnants of a once-proud church sandwiched between tall, featureless warehouses.

'What a godforsaken spot,' said Watson as they passed through the sagging gates and moved towards the shell of the church.

'A strange phrase indeed to bestow upon what once was God's house,' Holmes replied.

They entered the desolate building. It was eerily silent and strangely claustrophobic; in daylight the original fire damage was much more obvious. The walls were smudged with great black patches that the elements had been unable to scour away. Here and there still lay the aged, charred remains of old pews and rafters.

Holmes used his cane to indicate the position of the crypt entrance, which Houdini's captors had concealed with dirt and rubbish before leaving. Then they went to the far end, crossing what Holmes could see now had once been a vestry. A moment later they stepped through the curtain of ragged ivy and out into the narrow dead-end alley through which the kidnappers had made their exit.

In daylight the cobbled thoroughfare looked every bit as dismal and empty as it had the previous night. The thin strip of road ran arrow-straight until it reached a corner some hundred yards away. Every so often traffic passed in one direction or the other, but it seemed that there was no longer any need for anyone to pass along this lonely lane.

While Watson watched, Holmes knelt and began to examine the icy ground. At length his attention was taken by a small, dark puddle little bigger than a two-*coronae* coin, which had gathered in a dip between the cobbles. He removed one glove and was about to dip the tip of his right forefinger into the liquid when he seemed to change his mind, and bent forward to sniff it instead.

He looked over one shoulder. 'Here, Watson. What do you make of this?'

Watson joined him, resting his weight on his cane as he lowered himself to the ground beside his companion. 'What *should* I make of it?' he asked.

'The smell.'

Watson put his face close to the small puddle and sniffed. 'Ammonia,' he decided, and then wrinkled his nose. 'Possibly some cat . . . maybe even that fox you told me about . . . ' He sniffed again. 'It has a sort of . . . sulphur-like smell to it, as well.'

'And what could account for that?'

'I don't know . . . some sort of bacteria? A natural gas of some sort?' He straightened up. 'Given that it is coming from that liquid, I would hazard a guess at some sort of leak from the sewers below. There is a road gully just over there.'

Holmes considered the possibility, but then shook his head. 'I think not. I have spent enough years at my chemistry to recognize the unmistakable odor of sulphuric acid when I smell it.'

'Acid! Where the devil did *that* come from? And what's it doing here?'

'I believe I know,' Holmes said thoughtfully. 'Come, let us follow this lane to its conclusion.'

But the lane yielded no further information, and as they returned to the church, light snow began to fall again.

It was just as they were pushing through the wall of ivy and back into the church that Watson was suddenly grabbed by the right bicep and roughly dragged forward. He let out a startled yelp and stumbled several paces. As Holmes reached out to help him, the ice-cold barrel of a handgun pressed hard against his temple, and a heavily accented voice hissed, 'The decision as to whether you live or die is yours, *stranac*.'

231

Holmes froze immediately and raised both hands. 'We choose to live,' he said quietly.

Their attackers moved forward from where they had been hiding against the inner wall, and in seconds Holmes and Watson found themselves surrounded by five men, all heavily dressed against the inclement weather. One of them, a vaguely familiar-looking boy of no more than sixteen, shoved Holmes in the chest with both hands. As Holmes staggered back, the youngster snatched the cane from his hand and flung it as far as he could.

'*Stranac*,' he said with a disparaging curl of the lip.

Holmes recognized him at once. Here was the hot-headed rioter whom he had encountered during their meeting with Freud at the Beserlpark Alsergrund. Holmes had shoved a chair into his path before he could reach them, and the resulting collision had sent the youth sprawling, but when he attacked again Holmes had been forced to employ *baritsu* to knock him unconscious.

One look into the boy's eyes told Holmes that recognition had been mutual. He also saw that what the boy lacked in height he more than made up for in sheer hatred. Pushing his face close to Holmes's, he chattered for a few moments, then pulled his right hand back as if to administer a slap.

'*Princip!*'

The boy halted, turned to the man who had called his name and stopped himself. Holmes turned to regard the speaker, and again recognition was instant, for here was the black-bearded rabble-rouser who had been stirring up the crowd in the park that same day. He gave the youth, Princip, a firm shake of the head, and then put the pistol he had just held at Holmes's temple back into the pocket of his pea coat.

'Come,' he said, and draped an arm around Holmes's shoulders so that he could lead him out of the circle his men had formed around him. With his free hand he gestured to Watson. 'You too, Herr Doktor.'

Watson glanced at the bearded man's companions. A rougher lot he had never seen. Then he eased past them to join his friend.

'You must forgive Gavrilo,' said the bearded man, referring to the youth. 'Gavrilo is young and he has all the passion of youth, as well as all its recklessness. He is angry, and with some justification. He had to watch his parents struggle in the grip of poverty from which there was no escape. He saw six of his brothers and sisters die because there was no money for food. Ha! There was no food anyway, even if there had been money. And certainly there were no medicines available to save them when they weakened and fell sick. All Gavrilo could do was watch and know he could do nothing to prevent the inevitable.

'When Franz Joseph — about whom you appear to have been making enquiries — annexed Bosnia and Herzegovina for the Austro-Hungarian Empire, that was the last straw for Gavrilo; as it was for a great number of the Slav people, who did not wish to be part of the empire. So Gavrilo ran away from school and ended up here, determined to do something about it.'

'And he fell in with the Black Hand,' said Holmes.

The bearded man stopped and studied him shrewdly. 'It still takes some getting used to, that name,' he said. 'The Black Hand, as it has become known, was only formed a few months ago. Before that we were Mlada Bosna, and before that Narodna Odbrana. But always our aim has been the same — to liberate the Serbs under Austro-Hungarian rule.' Abruptly he held out his right hand. 'Forgive my manners, Herr Holmes, Herr Doktor. I am Javor Vasiljavic. Now we know each other.'

As Holmes shook hands, he said, 'You seem to have the advantage of us, *Gouspodn* Vasiljavic.'

Vasiljavic raised one bushy eyebrow. 'You

234

speak my language?'

'I am afraid *Gouspodn* is the extent of my Serbian,' said Holmes. 'This is clearly no chance meeting, sir. You obviously followed my companion and me from the home of Herr Lenhard.'

Vasiljavic nodded. 'His days as a reporter are more or less over, I fear. But he remains a man of many . . . *useful* . . . connections. Through him we can spread our message for a free Serbia, and every so often confound the Austro-Hungarian authorities with what we are pleased to call *misinformation*. But we are not so naïve as to imagine we are the only people who use Lenhard. And so we keep an eye on him, to see who else visits him. And when no less a figure than the great Sherlock Holmes *himself* visits Lenhard . . . well, I want to know why.'

'And yet you have already answered your own question,' Holmes replied. 'You said I had been making enquiries about Franz Joseph. So I have.'

'That was little more than an educated guess,' Vasiljavic said. 'Karl Lenhard is a man of many interests and he is knowledgeable about all of them, but he has one particular . . . is the word *forte*?'

'It is.'

'And that *forte* is the political situation

here in Austria. I cannot think of any other man who knows more about the intrigues of this country . . . and can thus think of no other reason why you would have visited him, Herr Holmes.'

'I have reason to suspect that someone may be plotting the Emperor some harm.'

'And you suspect the Black Hand?'

'So far I have found no reason *not* to suspect the Black Hand.'

'And I suppose you would like me to confirm such a fact for you?'

'On the contrary, *Gouspodyn* Vasiljavic, I expect you to deny it and with good reason.'

'I do deny it. Now, if we were under the command of a hot-head like young Princip Gavrilo over there, well . . . I think you might have some justification in suspecting the Black Hand. Left to his own devices, he would start a world war, that one. But he is nothing more than a foot soldier, and I suspect he will remain one, for his impulsive and sometimes violent behaviour is something I believe he will never grow out of.

'But for now, older and hopefully wiser heads rule our group and those older and wiser heads have only one aim. The Black Hand wants a free Serbia and to get that it needs *support*. A political assassination is one thing. To destroy part of Austria's heritage and kill many innocent members of staff in the process would only lose us whatever support we already enjoy. Besides, Herr Holmes, we are *men*. *Proud* men. If we kill, we do so in public, not behind closed doors.

'As for Franz Joseph himself . . . he is almost untouchable as far as we are concerned. Were we to do anything to destabilize this already destabilized country it might indeed end in war . . . and that is something none of us wants.'

He stopped and chuckled. 'Of course, I don't expect you to take my word for it. I am, after all, just a common anarchist.'

'You strike me as a rather *uncommon* anarchist,' Holmes said. 'If you give me your assurance that you are not engaged in anything involving the Imperial Palace or its inhabitants, then I will accept it.'

'A wise thing to do when the man giving you that assurance carries a gun.'

Holmes had no idea whether or not he was joking.

Then Vasiljavic turned and called, 'Princip! Fetch Herr Holmes's cane!'

The young Serbian had been lounging against the wall with the others. Now he stepped forward and took up a challenging posture, his fists clenched. 'Let him fetch it himself,' he called back.

Vasiljavic's wide shoulders moved beneath the dark material of his jacket. 'I gave you an order, Princip. You will carry it out, like a good soldier.'

It was clear from his stance that Princip Gavrilo had no intention of obeying. He refused to move and continued to glare at his leader. But Vasiljavic only held his stare, accepting the contest of wills to which he had been invited and knowing that the boy would never ever beat him.

Seconds passed. Snow continued to feather down around them. Then Gavrilo's eyes dropped away from those of his commander, and grudgingly he slouched across the church until he located Holmes's cane. Picking it up, he brought it over, his head down, his shoulders hunched, hating the humiliation that Vasiljavic was forcing him to endure.

'Here.' He thrust the cane at Holmes.

Holmes took it.

'Satisfied?' Gavrilo demanded of his leader.

Vasiljavic nodded. 'But next time I tell you to do something, Princip, you do it immediately. Understand me?'

Gavrilo looked up at him from lowered brows, his expression as surly as his tone. 'I understand.'

'Good. Now go back to the others.'

As Gavrilo obeyed, Holmes said, 'May I

238

take it that Dr Watson and I are free to go?'

Vasiljavic turned to him, surprised. 'Of course. But remember this, Herr Holmes. You and I, we have no quarrel. You have your business to attend and we have ours. But should you ever turn your attentions to the Black Hand, we will have no option but to stop you by any means we deem necessary.'

Holmes's mouth tightened at the threat. Still, there was little point in taking issue with Vasiljavic now. He had delivered his warning and was already turning away, making quick gestures with his enormous hands and barking orders at his men. As one they filed through the ivy curtain out into the dead-end alley beyond. Gavrilo was the last to go, and then only after he had given Holmes one final, murderous glance.

'How dare they treat us like that,' Watson said angrily. 'Especially that boy! He is well on the road to ruin, mark my words!'

'Probably so,' Holmes agreed. 'Nevertheless, this meeting has been an enlightening one.'

'How so?'

'It has convinced me that our present line of questioning is unlikely to produce anything of use to us. Therefore the time has come to approach the problem from a different direction.'

He turned and followed the path back toward the church gates. Around them, snow began to heap itself on the worn crosses and headstones still visible through the tall grass to either side.

'And which direction is that?' asked Watson as he caught up.

'Suppose this business serves a dual purpose? Suppose it is not just about gaining entry to the Imperial Palace? Suppose it is also about Houdini himself?'

'Now you've lost me, Holmes.'

'There seems to me to be something personal about this affair. From what I overheard here last night, the man behind this business wishes to *punish* Houdini for some reason, to break his spirit just as St Romedius broke the spirit of the bear that attacked him. Why should this be? What is the connection between them — a connection of which even Houdini himself seems unaware? If we can discover that, we may well be able to uncover the identity of our enemy. His identity, and his whereabouts. Come, old friend — let us rendezvous with Purslane and take this investigation one stage further.'

23

The King of Clubs

Purslane was waiting for them in the lobby when they arrived back at the Grand. As soon as they came through the doors he jumped up and hurried over to intercept them.

'You have found our silent car,' guessed Holmes.

'I have indeed, sir. It's known as a Waverley, and the reason it runs silently is because — '

'It runs on electricity,' finished Holmes.

Purslane looked crestfallen. 'How did you discover that?'

'Watson and I found a small pool of sulphuric acid in the alleyway behind the church. And since I could find no other logical reason for it to be there, I could only conclude that it had leaked from a battery, or a series of batteries . . . used, perhaps, to power a silent automobile.'

'Well, you are right,' said Purslane. 'The Waverley Electric, to give it its full name, is powered by no fewer than thirty batteries.'

'There cannot be many such vehicles

around,' mused Holmes. 'Is there any way we can locate a list of owners?'

'There is one, I believe, but it is based at the Waverley company's offices in the United States. I have already telegraphed them, requesting a copy.'

'Then all we can do is wait for it to arrive. But no matter, Purslane. It is possible that we may put our time to better use by following a more promising line of enquiry.'

'Enquiry into what, sir?'

'Houdini himself,' said Holmes. 'And for that we shall require a newspaper archive.'

'There is no one, single archive,' Purslane explained. 'I imagine every newspaper maintains its own.'

'But they will all have reported on many of the same subjects. And our search will encompass only one — Houdini.'

'Very well. We'll start with the back numbers of the *Kronen Zeitung*. It is a somewhat sensationalist newspaper, but it has an interesting political stance and quite a bit of influence. It also reports on a wide variety of topics.'

Purslane stepped outside and bought a copy of that day's *Krone* — as it was more familiarly called — and turned to the back page to obtain the address of its offices. Shortly thereafter the three of them found themselves at the top of the Muthgasse, a busy street that was within walking distance of the city's northernmost railway bridge.

With Purslane smoothing the way ahead, they were eventually given directions to the newspaper's morgue, which was situated in the basement. It proved to be a large, airless room with a central aisle set between row after row of ceiling-high wooden shelves; each of these was stacked with cartons upon which had been written a brief summary of their contents and the dates to which those contents related.

A petite woman seated behind a cluttered desk at the far end of the basement looked up as they approached. About the same age as Purslane, she had lovely skin, serene blue eyes and a small, heart-shaped mouth. She wore her dark hair to nape-length, with a side parting and tight curls. As they drew closer, they saw that the nameplate on her desk identified her as Eveline Bauer.

'*Guten Tag, meine Herren,*' she said, smiling. 'How may I help you?'

Purslane made their request, speaking German so quickly that it was all Watson could do to even catch the name 'Houdini'.

Miss Bauer told them to be seated at one of the tables reserved for researchers, only one of which was currently in use, and then went off to check the shelves. She soon returned with a box folder, which she set before Purslane.

He smiled at her. '*Danke sehr.*'

Once she'd returned to her desk, Purslane opened the folder and quickly perused its contents. 'This is all primarily concerned with the recent cancellations of Houdini's shows,' he said in disappointment. 'There has been no shortage of rumours, by the look of things. Houdini's producers have apparently run off with all his money ... Houdini's temperamental rages have caused a rupture between him and his company ... Houdini is awaiting the arrival of a brother named Dash, who performs all his stunts for him ... but nothing else of any import.'

He stood up, returned the folder to Miss Bauer and in German said, 'I'm sorry, but ... is this all you have on Herr Houdini?'

'I am afraid so. To be honest with you, I didn't even know we had that much.'

'Well ... thank you, anyway.'

'You did not find what you were looking for?'

'No.'

'What *are* you looking for, exactly?'

'That's the problem,' Purslane replied with a boyish grin. 'We don't *know*, exactly. We won't know until we find it.' He caught her look and added, 'I know it sounds mad. But then, we *are* British.'

She laughed and took the box folder from him. 'I'm sorry we couldn't help you.'

'You are forgiven.'

He, Holmes and Watson were about to leave when Miss Bauer said, 'I wonder if there's anything in the Eder file.'

'I beg your pardon?'

'The Eder file,' she repeated. Then as Purslane continued to look blankly at her: 'The King of Clubs.'

He, Holmes and Watson exchanged a look. 'I'm sorry,' he said. 'I don't understand what you mean by 'The King of Clubs'.'

'Yes. It was his stage name. He was Austria's very own Houdini. If you'll wait a moment, I'll show you.' Rising, she hurried away to find the file she wanted. A few moments later she came back and set down a box. 'You never know. It might be of help.'

'Thank you,' Purslane said. She smiled and returned behind her desk.

Purslane continued to stare at her until Holmes, losing patience, rolled his eyes and cleared his throat loudly. Purslane turned back to the table with some embarrassment, although, Watson wryly observed, not without some further glances in Miss Bauer's direction. A moment later Purslane's brow was furrowed in concentration as he sifted through the contents of the new file.

The box was filled with newspaper clippings, all arranged chronologically. Some were small fillers or press releases, but many of the larger ones were accompanied by a photograph of a lean but well-developed man in his forties, wearing a leotard and brandishing a scimitar. He was smiling hugely, revealing large, white teeth. He had fair, tousled hair, personable eyes, a long straight nose and a square, manly jaw.

Purslane continued to examine the clippings until finally, after several minutes, he summarized what he had just read.

'The subject of all this material is one Nikolaus Eder, best-known by his stage name, 'The King of Clubs'. He was a sort of . . . comedy conjuror, I suppose you'd call it, who also employed a little ventriloquism in his act. It says here that he would throw his voice quite convincingly to make it appear as if different members of the audience were constantly challenging him to perform ever more outrageous tricks, all of which he then, of course, performed flawlessly.

'By all accounts he was a very gifted magician. One of his specialities was to make a chicken vanish from a box that was in full view, only to have it reappear beneath the seat of a member of the audience. But principally he was an extraordinary juggler.'

He quoted, ''The most startling feats and tricks in the world are those performed by numerous professional jugglers from India and these have been unvaried since the days of Baber, the descendent of Timour, in the sixteenth century. Nikolaus Eder has clearly derived inspiration from the same source, and performs feats of *legerdemain* superior to anything this reviewer has seen before. With seeming ease, Eder holds no fewer than nine Indian clubs in play with his hands and feet and the muscles of his arms and legs, each club weighing not less than three pounds. He then astounds his audience by adding six more clubs to those already in the air, so that he somehow manages to create the impression that he is surrounded by fifteen ivory-white clubs with a combined weight of forty-five pounds, each with a will of its own.

''Before his audience can pause for breath, however, Eder deposits all fifteen clubs neatly into a rack, then takes from his red trunk the most impressive club I have ever seen. It is at least three feet in length and cannot weigh less than fifty pounds. Indeed, to prove as much, Eder requests a man of large build to join him on stage, and the poor man can barely lift the club.

"And yet Eder then begins to swing the club back and forth, until at last he has sufficient momentum to fling it some twenty feet in the air. It turns end over end, light flaring from the small, circular mirrors with which its tip and tail are adorned, and then he catches it with an air almost of nonchalance and throws it high again. He works his way from stage left to stage right and back again, making this massive club appear more like an extension of his arm; and though he was breathing hard by the end of his performance, he was able to enjoy the great show of appreciation of the crowd and come back for an encore, during which he juggled a dozen razor-sharp knives."

'Fascinating, I am sure,' said Holmes testily. 'But what does it have to do with Houdini?'

Purslane continued to read through the clippings, then stiffened. 'Here . . . '

Watson leaned closer. 'What is it?'

"Inspired by Houdini," Purslane translated, "Eder has started to incorporate ever more dangerous elements into his act. He allows himself to be bound hand and foot and placed beneath an ever-descending pendulum blade as he attempts to free himself from his bonds. He also lets himself be locked inside a milk can filled with ice-cold water, only to escape at the last moment, and performs Houdini's famous Needle Trick not with needles, but with razor blades.''

'So he was Europe's answer to Houdini,' said Holmes.

'There's more,' said Purslane, quickly reading on. 'And ... yes, I believe it's relevant.' He continued reading. 'About a year and a half ago the King of Clubs was said to be working on a new sensation, something he referred to as the *Underwater Box Escape.* The idea was that he would be bound hand and foot, and locked into a crate that was then chained and padlocked. The crate was to be thrown into a lake or river and only then could he begin his attempt at escape. Unfortunately he got word that Houdini was working on a similar stunt and in order to trump Houdini he brought the date of his own performance forward by two months. It was a complete disaster.'

'What happened?' asked Watson.

'The trick was well publicized. It was billed as a challenge to Houdini — that anything Houdini could do, or *thinks* to do, the King of Clubs could match and indeed surpass. Pure showmanship, of course. I doubt that Houdini even knew who Eder was. But it did the trick. The performance was a sell-out. It was staged on Ascension Day — that's quite a popular holiday here — and Eder's manager received permission to close off a section of the Danube at its narrowest point — a span of about three hundred metres from shore to shore, or thereabouts — so that only ticket-holders could actually watch the performance. Eder was handcuffed, his feet were shackled and he was then locked into the box, which was subsequently chained and padlocked before finally being thrown into the river.

'There followed a wait of some minutes. The tension continued to grow . . . but it was only after *ten* minutes that Eder's manager realised that something had gone wrong. Members of a local swimming club, who had been hired for the purpose, dove into the river and located the crate. The chains were removed, the box unlocked and Eder was brought to the surface, unconscious. Back on dry land, a doctor tried to revive him.'

'But it was too late,' Watson murmured, caught up in the story.

'No, they *did* manage to revive him,' said Purslane, 'but he had been starved of oxygen for too long. Apparently the man suffered a . . . ' he paused, stumbling over his translation, 'a massive cerebral . . . '

'Infarction,' Watson finished grimly. 'In other words, a stroke. It must have virtually destroyed the poor devil's brain.'

'According to this report, it did. Eder ended up in a vegetative state, neither dead nor alive but simply . . . existing.'

He read on. 'There was an investigation into what went wrong, and it concluded that Eder had hit his head when the crate first struck the water, and lost consciousness. Today he resides in a *Palliativestation* in Engelhartstetten.'

Watson said, '*Palliative* — you mean, a hospice?'

'Yes.'

'What do you make of it, Holmes?'

Holmes shrugged. 'We need to make further enquiries and I can think of no better place to start than at the hospice.'

'Well, it's too late to do anything now,' said Purslane, consulting his pocket watch. 'Engelhartstetten is about thirty miles from here, perhaps a little more.'

'And with or without a prior appointment,' argued Watson, 'I doubt they'll allow us to see Herr Eder, and they *certainly* won't release any personal details regarding their patients.'

'We shall see,' Holmes said.

While he and Watson donned their coats, Purslane returned the box to Fräulein Bauer. Watson watched the two young people talking softly and gave a melancholy smile. He missed being young, but more than that he missed his beloved wife and the simple joy of being in love. In the early years at Baker Street his bachelor existence had suited him. He had had the freedom to come and go as he liked, and to join Holmes on one adventure after another. But following his marriage to Mary Morstan in the late spring of 1889, he had changed. At first he had missed those heady days in Holmes's company. Now he missed those quiet evenings at home and the company of a woman just as much.

'Come along, Purslane,' called Holmes with new purpose. 'We still have much to do.'

Reluctantly Purslane bade goodbye to Miss Bauer, with whom he was obviously smitten, and hurried to join them as they left the building.

Outside, darkness was already approaching, and the snow that had been falling lightly all day now started to come down harder. They tugged their collars up and left the offices of the *Krone* behind them. But as they were about to cross the busy road and find a cab to take them back to the Grand, there was a noise not unlike a car backfiring. In the same moment Holmes grunted, stumbled forward, his hat flying off, and dropped to his knees.

Purslane saw blood darkening Holmes's collar and his stomach lurched unpleasantly.

'Doctor!' he cried. 'He's been shot! Mr Holmes has been shot!

24

Tomorrow is Another Day

'Holmes!'

The concerned cry was wrenched from Watson. He quickly grasped his companion around the shoulders to stop him from collapsing completely. In that instant he was so concerned for Holmes that he hardly noticed a man bursting out of the alley behind them where he'd been hiding. Knocking Purslane aside, the fellow raced across the road, dodging traffic as he ran.

'Holmes . . .'

Purslane said something but Watson, in shock, barely heard the words. As Purslane ran off after the gunman, all Watson could think to do was hold his friend close and at the same time try to examine his wound.

The right side of Holmes's face was streaked with blood. It seemed to be seeping from an area just above his ear. His breathing was coming in great, gasping clouds of vapour.

Though he looked pale as the snow falling all around them, Watson knew better than to write Holmes off immediately. Even as he tossed his cane aside and reached for a handkerchief with which to staunch the flow of blood, Watson saw Holmes open his eyes, blink a few times, then focus.

'It's all right, Holmes,' Watson assured him. 'You're all right now . . . '

'Of course I am,' Holmes replied irritably. 'Let me up.'

'I don't think you understand,' said Watson, aware of the curious spectators who were gathering about them. 'You've been shot, old chap.'

'No . . . '

'With all due respect, Holmes, I am the doctor here — '

But Holmes would have none of it. 'I was *nicked*, Watson. Anything more and I would be unconscious, if not worse. It is . . . nothing.'

'You're *bleeding*,' Watson insisted.

Holmes seemed to realize this fact for the first time. He took Watson's handkerchief and pressed it gingerly to the right side of his head. Pain briefly crossed his face before he regained control of himself, despite looking decidedly nauseous.

'It is little more than a shallow furrow,' he said.

'But . . . but that fellow . . . he *shot* you! I

heard the report myself, though I didn't immediately recognize it for what it was!'

'Fortunately for me,' Holmes said, shaken but still in conrol, 'my would-be assassin obviously made his shot in haste and missed me . . . though not by much, I confess.'

Relief washed through Watson. He and a couple of onlookers helped Holmes back to his feet. He looked decidedly unsteady, but for a man who had just cheated death, also remarkably composed.

'We need to get you to a hospital,' Watson said, retrieving Holmes's hat and cane.

'Nonsense. You are a perfectly adequate physician. You can clean the wound when we get back to the Grand.' Holmes looked around. 'May I assume from his absence that Purslane went after the gunman?'

'Yes. As soon as he fired his shot, the fellow belted off across the road there like a scalded cat!'

'Then Purslane will do well to take care because his quarry is not of sound mind.'

Watson showed surprise. 'You *know* him? It was too dark and too snowy to get much of a look at him. The best I managed was a brief impression, someone bundled in an overcoat.'

'I didn't even see that much,' Holmes admitted. 'But it is unlikely that Houdini would betray us to his kidnappers, and we have no reason to believe they are onto us. Which leaves only one candidate.'

'The Black Hand?' muttered Watson, taking Holmes by the arm as they crossed the road in the footsteps of their young companion.

'I doubt it.'

'But — '

'Vasiljavic certainly warned us against interfering with the activities of his group. But since we have done no such thing and Vasiljavic is canny enough to know that any attempt to harm us would inevitably invite the wrath of the British government, I think not.' He went to shake his head, then thought better of it, for it was aching fiercely. 'No, Watson, not the Black Hand, but certainly one of its members — young Princip Gavrilo.'

'*That* scoundrel!'

'Yes. A boy whose emotions are ruled by anger and whose actions are as impulsive as they are ill-conceived. He clearly bears a grudge for what happened during our first encounter at the Beserlpark Alsergrund. Being similarly humiliated during our second did nothing to appease him.'

'Then I hope Purslane *does* catch him,' Watson said grimly. 'Because then I shall teach him a lesson myself.'

'You may get your wish, old friend,' said

Holmes as they turned a corner and saw two figures grappling beside a low wall in the shadow of the railway bridge that spanned the river, 'for Purslane has indeed caught our man.'

The British agent now had Gavrilo Princip pinned against the wall, his free hand holding the gun with which Princip had tried to murder Holmes.

Hearing them approach, Purslane looked surprised to see Holmes back on his feet. Gavrilo also glared at Holmes, angry and disappointed that he was not dead.

'You have had a very lucky escape, Gavrilo,' said Holmes, when they were close enough. 'I do not think Javor Vasiljavic would have been pleased had you succeeded in your endeavour.'

The boy spat his defiance at Holmes's feet. However, it was obvious that the mention of Vasiljavic's name had unnerved him.

'Javor would thank me for killing the enemies of the Black Hand,' he managed in hesitant English.

'Enemies, yes,' Holmes agreed sternly. 'But we are *not* enemies of the Black Hand, as Vasiljavic knows very well. He has no quarrel with us, just as we have no quarrel with him. And for that reason he would not wish us any harm . . . but would most certainly be quick to punish the man who *did* harm us.'

Despite his surly expression, it was obvious Gavrilo knew Holmes was right. But still he said defiantly, 'We'll see.'

'Are you really willing to take that gamble?' asked Holmes, raising one blood-smudged eyebrow. 'Have you any idea what would have happened had you succeeded in killing me? My government would have demanded that the authorities here spare no effort in bringing my killer to book. And to maintain diplomatic relations with Great Britain Vienna would have done so, too. They would not have had to look too far to find the guilty party.'

Curious, Gavrilo said grudgingly, 'Why not?'

'Because Vasiljavic would have taken no small delight in serving you up to them. Anyone who puts the Black Hand at risk becomes an enemy of the Black Hand and is dealt with accordingly. You would have been handed over to the authorities sooner rather than later . . . and not necessarily alive.'

'No!'

'Yes. But I won't tell Vasiljavic — *this* time. However, this very evening I will see to it that, should anything else untoward happen to me during my stay in Vienna, he will be informed *immediately* of your actions here today. What happens to you then will be up to him, but I do not imagine it will be particularly pleasant for you.'

By now the fear in Gavrilo's eyes was all too obvious, though he tried to hide it. Holmes took the gun from Purslane, examined it cursorily — it was an antiquated pepperbox pistol — and then tossed it over the wall into the river. Gavrilo started to curse him, then fell silent. His hatred of Holmes appeared undiminished, but the slump of his shoulders showed that he knew he had been defeated.

'Let him go,' Holmes told Purslane. 'And remember this, Gavrilo. Should we ever meet again, you will be poorer for the encounter.'

Gavrilo glared at him for another moment, then stuffed his hands into his too-large overcoat and stamped off into the gloom.

Only when he had vanished from sight did Holmes allow himself to sag. He'd been successfully fighting the effects of the head injury which were making him weak and nauseous and had been unaware of how dangerously close he was to complete collapse until Watson suddenly grabbed him by the arm. 'Steady, old chap.'

Purslane quickly moved to Holmes's other side to help support him. 'What happened? I was afraid that — '

'Fortunately it was nothing more than a nasty graze,' said Watson. 'Still, he's lost quite a bit of blood and must surely have a prince among headaches.'

'You needn't talk about me as if I'm not here,' Holmes grumbled.

'Well, one thing is certain. You're not going to Engelhartstetten or anywhere else today.'

'But — '

'Be sensible, Holmes! Another inch to the left and you'd be dead now. As it is, there's no need to use up whatever luck you still possess. Listen to me,' he continued, his tone softening. 'If what we suspect about the King of Clubs turns out to be right, then we have already made more progress than we had any right to expect. We'll resume our investigations tomorrow. What you need now is some food, a stiff drink and a good night's rest.'

Holmes started to protest. Then, knowing that Watson was right, he reluctantly nodded. 'Very well. I shall rest tonight. But tomorrow . . . '

' . . . is another day,' finished Watson.

25

The Willing Accomplice

'This,' Watson exclaimed as their cab clattered through the streets of Vienna, 'is utter madness and quite beyond all the bounds of propriety.'

It was the next morning and Holmes, somewhat recovered following a good night's rest and with his wound cleaned and neatly bandaged, looked at Watson and Purslane and said, 'Nevertheless, it is the best and easiest way to obtain the information we require.'

Watson rolled his eyes in despair. 'By enlisting the help of Sigmund Freud? My God, Holmes, are you forgetting that he's considered to be one of the most eminent psychologists in the world, a man whose ability to see into the complexities of the human mind are shown almost utmost respect?'

'That is precisely why he is the best man for the job. No other is more likely to persuade the staff at Engelshartstetten to assist us in our enquiries.'

'But that is exactly my *point*, Holmes! What you intend to do — enlist Freud as a means to get access to Eder — is highly unethical. It could damage Freud's reputation irreparably if it were to get out.'

'Then we must make sure that it does *not* get out.'

'Dear Lord.'

'Besides,' Holmes continued, 'he may yet refuse our request.'

'*Your* request,' said Watson petulantly. He turned to Purslane, who had met them earlier and was now sharing their cab as it headed for Freud's apartment. 'Well, don't just sit there, man. Say something!'

'Would it do any good?' Purslane replied. 'It would appear that Mr Holmes's mind is made up. If we are right in our suspicions regarding the King of Clubs and if by bringing this gang to justice we can prevent the international incident that Mycroft Holmes fears, then in my opinion, the end justifies the means.'

'"The end justifies the means",' Watson mimicked. 'I am growing heartily sick of that proverb.'

But Holmes offered a rare smile. 'Well said, Purslane. I knew you were a man of great common sense.'

Shortly thereafter the cab arrived at

Freud's apartment. They were shown into the psychologist's study, where Freud — delighted to see them again — alternately puffed at his ever-present cigar and stroked his grey beard as he listened to Holmes's request.

Freud thought a moment before answering. 'I am, of course, flattered that you think my participation will carry some weight, but . . . you do realize you are asking me to do something highly unethical?'

Watson pounced. 'My own words exactly, Herr Doktor!'

'Nevertheless,' Freud continued, still studying Holmes thoughtfully, 'I believe it would be irresponsible of me not to assist a man of your stature in his investigations, especially since it may well, as you say, become a matter of life and death.' He smiled. 'I will telephone the *Palliativestation* at Engelhartstetten at once, gentlemen.'

He went to one of the bookshelves that lined his office and searched until he found the medical directory he was after. Then, bringing it back to his desk, he opened it and quickly found a reference for the hospice. He picked up the handset of the brass telephone on his desk and asked the operator to connect him with the *Palliativestation*.

After a long wait he finally said, 'Ah, good morning, Doktor Meisener. It's Sigmund

Freud. We met briefly at the conference in Steyr, if you remember . . . Yes, yes, I am fine; and you? . . . Good. I wonder if you can help me, Herr Doktor? I am presently researching the mental faculties of the injured brain . . . Yes, yes indeed. I was especially interested in getting the opportunity to study a patient of yours, a man by the name of Nikolaus Eder. That's right the King of Clubs . . . No, I understand that. But do you think his next of kin would be willing to grant permission . . . ? Ah, I see. Do they, indeed? . . . Yes, it is very difficult to underestimate the importance of a loving family . . . but still, if you could let me have their address . . . ? It will certainly do no harm to ask.'

He waited a moment, then scribbled an address on the pad in front of him. After exchanging a few final pleasantries, he rang off, tore the page from his pad and handed it to Holmes.

'Apparently the family live in Pottenmauer.'

Holmes glanced questioningly at Purslane, who said, 'It's out on the Slovakian border, I believe, about forty kilometres away.'

'Are you sure you believe you have the right people, Herr Holmes?' Freud asked with concern. 'Doktor Meisener says the family are very protective of Herr Eder, and absolutely devoted to him. They visit him often and sometimes, if the weather is clement, take him for drives in their motor vehicle.'

'We cannot say for sure,' Holmes replied honestly. 'Did Doktor Meisener give you any further information about them?'

'Only that Eder's brother, Florian, also happened to be his manager. A positive saint, to hear Meisener tell the story. Following the accident, he took Herr Eder's children under his wing and has looked after them ever since.'

'His children?'

'Yes; though he was a widower, the King of Clubs has a son and a daughter.'

Holmes looked Freud in the eye. 'Did he by any chance mention their names?'

'Yes, I believe he did.' The neurologist frowned as he searched for an elusive memory. 'What was it he called them . . . ?'

'Wolf?' prodded Holmes. 'Annalise?'

Freud snapped his fingers. 'That's it!'

'Then there can no longer be any doubt at all,' Holmes said grimly. 'Thank you, Herr Doktor. You have been of more help than you will ever know.'

As they shook hands, Freud said, 'How do you intend to get to Pottenmauer?'

'We shall hail a cab.'

'I doubt you will find any cab willing to

make such a long journey. But perhaps I may be of one further service to you.' He looked at Purslane. 'Young man, do you know how to drive a motor vehicle?'

'Yes, sir.'

'Then take this,' said the neurologist, reaching into his waistcoat pocket. 'It's the key to my own private motor carriage.' He looked self-consciously at his visitors. 'It is one of my few extravagances, a Daimler only five years old. My friends told me I could not possibly be without a motor vehicle in these modern times, and so I indulged myself . . . but in truth I rarely use it. It is parked downstairs; you are more than welcome to it.'

Purslane took the key. 'Thank you, Herr Doktor.'

'Thank you, indeed,' said Holmes. 'Now, come along, gentlemen. I do believe we have some kidnappers to expose — and a brace of Houdinis to rescue.'

26

Meanwhile . . .

Houdini believed he had conquered claustrophobia years ago. Such a fear would have been disasterous for a man who allowed himself to be locked into a filled milk can; or who spent as long as possible in a tub, under water, to increase his lung capacity. But now, as he looked around the small attic room in which his captors had imprisoned him, he began to feel, for the first time, that these dark, angled walls were crowding in on him and squeezing all the air out of their meagre confines.

He had always gone his own way in life. He had set goals and gone after them with utter dedication and complete focus. He had never before been forced to submit to any will but his own, but now he was at the mercy of another, a man whose name he still didn't know, and it was . . .

God, he hated to confess it, even to himself, but it was true: it was *breaking* him.

More of a torture still was the knowledge that Bess, his beloved Bess, was also being held prisoner in the cellar of this very house. And equally frustrating was the realization that there was not a single thing he could do about it.

He got up irritably from the architect's drawing board where he had been studying the blueprints of the Imperial Palace. This was crazy! Here he was, the world's greatest escapologist, unable to do the very thing he was so famous for.

He went over to the skylight set high in the north-facing section of the roof. It wasn't much, a window barely sixteen inches square. He reached up, pushed it open and cold air immediately rushed inside.

He inhaled deeply and felt invigorated; he tried to bring sharpness and order to his thoughts. After a moment he dragged a box across the floor, climbed onto it and looked out at his surroundings.

The three-storey house in which he and Bess were imprisoned was set in acres of forest. Leafless oaks and black pines stretched as far as he could see on this bleak winter's day, with its low, heavy clouds and light, breeze-blown snow.

After leaving the church, his captors had shoved him into a narrow alley where a square-looking car built along the lines of a four-seater brougham was waiting for them.

The younger man, the one called Wolf, had then driven them through Vienna. There had been no conversation, except for the fat man with the tortoiseshell glasses occasionally telling him to keep looking down, presumably so he wouldn't have any idea where they were taking him.

The car had made barely any noise; Houdini had wondered what kind of a car could travel so soundlessly.

As near as he'd been able to tell, the journey had taken them across the Danube and then through a sparsely populated area. Soon the lights of Vienna fell behind them and darkness filled the car. Houdini tried the cuffs with which they had bound his hands behind his back, but these people really *did* know all the tricks. He had tried to make them cuff him more on the forearm than the wrist, so that he could later slide the cuffs down his arms and slip out of them, but that was an old dodge and one with which they were all too familiar.

So he was theirs for the taking.

He estimated the journey had lasted perhaps an hour. Then the car crunched along a gravel drive until at last it braked and came to a halt. While Wolf turned off the engine, the girl, Annalise, got out, hurried around the car and opened Houdini's door.

Sleet lashed at the exposed side of his face. The muzzle of the gun in the fat man's hand pressed into his side. 'Get out,' he was told.

Houdini obeyed, finally looking up in order to examine his surroundings. It was a wretched night and visibility was poor, but as he glanced around he noted that they had halted before a large, dark and seemingly isolated house.

Wolf climbed out of the car, closing the driver's door, then walked hurriedly to the front door, unlocked it and went inside.

Houdini wondered about Wolf. He talked tough, but Houdini sensed that it was just an act. He wondered if he might be able to exploit that in some way. During the cab ride from his hotel to the church, Wolf had even apologized for what had happened to Frankie, saying that this hadn't been part of the plan, but that it had been an accident. Houdini found this of no comfort at all.

A few seconds later lights began to show inside the house.

'Go inside,' said the fat man.

Again, Houdini did as he was told. He went through the front door and into a spacious lobby, now hardly able to feel his frozen feet. Electric lamps showed him a comfortable area with old, expensive-looking paintings and fine furniture. Whoever these people were, they clearly had money.

'Now,' said the fat man, confronting him, 'you will be quartered upstairs, in a room from which I fancy even *you* will be unable to escape. And it is there that you will work upon the problem that has caused me considerable vexation.'

'How to get into and out of this building of yours, undetected, right?'

'Precisely.'

'No,' said Houdini.

The fat man arched an eyebrow. 'No?'

'No.'

Without warning, the fat man lashed out with the butt of the gun, slamming it across Houdini's jaw. Houdini dropped to his knees and lights exploded inside his head. It had been his understanding that the jaw was one of the strongest bones in the human body, but just then it didn't feel anything like strong enough.

'Listen to me,' he gasped, lurching back to his feet.

The fat man, Annalise and Wolf all gathered before him.

'I'll do whatever you want,' Houdini continued. 'But I won't do a single damned thing until I see my wife.'

'She is here and she is safe,' said the fat man. 'That is all you need to know.'

'And am I supposed to take your word for that?' asked Houdini. It was hard to talk now because his jaw was as numb as his feet.

'You have no choice.'

'Well, let's just see, shall we?'

'Don't try my patience — '

'Then don't try *mine*,' Houdini warned. 'Now, I've told you, whoever you are, that I'll do as you ask. I'll play square with you right down the line . . . but I won't do the first damned thing until I know Bess is all right.'

The fat man looked at him. His expression said that he wanted to use the gun on Houdini again, but finally his damp shoulders rose and fell in an irritable sigh. 'Very well. Come this way.'

Wolf led the way and Annalise followed. Houdini didn't know why, but she was the one he felt he should fear the most. There was a hardness to her that was missing from Wolf. A hardness he suspected was missing even from the fat man. Her silence was unnerving, too. But then, she didn't seem to need speech. One glance from her flat hazel eyes clearly conveyed any message she chose to send.

At the fat man's urging Houdini followed the others to a door at the far end of the hallway beside the staircase. Wolf turned on lamps as he went. Houdini's throat tightened

and his heartbeat picked up expectantly. *Bess
. . . Bess . . .*

The door led through to a kitchen. It was
large and functional, but also curiously
sterile. Houdini decided that precious little
cooking went on here. In the middle of the
flagstone floor Wolf bent and slipped gloved
fingers through a metal ring, then lifted a
hinged trapdoor, showing a series of wooden
steps descending into the twilight below.

'She's down there,' said the fat man, and
when Houdini hesitated, 'Go on. You wanted
to satisfy yourself that she's all right.'

Still Houdini didn't move. Was this some
kind of trap? Was this the room from which
he couldn't escape, the *cellar?*

Then he heard it and all further thought
simply ceased.

A sob.

He went down the creaking steps into a
cluttered cellar lit by a single hissing carbide
lamp resting on an overturned tea chest. At
first he didn't see Bess. Then his eyes
adjusted to the semi-darkness and he saw her
sitting on an old dining chair in the far
corner, her head bowed, face buried in a
small, embroidered white handkerchief.

She looked up at the clatter of footsteps.
Houdini saw her face as something ghostly;
her eyes seemed dark in a bloodless oval and

then she jumped up, saying in absolute disbelief, 'H-Harry . . . ?'

'Bess!'

He went to her, words tumbling out of him as he did so, dirt from the earthen floor sticking between his toes. 'Are you all right? Tell me they haven't ill-treated you?'

She came to meet him. But even as she moved there was a cold, metallic clanking sound and when she stopped moving forward, he realized with mounting fury that she had been shackled.

Houdini could barely control his fury that these *animals* had shackled one of her ankles and that she was unable to move more than a few feet from her dirty, depressing, garbage-filled corner.

Then Bess was holding him, pressing herself against him, and he could feel her crying. It broke his heart that he couldn't hold her because of the cuffs. 'Tell me you're all right,' he said in anguish.

She stood back, holding his arms, looking up at him. It seemed like an eternity since he had last seen her and it was all he could do now not to break down completely.

'I . . . I'm all right, Harry,' she said, fighting back her tears. 'But who *are* these people? What do they want?'

'A favour.'

'Favour?'

'Yes. They want me to do something for them. Once it's done they'll let us go.'

He tried to sound as if he believed it, but of course he didn't. The only way he and Bess would gain their freedom would be through their own efforts. And that was something he had been thinking about all the way from Vienna.

Bess frowned at him. She looked exhausted, her face smudged, her hair in disarray. 'What do they want you to do, Harry?'

'I don't — '

'What's happened to your coat?' she asked suddenly, noticing the torn lapels.

'Oh, nothing . . . They roughed me up a little is all.'

More footsteps echoed on the wooden staircase behind them. They broke apart and Houdini turned to face the fat man.

'She is unharmed,' he said, 'as you can see.'

'You didn't have to shackle her.'

'That's a matter of opinion. Now, come along. Time to lock *you* away, too.'

Houdini managed one last look over his shoulder as they led him back upstairs. His wife was watching him go through eyes that swam with tears.

'It'll be OK, Bess,' he called. 'Just hold your nerve. Everything's gonna be OK.'

27

Escape!

After that they had taken him up three flights of stairs until they reached a small landing. The narrow, ill-lit passage ended in a sturdy, bolted door. Wolf went ahead, threw back the bolts top and bottom, then took out a key and unlocked the door. It opened into a dusty attic room.

Houdini was pushed inside.

The dark interior smelled of damp and dust, but after a few moments his eyes adjusted to a small square near his head that was somewhat lighter than the rest. Then came the scratch of a match and a storm lantern was lit. Amber light ghosted through the room. He realized that the square was a small skylight. Beyond it, the inky shades of night were shot through with slanting snow.

'Until you have completed your task,' said the fat man, 'this will be your home. The sooner you present me with the solution I require, the sooner you regain your freedom.'

Again, Houdini knew he was lying. And the

fat man knew that he knew, and cared not one whit.

'I shall bring you the blueprints tomorrow morning,' he continued. 'Then you will set to work.'

At last they uncuffed him, threw his shoes and socks into the corner and left him alone. He heard them locking and bolting the door from the outside, then sat on the edge of a mean little truckle bed that had been set up for his benefit. The attic was cold and cheerless. The only other furniture was a sloping drawing board, a stool and an empty crate upon which sat the lantern.

How are you going to escape from this place, Harry? Think!

Although Houdini had been certain sleep would prove impossible, he eventually dozed off, shivering beneath a thin grey blanket, only to be woken at seven the following morning by the sound of the bolts being drawn back. A moment later the door was opened and there stood Wolf and Annalise. While Wolf kept him covered with the revolver, the girl entered and set down a bowl of oatmeal. The sight of it reminded Houdini how long it had been since he had last eaten. Hunger and the cold had made him sluggish — if he were to find a way out of this predicament he knew he must be as sharp as possible.

Soon they left, locking and bolting the door behind them. Houdini rose, picked up the bowl and began to eat. The oatmeal was tasteless, but it was hot and he was determined to get as much nourishment from it as he could.

He had just finished when he heard footsteps on the landing outside, and then the fat man entered with a roll of papers tucked under one arm.

'Here,' he said, offering them to Houdini. 'These are the plans of the Imperial Palace. You will examine them and then — '

'I know,' Houdini interrupted. 'If it's possible, I'll find you a way in and out.'

'Precisely.' The fat man smiled, but it was a cold, fleeting smile that never reached his eyes.

After that Houdini was left alone again, the door locked and bolted.

He walked around the room to loosen his cramped muscles. Beyond the skylight the Austrian countryside was bleak, the new day's sky still heavy with snow. He shivered, then unrolled the blueprints on the drawing board and began to study them.

But concentration was next to impossible. All he could think about was Bess; Bess shackled in the cellar, alone with the shadows, and the cold and the damp stench of worm-riddled earth . . .

As difficult as it was to do so, however, he

knew he had to set thoughts like that aside. He and Bess weren't finished yet. Holmes was still out there somewhere, and if anyone could find him and somehow set him free, it was that Limey detective.

He forced himself to focus on the plans, and gradually his analytical mind began to work. His fingertips traced the lines of passages and tunnels; the lines of sewers and access routes, and somehow the day passed in oppressive silence.

Evening arrived. The bolts were drawn back again, the harsh grating sound unnaturally loud in the hitherto unbroken quietude. Wolf opened the door, his revolver trained on Houdini's stocky torso. His sister, Annalise, was with him — as unnervingly silent as ever. She came in, set a plate of what appeared to be rabbit stew on the crate beside the lantern.

'Do you have anything for us yet?' asked Wolf.

Houdini shook his head. 'No. I can see why you had problems yourselves.'

'Well, don't keep us waiting too long, *Amerikaner*.'

Darkness came early and with it a white blanket of snow that covered the skylight. Houdini doused the lamp, curled up beneath his blanket on the truckle bed and dozed the night away.

The following dawn he awoke with new purpose. He had been cloistered here in this unknown location for long enough. Today he was going to escape and take his beloved Bess with him.

Around him, the isolated house creaked in the biting wind. He dragged the crate over to the skylight, hopped up onto it and looked out into the dawn: skeletal trees waved back and forth as an icy breeze chased swirling snow across the lawns.

Now that he had made up his mind, he was eager to get on with his plan. But he also knew that, as with everything in life, it would rely on timing. And so he forced himself to wait, to let them deliver his bowl of oatmeal and lock him in again, and then he went back to the skylight and continued to wait.

Eventually his patience was rewarded. There was a sudden crunching of gravel. He scrambled onto the crate and opened the snow-covered skylight. He looked below. And . . . yes . . . there! The boxy little maroon-coloured car was driving silently off along the lane, making for the narrow road they had followed to get here.

Houdini squinted, trying to see who was inside. He thought he could discern the silhouettes of two figures. One, he thought, would almost certainly be the girl.

Knowing there was not a moment to lose now, he jumped off the crate, composed himself as best he could, squared his shoulders and thumped at the attic door.

'It's done,' he called. 'I've found you your safe passage in and out of the palace.'

He stepped back and waited. Nothing happened. He went back to the door and was just about to hammer at it again when he heard footsteps coming along the hallway outside. He waited, his pulse racing.

The bolts were dragged back; a key turned in the lock. The door opened and Wolf stood within its frame, the revolver as always in his hand, held tight against his right hip, so there was no chance that Houdini could make a successful grab for it.

'What was that you said?' he asked.

Keeping himself subdued, Houdini said, 'I've worked it all out, I think.'

'What do you mean, you *think?*'

'I mean I believe it will work, but I can't be sure. No one can, until you attempt it.'

Wolf's eyes flickered briefly to the blueprints. Houdini said wearily, 'Here, I'll show you what I mean.'

He gestured at the blueprints, hoping Wolf would join him. Houdini's plan hinged on Wolf's natural curiosity dictating his actions. It was the only thing that might stop him from leaving, from locking and bolting the door and awaiting the fat man's return.

Houdini held his breath, trying not to look as desperate as he felt. Another moment passed, and then Wolf said, 'All right — show me.'

Houdini almost wilted with relief. He stood back, keeping his hands raised. Wolf entered, closed the door behind him and locked it without once taking his eyes off his prisoner. Then, slipping the key into his pocket, he came closer, glancing at the blueprints as he did so.

'The key to it all is this tunnel here,' said Houdini, indicating a point on the plan.

Instinctively Wolf looked at the spot and that was when Houdini struck.

He threw himself at the younger man and grabbed Wolf's gun-hand.

Wolf cried out, tried to jerk his wrist free and inadvertently pulled the trigger.

The gun boomed. Houdini had no idea where the bullet went. He wrenched the gun from Wolf's grasp, but before he could get control of it, Wolf hurled himself at Houdini.

As they collided Houdini lost his grip on the gun. It hit the floorboards and before he could try to retrieve it Wolf started swinging wildly at him.

Houdini fell back under the onslaught.

Wolf was like a madman, battering him with a desperate rain of punches. Houdini did his best to swat all the blows aside, then punched him in the face. Wolf staggered back and dropped to the floor. Dazed, he groped around for his gun.

Houdini quickly kicked the weapon out of reach. It slid across the floor into a corner festooned with spider's webs. Houdini dragged Wolf to his feet and drew back his fist to hit him.

Wolf twisted free and kicked Houdini in the shin. Houdini yelped with pain and stumbled back. Wolf ran to the door, where he fumbled the key out of his pocket.

Houdini was on him instantly. He wrenched the younger man back around, grabbed his throat and squeezed hard.

'Give it up!' he rasped. 'Drop the key!'

Bug-eyed, Wolf shook his head, knowing he was beaten but knowing also that he couldn't allow his prisoner to escape.

'I'm warning you,' Houdini yelled at him. 'I'll kill you, if I have to!'

Wolf struggled to break his hold, but couldn't. He tried to butt Houdini in the face. When that didn't work he did the one thing Houdini hadn't allowed for.

He threw the key toward the open skylight.

Horrified, Houdini watched the key turn

end over end, reflecting the weak morning light as it flew out the window.

Enraged, Houdini slammed Wolf on the jaw. Wolf's head snapped back and he collapsed at Houdini's feet.

It was suddenly deathly quiet in the attic.

Then Houdini grew aware of his own ragged breathing, of the sweat trickling down his face, of his blood on his raw knuckles, the throbbing of his bruised shin.

He ran his fingers through his tight curly hair, went over and picked up the revolver, then stepped over the unconscious Wolf and hunched down to examine the lock.

He was extraordinarily well educated in the workings of locks, enough to know that any attempt to use the gun on this one would only buckle the mechanism and make it even harder to open.

He tucked the pistol into his waistband and returned to the unconscious Wolf. He searched Wolf's pockets, but the young man carried nothing that Houdini might use to pick the lock.

Houdini slumped, mentally near defeat. He had come so close to escape . . .

But his will to survive wouldn't let him quit. He knew this was too good an opportunity to waste. He *had* to escape, for it would go even harder for him and Bess now, after the fat man discovered what he had just attempted.

He stared at the skylight. Whether he liked it or not, this was now his only means of escape.

Heights had never frightened him. Before this he had regularly hung upside-down from tall buildings whilst escaping from chains and straitjackets. If he'd had any fears in that regard he would never — *could* never — have attempted such feats, but climbing down the outside of a house in such inhospitable conditions? He imagined the icy ledges out there, the frost-covered drainpipes that were so cold his skin might well stick to them as he tried to lower himself to the ground.

Then he gave a sour laugh. Anyone would think he had a *choice* in the matter.

In any case, the longer he remained there, undecided, the more time he was allowing the fat man and Annalise to return from wherever it was they had gone. He had to leave *now*.

He shrugged into his overcoat and tugged on his hat, then set the lantern down and dragged the crate over to the skylight. Climbing onto it, he pushed the little window open as wide as it would go. It still wasn't as wide as he would have liked, but he drew a breath, composed himself and reached one arm up and through the skylight.

28

The Descent

It was going to be even tighter than he had imagined. Unless . . .

He stood absolutely still for a moment, then gave a sudden shake that resembled an exaggerrated shiver. He closed his eyes, wincing with pain . . . But then it was done. He had successfully dislocated his left shoulder.

Now it was somewhat easier for him to slide through the skylight frame.

When he had squeezed halfway through, he found himself looking out over a gently sloping gable roof that was slippery with a thin coating of icy snow. A cold wind whipped at him and he began to feel his fingers losing all sensation. He craned his neck to check his surroundings. The gable end shelved away some twelve feet to the edge of the roof. Just visible beneath it was a line of leaf-clogged guttering.

It would have been easy to tell himself that this was hopeless. Worse, that it could only end one way. But he wasn't trying to escape just for himself. Bess's life also depended upon his actions.

So think, Harry . . . think!

The safest way to reach the corner of the roof and the drainpipe was by the ridge of the roof itself. He couldn't trust the guttering to hold his weight, but he *could* trust the ridge to take him that far.

First, though, he had to replace his dislocated shoulder. Carefully bending his left arm at the elbow, he kept it braced tight against his side, trying as he did to ignore the pain. Slowly he rotated his arm until he could feel the beginning of resistance in his left shoulder socket. He then reached across his chest with his left hand until it touched his opposite shoulder. A moment later the shoulder relocated and, as if by magic, the pain was gone. Only a dull ache remained.

He then stretched his right hand up as high as he could and felt around. After a few moments his fingers closed on the curving ridge tile directly above him. It was like grabbing a chunk of ice, but Houdini willed himself to hold tight and then reached up with his left hand.

When he was satisfied that his grip was secure, he dragged his legs out of the skylight and hauled himself up onto the top part of the two sloping roof planes.

With nothing to blunt it, the wind was stronger up here. It tugged at his torn lapels and the brim of his slouch hat. He shivered and tucked his frozen palms deep into his armpits. Around him the Austrian countryside, seen now from a bird's-eye view, seemed to go on forever, as did the slate-coloured sky above it.

Realizing he was running out of time, Houdini got to his feet and steadied himself. He was now balanced on the curved ridge tiles much as a tightrope-walker might balance on a length of cable. Swaying a little in the buffeting wind, he held his arms out to either side for balance and looking straight ahead, began to walk slowly toward the gable end.

It seemed to take forever, but he knew this wasn't the kind of thing you could rush. Snow blew in his face. He kept blinking, trying to keep it out of his slitted eyes. His concentration was total now, it *had* to be. He had nerve and nerve to spare; this he knew, but he had never tested it as he was testing it now. Before, only his life depended on his success. Now he had the extra burden of Bess's life to consider and that weighed on him like the weight of the world, stretching his nerves almost beyond his endurance.

Step after step after step ... and all the

time trying not to think of the buffeting wind, or the slippery ice underfoot . . .

And then, somehow, he was there, at the gable end.

He knelt down, straddled the ridge again and caught his breath. He was freezing and sweating and shaking all at the same time.

He looked down and saw that he would have to descend one of the two sloping gable ends until he reached the guttering.

He knew the best and safest way was to lower himself on his stomach. He was painfully aware, though, that gravity would have something to say about that, not to mention the snow-covered ice. Should he fall there would be no handholds to grasp or other means of slowing himself once he'd gained momentum.

He needed a ladder.

He peered down at the slates nearest his right foot. Even with the steel-toe-capped shoes he was wearing, these tiles weren't going to break unless he concentrated his blows on their weak points — the lines of grain. Choosing his spot with care, he kicked at the ice-cold tile immediately beneath his foot. He had to kick twice more before it finally cracked. Another kick and a hole appeared — a hole into which he slid his foot up to the heel.

Lowering himself a little, he repeated the procedure with his left foot. As weathered as they were, the slates did not break easily. But desperation gave him strength. *Keep at it*, he told himself. *Don't give up.*

Without warning the next tile broke and Houdini slipped his left foot into the hole.

Carefully, cautiously, he lowered himself by six, perhaps eight inches. Then he started kicking at another tile. Once he almost lost his precarious hold, but somehow he managed to catch himself at the last second.

Doggedly he kept working his way lower, kicking holes into the tiles until they formed footholds and then, as he climbed lower, each foothold became a handhold. Their edges were sharp; more than once they sliced his hands. Each time this happened he had to wipe the blood from his fingers, knowing it would undermine his grip if he didn't.

An eternity passed until finally he felt the guttering beneath his feet. Cautiously he set his weight down on it. The guttering sagged under him, but held.

Breathing hard, he turned and peered over the edge. The snowy ground seemed impossibly far below him; much further away than it really was. He steeled himself and slowly leaned forward, now glimpsing a drain pipe leading down to the ground. Hopefully it would be strong enough to hold his weight.

Trying to imagine that this was just another performance, he lowered himself over the edge of the roof. From there it was reasonably easy to swing down and around so that he was hugging the drainpipe. The pipe glistened with ice that numbed his palms and burned his skin. Fighting the impulse to hurry, he began to lower himself inch by frosty inch down the pipe.

The wind picked up again, this time blowing hard enough that it threatened to dislodge him from the pipe. He clung on desperately, forcing his numb hands to grip the pipe even harder. *Just keep going, Harry. Hand over hand, hand over hand . . .*

Without warning the drainpipe gave a sudden lurch and bits of brick and cement showered on to his head from above. Damn! His weight was proving too much for it. Realizing that any minute it might break away from the wall altogether, he kept going, down, down, down, reminding himself that every foot he descended was a foot less that he would have to fall . . .

It was a slow, dangerous descent. Little by little he could feel the pipe pulling away from the wall above him and each time it did he was showered with debris. He waited until he was about ten feet from the ground, then deciding not to push his luck any further, he let go of the pipe and jumped.

Catlike, he landed on his feet, stumbled, rolled and came up unharmed.

Terra firma had never felt so good.

29

Saved by the Bell

He leaned against the wall for a moment, the cold having finally caught up with him. All at once he started shaking almost uncontrollably.

He blew on his fingers, flexing them to get the blood flowing again, then suddenly stopped. He thought he heard the fat man and the girl coming back.

He hurried anxiously through the snow towards the front door. Mercifully the gravel driveway was still empty.

He retraced his steps along the house and stopped at the first sash window he came to. Still shivering and exhaling great white clouds of breath, he took off his overcoat, wrapped it around the hand holding the gun and smashed the glass. In the winter hush the breakage sounded more like an explosion.

He tapped out the jagged edges, quickly put the overcoat back on, tucked the gun into his waistband and reached through. He found the catch, turned it and raised the lower half of the broken window, then climbed inside.

He was in a modest sitting room.. Hardly noticing it, he crossed the room, opened the door and stepped out into the hall. How much longer did he have before the fat man and the girl came back? It might be hours, for all he knew, but equally it might be no more than minutes now. He entered the kitchen, opened the trapdoor and went down the steps.

Bess was still seated in the corner. She looked up, her face bloodless; her eyes, usually so alert and vital, were now tired and dull. At first Houdini wondered if she even recognized him. Then she said, almost brokenly, 'Harry.'

He had no memory of crossing the cellar and yet he must have, because suddenly he was holding her close and telling her that everything was all right, that he was going to take her away from this terrible place.

'What . . . Harry, how did you get free?'

'That's not important right now.'

'But . . . look at your hands. You're bleeding!'

'There'll be plenty of time to tend to that later,' he assured her. 'For now, just sit down.'

As she did so, he dropped to one knee so that he could examine the shackle that bound her ankle. It was of a fairly basic design and he asked her if their captors had allowed her to keep her hairpins.

She shook her head. She then gave a nervous, eerie little giggle that verged on hysteria. 'Perhaps they thought I had your skills at picking locks.'

'Perhaps they did,' he said distractedly. Rising, he quickly examined the contents of the cluttered shelves for any implement he might be able to use to force the lock.

He found what he was looking for in a set of Allen keys on the top shelf. Choosing the smallest he made short work of forcing the lock. He removed the shackle from Bess's ankle, leaving a red mark that was sore to the touch, and threw it aside.

'C'mon, let's get out of here,' he said.

That was when a voice behind them said softly, 'You're not going *anywhere*, Herr Houdini.'

Houdini recognized the fat man's voice immediately. He was reaching for the pistol in his waistband when the fat man raised his own handgun and snapped, 'Don't! My first bullet will kill your wife!'

Houdini froze.

'Annalise,' said the fat man, 'go and fetch the gun from Herr Houdini.'

The girl descended the steps and came up to Houdini. She took the gun from his waistband and backed away from him until she reached the foot of the steps.

'I congratulate you,' said the fat man. Snow still glistened on their hats and the shoulders of their overcoats. 'It really *does* seem that no cell can hold you for long.' He paused, then as if it had just occurred to him added: 'Where is Wolf?'

'Upstairs.'

'For your sake I hope that he has not been harmed.'

'He'll be fine,' Houdini said.

'Give me the key.'

'What key?'

'The key to the attic room.'

'Wolf threw it out the window.'

The fat man eyed him curiously, trying to decide whether Houdini was telling the truth. 'Evidently that didn't stop you from escaping. How did you manage it?'

'How do you *think?* Out the skylight and down the drainpipe.'

'What a resourceful person you are.' The fat man turned to Annalise. 'Take the spare key and make sure Wolf is all right.'

'Must I?' she asked. The fat man's glare was answer enough.

With a shrug, Annalise climbed the steps and left the cellar.

★ ★ ★

'I think this is it,' said Purslane. He stopped Freud's Daimler at the head of a gravel drive that curved between tall trees until it reached a three-storey house that was just visible in the murky distance.

Holmes leaned forward in the back seat. 'Excellent. You may drop me here. Then drive on to the nearest property that has a telephone and call the authorities.'

'Shouldn't we have called the police before we left Vienna?'

Holmes's lips tightened. They had been through this earlier. 'Should the police be seen approaching the house, it would put Houdini and his wife in even greater danger, for the Eders would almost certainly use them as hostages to buy their freedom. If one man calls at the property, though, it might be possible to maintain the element of surprise. Just do as I ask, please,' Holmes said.

'I don't like it, sir. Your brother's orders were quite specific. I was to keep an eye on you and Dr Watson to ensure — '

'Oh, for God's sake, Purslane, just go and summon the police,' Watson snapped. 'When you have known Holmes as long as I have, you will learn that argument — no matter how logical — is useless, once his mind is made up.' He produced his Webley Mk II and held

298

it up. 'Here. This will protect us in your absence.'

'You don't have to play a hand in this, Watson,' said Holmes.

Watson smiled. 'Oh yes I do.'

Holmes, knowing his friend was thinking of Frances Lane, said: 'Come along, then,' and climbed out of the car. 'Get back here at your earliest convenience, Purslane.'

Purslane started to make one final protest, realized he wasn't going to change Holmes's mind and kept silent. He waited until Holmes and Watson set off along the gravel drive toward the house, then started the engine again and drove on, hoping that one of the houses in this isolated area would have a telephone.

★　★　★

Silence filled the cellar for a long moment as Houdini and the fat man traded stares, and Houdini tried desperately to find some way to turn the tables on his captor before Annalise returned with Wolf.

'Have you even looked at the plans I left you?' the fat man asked suddenly. 'Or were you just biding your time until the opportunity for escape presented itself?'

'I looked at them.'

'And?'

'It can't be done.'

'You're lying.'

'I can't make you believe me, but whatever your plan is, I should give it up.'

'The great Houdini concedes defeat? Is that what you're telling me?'

'That's what I'm telling you.'

'Then give me one good reason why I shouldn't kill you both directly.'

'*I'll* do it,' Annalise said, returning. With her was a thoroughly bruised and battered Wolf. She glared at Houdini, her low, husky voice filled with venom. 'After what he did to my father it'll be a pleasure.'

Houdini frowned. 'And what am I supposed to have done to *him*, whoever he is?'

'You destroyed him.'

'I *what?*'

'Oh, maybe not directly,' the fat man conceded. 'But you were certainly responsible.'

'How?'

'Our father is Nikolaus Eder,' Annalise said. 'The King of Clubs.'

Houdini's eyes narrowed. 'Eder? You're *Eder's* kids?'

'That's right.'

Houdini sucked in his breath as it all came back to him. 'Sure, I correspondended with

Eder. He was hoping to perfect the Underwater Box Escape, but it proved harder than either of us thought. I told him not to rush it, that it wasn't a race. One or the other of us would work it all out in time.'

'Liar!'

Ignoring her, Houdini looked at the fat man. 'What's your name?'

'Does that matter?'

'If you're Florian Eder it does matter.'

The fat man frowned. 'What does that mean?'

'It means that you were the one coercing your brother to perfect the trick.'

'That's absurd.'

'Is it? Then why did he tell me that? One of the first things he ever said in his letters was that I shouldn't take any notice of all the talk of rivalry between us, that it was just an invention of his brother's, a way to sell more tickets.'

'Are you trying to say you *weren't* his rival?'

'I was too damn' professional for that and so was he. Neither of us would willingly have risked his life just to get one over on the other. There's too much at stake — as Nikolaus found out.'

'And yet you announced it,' said the fat man. 'And the minute you announced it, it became a race, as you must have known it would.'

'I might have announced that I was *working* on it, but that's all I did. I didn't even perform it until earlier this year and then only after I was as sure as I could be that nothing would go wrong.' He glared at Florian. 'You dreamed up that rivalry, mister. And you forced your brother to push forward with the escape even though he knew there were still too many things that could go wrong. But when it *did* go wrong, you needed a scapegoat and I guess I fitted the bill.'

Turning to Annalise, he added, 'Is that what he told you? That your dad would still be here if it wasn't for Big Bad Houdini?'

'You're wasting your breath,' Annalise said. 'I don't believe you and I never will.'

Nearby, Wolf was watching Houdini with a strange expression on his battered face.

'I'm not so sure . . . ' he said, coming forward. 'What if he's telling the truth?'

'That's ridiculous!' said the fat man.

'What does it matter, anyway?' said Annalise. 'He says there's no way into the Palace. If you believe him about that, as well, then you have to agree — he is of no further use to us.' Again she looked up at Florian Eder. 'Let me kill him,' she said. 'For Father.'

The fat man gave no immediate reply. He

had known all along it would come to this eventually, no matter how things turned out. Still, murder was not a thing to be taken lightly, especially the murder of such a well-known celebrity. The American woman, Lane, she had brought it upon herself. Her death had not been premeditated, it had just happened. But now, as he looked at Annalise, he realized that something else had happened during their struggle. The girl had developed a taste for the taking of life and it shamed him.

'I'll do it,' he said firmly.

Houdini's throat tightened. 'Listen, Eder. Please. I don't care about myself, but for the love of God spare my wife.'

'That is impossible, I'm afraid. You know it is.' He raised the pistol and steeled himself to pull the trigger.

At the foot of the steps Annalise hissed, '*Do* it, Uncle. Let them join their pretty Fräulein Lane in hell.'

Bess looked dismayed. 'W-What?'

'Frankie's gone,' Houdini said grimly. 'They killed her.'

'*I* killed her,' said Annalise. 'And I *enjoyed* killing her, the bitch!'

'I bet you enjoyed dumping her body in the river, too,' Houdini said angrily.

Beside him, Bess started weeping.

'She was nothing,' Annalise said coldly. 'Nothing more than rubbish to be discarded. But in death she served her purpose. She served to warn you that we were determined.'

Houdini looked at Florian. 'What have you done to these kids? My God, you've twisted their minds out of shape.'

'Annalise is what *you* made her,' Florian said.

'Aw, come off it! You don't believe that any more than I do.'

'*Do* it, Uncle,' Annalise repeated. 'Shoot him. For Father.'

As the fat man's finger tightened on the trigger, Houdini heard Bess whisper his name. It galvanized him. Keeping his eyes on the fat man and knowing that his and wife's escape was all going to come down to timing, Houdini said, 'I love you, Bess.'

Florian's pudgy finger continued to squeeze the trigger. Behind his glasses his chocolate-coloured eyes filled with resolve.

'Goodbye, Houdini,' he said.

Just then, from the front of the house, came the shrill ring of the doorbell.

30

It's Over

The sound made Eder swear softly under his breath. 'Answer it,' he told Annalise.

'Let them go away, whoever they are.'

'Answer it,' he repeated. 'And deal with whoever it is.'

'But — '

'We haven't survived as long as we have by drawing undue attention to ourselves,' he reminded her.

Annalise indicated Wolf with an imperious flick of the head. 'Let *him* go.'

'With his face looking the way it does?' snapped Florian. 'Just do as I say. And give that gun back to Wolf.'

Annalise stamped angrily back upstairs, thrusting the gun into Wolf's hands as she passed him.

As she approached the door she tried to compose herself. She would tell their caller politely but firmly that they were not buying from vendors today, then return to the cellar and finally see her father avenged.

The thought sent a thrill of anticipation through her.

She opened the door to find two strangers standing outside, muffled against the foul weather.

'Yes?' she asked.

'Miss Annalise Eder?' asked one of the men. He was thin of face, with incisive grey eyes.

'Yes. May I help you?'

'You may,' said Holmes — and even before he finished speaking, the grim-faced man to his left produced a handgun and pointed it squarely at her.

'You may step aside,' Holmes continued. 'And you may consider yourself held until the authorities get here.'

Caught off guard, Annalise stumbled back. Holmes brushed past her and looked around the lobby. Behind him, Watson kept his Webley trained on the girl.

'You . . . you have no right to hold me!' she exclaimed.

'In Austrian law I *do*,' Holmes replied. 'Until such time as the police can make a formal arrest. Now, where are they?'

'I don't . . . who are you men? What do you want here? How dare you try to intimidate me!'

'I rather fancy you are not easily intimidated,' Watson replied.

There was no longer the slightest shred of

doubt in his mind as to the Eders' guilt. The distinctive Waverley Electric parked outside told its own story, while the shattered ground-floor window they'd seen as they approached suggested something untoward.

'Where are you holding Houdini and his wife?' he demanded.

Annalise's manner changed. These men, whoever they were, had somehow discovered enough to know that Houdini was here.

In desperation she threw herself at Watson, screaming at the top of her lungs as she did so.

'*Uncle!*'

Before Watson could stop her, she knocked the Webley from his grasp and tried to rake his face with the nails of her other hand. It was all he could do to hold her off.

Holmes grabbed the girl by her shoulders and tore her away from Watson. Before Watson could cross the hall to retrieve the fallen weapon, footsteps came pounding from the rear of the house. Seconds later Florian Eder stormed into the lobby, gun in hand.

'They know about Houdini!' Annalise screamed. 'They say the police are coming!'

'That's not possible!' Eder raged. Then: 'Get your hands up, gentlemen! You're not policemen, I know that much!'

'But they know about *Houdini*,' said

Annalise, retrieving Watson's revolver.

'We know more than that,' Holmes added coolly. 'And the authorities are being told everything at this moment — about the robbery at Christie's in London; about the abduction of Bess Houdini; the murder of Frances Lane by *you*, Miss Eder; the subsequent abduction of Houdini himself and your desire to gain access to the Imperial Palace. The only thing we don't know, Herr Eder, is what you hope to gain once you're inside.'

'And you'll never find out,' Florian snapped, but Holmes's threat had shaken him. He couldn't understand how this man — whoever he was — knew so much about his plans. It was all too clear that he knew enough, though, and if Annalise was right, then it was only a matter of time before the police arrived.

Fighting down his mounting panic, he demanded, 'Who are you?'

'My name is Sherlock Holmes.'

Eder recognized the name immediately. '*The* Sherlock Holmes?'

'To the best of my knowledge there is no other.'

'That it is something of a consolation, Herr Holmes. For there is no shame in being bested by the most famous detective in the world — even if only temporarily.' He gestured with the pistol. 'Now, go through to the kitchen, if you please.'

Holmes didn't move. 'It is over, Eder, but it may go in your favour if you and your wards surrender yourselves willingly.'

Eder scoffed. 'A wise man knows when to cut his losses. But sometimes wise men can also become desperate men — and it is best not to try the patience of a desperate man.'

Holmes knew he was right. Knowing that he now had nothing to lose could only make Florian Eder more dangerous. Holmes and Watson marched reluctantly ahead of Annalise, entered the kitchen and from there went down to the basement.

They found Wolf nervously watching Houdini and Bess. Earlier, Houdini had sensed once again that Wolf's heart really wasn't in this enterprise, whatever it was. Before he could do anything about it, though, Holmes and Watson, with Annalise behind them, came down the steps.

Houdini's spirits dropped still lower. Holmes had represented his last, slim chance.

'I see they got you, too,' he said.

Holmes nodded. 'But we may yet triumph. A man called Purslane, who is highly placed within the government of my country, is presently telling the police everything. It is only a matter of time before they get here.'

'They will be too late to do *you* any good,' Annalise hissed, raising Watson's gun.

'Don't be a fool,' Holmes told her. 'The game is up. Killing us will do nothing to change that. Indeed, if you kill us the police will only become more determined to bring you to book for your crimes. The British government will insist upon it, as will its counterpart on Capitol Hill.'

'You're bluffing,' said Annalise.

'Then call that bluff,' said Holmes. 'The net is closing, Eder. Murdering us will only add to your crimes. If you go now, you might still escape; the difference between freedom and capture may depend upon a matter of minutes, either way.'

Eder considered Holmes's reasoning, and was forced to admit the unpalatable truth. 'You are quite right, Herr Holmes. As things stand, we can no longer spare the time to argue with you and for that reason, we now bid you good day. We shall not meet again, gentlemen, Frau Houdini . . . but if we ever do, it will be to your great misfortune. Come, children!'

He stood back, keeping the prisoners covered, while Annalise and Wolf left the cellar. Then Eder followed them, closing the trapdoor behind him.

'Holmes — ' began Houdini.

Holmes raised a hand for silence. They all listened as an ominous scraping sound moved across the ceiling over them. A few seconds later the sound stopped and silence once again claimed the large, isolated house.

'What the devil was that?' asked Watson.

'They're using furniture to weigh down the trapdoor.'

The silence dragged on.

'I think they've gone,' Watson said at length.

'Then let us go after them,' said Holmes, starting toward the steps.

Houdini got there before him. 'Leave this to me.'

He climbed the steps until he was close enough to turn and brace his back against the trapdoor. Then he pushed upward, grimacing with the effort. But the trapdoor remained stubbornly intractable.

'Dammit!'

With one more Herculean effort he pushed and the trapdoor moved, allowing a crack of daylight to appear, but that was as much as he could manage.

'It's useless,' he muttered, sitting on the step.

'Perhaps not,' said Holmes. 'Listen.'

31

A Choice That Was No Choice at All

The cellar was quiet save for the hissing of the carbide lamp.

Then, as they strained their ears, there was the faintest of noises.

'What was that?' Houdini whispered.

It came again, barely audible. 'Holmes! Dr Watson!'

'It's Purslane!' cried Watson. And then, raising his voice, 'Here, Purslane! In the kitchen! We are down in the cellar!'

Houdini and Bess started shouting as well.

After a little, they heard footsteps hurrying into the room above, then the sound of a cupboard being dragged away from the trapdoor. As soon as the door was clear Houdini pushed it open, climbed out then turned and reached down for his wife.

'What happened?' asked Purslane as he helped pull them up into the kitchen. 'I passed the Waverley Electric as I was on my way back here. It was headed east as fast as it could go.'

'The Eders are getting away,' said Holmes.

'You have alerted the authorities, I take it?'

Shamefaced, Purslane shook his head. 'I drove as far as I dared, but I couldn't find any other properties around this neck of the woods, so I turned around and came back. The Eders almost ran me off the road, they were going so fast.'

'And they were going *east*, you say?'

'Yes.'

'They are heading for the border,' said Holmes, 'and a country — Slovakia — with which Austria has no extradition treaty. Once they cross the frontier they will be free to go wherever they like.'

'Then they'll get away,' said Watson.

'Not if I can help it,' Houdini said through gritted teeth. He pumped Purslane's hand. 'I don't know who you are, mister, but thanks for rescuing us. Now, if you don't mind, I'm going to borrow your car.'

'Harry!' His wife grabbed his arm, pleading with her eyes.

'They kidnapped you and they've killed Frankie,' Houdini said. 'I'm damned if I'll let them get away with *that*.'

Holmes, knowing that Houdini would not be dissuaded, strode through the silent house toward the still-open front door. 'There is no time to debate the matter,' he told the others. 'Therefore we shall all go.'

Florian Eder leaned forward in the back seat of the Waverley and tapped Wolf on the shoulder. 'Faster, boy! We've got to go *faster!*'

Wolf, hunched over the steering wheel as he tried to see the road ahead through a wall of tumbling snow, called back, 'I daren't go any faster in these conditions!'

'You talk as if we have a choice,' said Annalise. She was seated beside her uncle, wrapped against the foul weather in her long, heavy coat. 'Just do it, curse you!'

For a moment Wolf took his eyes off the blizzard to look back at his sister. She was glaring at him, her eyes the eyes of someone he had never seen before.

She had never cared much for Wolf. He was her complete opposite. She had always been headstrong, a quality she inherited from her mother, who had always been ambitious for her husband and her children. Wolf, by contrast, had taken after their father. On stage the King of Clubs had been a commanding figure, someone who was truly larger than life. Offstage, however, he had enjoyed a quiet, domesticated existence. If it hadn't been for Uncle Florian, who had seen his brother's enormous talents early in life and moved heaven and earth to make him the

314

star he was at the time of his accident, he might never have reached those giddy heights at all.

Facing forward again, Wolf said miserably, 'Uncle . . . is it true? What Houdini said?'

'Houdini is a liar,' growled Florian. 'All *Amerikaner* are liars.'

'*Are* they? I was watching his eyes when he spoke about Father. They were the eyes of an honest man.'

'Are you calling *me* a liar, then?'

Although the urge to back down was strong, Wolf stood his ground. '*Did* you force my father into performing the Underwater Box Escape too soon?'

'Of course I didn't!'

'Then why did Father tell Houdini that you did?'

'You only have Houdini's word for that!'

'And we only have *your* word against it.'

Florian glared at him. 'Damn you, Wolf! Haven't I always looked after you? Didn't I take you in after your father's accident, see to it that he had the finest care, that he could live out his final days with as much dignity as possible?'

'You make them sound more like the acts of a guilty conscience, Uncle.'

'How dare you take that tone with me!'

'I dare,' said Wolf, 'because there was

something else you also *kindly* did for us — you introduced us to the world of crime and I no longer even care to *think* about what all your poisonous lies have done to Annalise!'

'What is that supposed to mean?' demanded his sister.

Before Wolf could reply, the car started bumping precariously, tossing its occupants about. Wolf stamped on the brake, and the Waverley skidded to a halt.

No one said anything.

Wolf, badly shaken, climbed out into the blizzard. A moment later he stuck his head back inside and said, 'Curse it, I've driven us off the road. Get out. You'll have to help me push the car back from the verge, Uncle.'

Florian and Annalise struggled out of the car. Annalise got in behind the steering wheel, released the brake and indicated that her uncle and brother should start pushing. They leaned into the ornately curved front bodywork and slowly — too slowly, as far as Florian was concerned — the car rolled back along its own snow-furrows until it was once again on the road.

'*I'll* drive from here,' said Annalise.

'You'll get us lost,' grumbled her brother.

'How can I get us lost? There is only one road to the border. And it is the matter of only a few miles now.'

316

'Stop bickering!' Florian snapped. 'Let her drive, Wolf. Annalise — just get us out of here!'

The car whirred back into motion, swerving drunkenly from one side of the snowy road to the other until Annalise got the feel of the steering.

Florian stared out at the passing trees distractedly. He still couldn't understand how everything had fallen apart so rapidly. But now was no time to dwell on the past. He had to concentrate on getting them across the border to safety. Only then could he attempt to understand what had gone wrong, the mistakes he had apparently made and, hopefully, learn from them. Once they were settled in the second home he had bought them in Slovakia, he would find ways to empty their many pseudonymous Austrian bank accounts and transfer the money to their new country of residence. He would fetch Nikolaus too, in time. He would find a way to have his brother removed from the hospice in Engelhartstetten and placed into the care of a good Slovakian equivalent.

He started to feel somewhat better about things. For one brief moment there he had believed it was all over. Now, as the Waverley continued to carry them east toward the frontier, he dared to believe that they might yet salvage victory from what had seemed like certain defeat.

'Uncle!'

Florian turned to Wolf. 'What is it?'

Wolf was looking back the way they had come. 'I'm not sure . . . I thought . . . '

'What is it, boy?'

'I think we are being followed. I saw a car back there . . . just for a moment, a fleeting break in the snow — '

'Are you *sure?*'

'No . . . But I'd sooner we didn't take the risk.'

Florian agreed. 'Go faster, Annalise. The border can't be that far now.'

Annalise stamped on the accelerator, but the batteries were already giving as much power as they could. The fact that they were now labouring uphill was also causing them to lose ground.

'*Look!*' Wolf pointed. 'There *is* someone following us!'

'We don't know that for sure,' Florian replied. 'They could just as easily be travelling this same godforsaken route.'

'But they're not,' Wolf said. 'I recognize it now. It's that car we passed just after we set out. The Daimler.'

The Waverley whirred on, struggling to find traction.

'Annalise,' Florian urged softly. '*Faster.*'

It was then the Waverley reached the crest of the hill. As it did, there was an unexpected slackening of the wind. The falling snow stopped blowing against the windshield, revealing an old beam bridge spanning the winding cobalt line of the Danube below.

The Danube . . . and the border.

On the far side of the bridge sat a cluster of wooden huts, their pitched roofs thick with accumulated snow. Nearby, two chilled Slovakian soldiers manned a barrier that was now down.

'There it is,' pointed Florian. 'Come on, we're almost there.'

Again Annalise pressed down on the accelerator and this time the car lurched into high speed, aided now by its slippery decline towards the bridge.

The Slovakian soldiers watched them approach, grateful for the distraction they would provide from the bitter cold. One of them ducked under the barrier and walked forward to meet them, raising his hand as he came. As they raced down off the slope Annalise slowed the vehicle before it could reach the Austrian side of the bridge.

'Don't slow down,' Wolf shouted. 'They're right behind us!'

This time Florian turned to look for

himself and saw a blood-red Daimler with white-walled tyres coming down the hill after them.

'Go!' he yelled. 'Once we're across the border they can't touch us!'

Annalise pushed the accelerator to the floor and the Waverley lurched onto the bridge with snow flying up from under its spinning wheels. The Slovakian border guard on the other side of the bridge, sensing some sort of threat, immediately brought his Steyr-Mannlicher rifle up to one shoulder, yelling: '*Zastavi! Zastavi!*'

'Uncle . . . ?' cried Annalise.

'Keep going!' Florian shouted. 'Don't stop for anything!'

Behind them, the Daimler raced down off the hill and drove onto the bridge just as the guard at its far end fired a warning shot over the oncoming Waverley. The electric car veered wildly. Its rear tyres hit a patch of ice. The car spun around, out of control, and smashed through the wooden palings that lined the left side of the span.

For one awful moment the car tipped toward the icy waters twenty feet below, then slowly . . . slowly . . . righted itself.

'Get out!' exclaimed Florian. He had hit his head in the collision, his glasses had cracked and blood was streaming down one side of his pasty face. 'You hear me? Get out!'

'Wait,' Wolf urged. 'Don't move so fast!'

But Florian, in his hurry to escape the precariously balanced car, had shifted its point of balance so that it began to tilt at an even greater angle toward the river.

'No!' wailed Annalise. '*No!*'

It was too late. The car slid forward and — fell.

It turned end over end and crashed roof-first into the freezing water. There was an enormous explosion of foam. The car bobbed there for a moment, the inside filling sluggishly with ice-laden water.

Purslane brought the Daimler to a skidding halt on the bridge. Everyone piled out. The Slovakian guard and some of his companions, alerted by the sound of the crash, came running toward them. Purslane immediately raised his hands and started to address them in halting Slovak, telling them not to shoot.

Holmes, Watson and the Houdinis, meanwhile, raced to the splintered edge of the bridge and peered down at the water. The Waverley bobbed several more times, sinking ominously lower with each successive dip, and then vanished below the surface.

Watson breathed softly, 'My God . . . '

Holmes glanced at Houdini. 'It is over,' he said flatly.

But even as he spoke, two figures broke the

surface, struggling to stay afloat — Wolf and Annalise. Annalise flailed around, screaming for help. But her heavy coat, now saturated, dragged her under even as they watched.

Horrified, Bess looked away. 'Oh, dear God . . . Harry . . .'

She buried her face in her husband's chest. But Houdini gently pushed her away from him.

'Harry? What — ?'

'Take this,' he said, removing his overcoat.

She stared at him, alarmed. 'Harry, you can't *do* this! It's madness!'

'Bess, I can't just stand by. Not when I can do something about it.' He draped his coat about her shoulders, removed his slouch hat, and hurried to the splintered fence. There, he kicked off his shoes, took several deep breaths and dived into the water.

By now Annalise's head had disappeared below the surface. Wolf, struggling against the cold, somehow managed to drag her back up. His sister was still screaming, slapping desperately at the water and at her brother, in fact at anything within her reach. One of her blows struck him in the face, dazing him. Instinctively he let go of her and fought to save himself.

He sank below the surface. Panicking, he felt his lungs filling with icy water, his vision blurring . . . darkening . . .

Then . . .

He felt someone behind him, hands sliding beneath his arms, lifting him back to the surface.

He and his rescuer broke the surface together. Annalise could no longer be seen. Still struggling, Wolf turned to see who was supporting him. Stunned, he saw it was the very man he and his family had tried to imprison and had intended to kill.

Houdini's blank expression gave nothing away. Taking care to keep Wolf's head above water, he broke into a powerful sidestroke.

Behind them, Annalise appeared again, screaming. Houdini paused and looked back at her. He knew he could probably save her too, if he'd wanted . . . but with Frankie's death so fresh and his emotions so raw . . .

He *didn't* want to.

Annalise glared at him; for an instant her hatred of Houdini was greater than her fear of drowning.

Houdini, seeing that glare of hatred, turned and continued swimming towards the Slovakian bank of the river.

Annalise's screams ended, permanently, long before he reached it.

32

A New Beginning

For some time afterwards chaos ruled. Houdini and Wolf were hurried away and given the opportunity to dry themselves and change out of their sodden clothes into some coarse hand-me-downs that the Slovakian border guards found in the adjoining barracks. The checkpoint's commanding officer — a gravel-voiced *stotnik*, or captain, called Široký — had everyone brought to his office. Here, he tried to question them, but it did not go well for him. There was a major communication problem, for Purslane's Slovakian was poor and the captain's Austrian-German not much better.

At last the captain gave up and mimed the sending of a telegram. It appeared that he was going to summon someone from the nearest headquarters who could speak either German or English. Holmes nodded to show he understood and the captain left.

Once he'd gone, Wolf joined Houdini and Bess beside the ancient pot-belly stove in the corner of the office. The three of them silently sat there, draped in blankets, each sipping a mug of hot chocolate that they held in their half-frozen cupped hands.

Finally, Wolf broke the silence. 'I must thank you, Herr Houdini,' he said in a subdued voice. 'Without your intervention I would have drowned along with my sister and uncle.'

Houdini shrugged indifferently, but said nothing.

'No one would have blamed you for not coming to my aid,' Wolf continued, 'especially after all the suffering you have endured at our hands. And my apologies to you, Frau Houdini, though I am well aware that I can never fully atone for the misery I've caused you these past few days.

'I also owe you a debt of thanks, Herr Holmes, for bringing this abhorrent period of my life to a close. Since my father's accident . . . well, certain things have happened that made me uneasy. My father was, as you know, one of my country's brightest stars, the epitome of a showman, and a hero of sorts. He was paid handsomely for the pleasure he brought to his audiences, and as a consequence neither Annalise nor I ever wanted for anything. We enjoyed a very comfortable existence and, I suppose, you could say we were spoilt. But when the day came that Father was no longer able to perform to the level expected of him, Annalise and I intended to take over and become the new King — and Queen — of Clubs.

'Alas, that will now never happen, but I am inclined to believe you, Herr Houdini, when you say that it was Uncle Eder who encouraged my father to attempt the Underwater Box Escape too soon. He was always ambitious for his brother — perhaps even jealous of him — and believed that if the King of Clubs were to some day become a star on the international stage, he would first have to eclipse his only true rival — *you*, Herr Houdini.

'And so it became a race to see who could perfect and perform the Underwater Box Trick first — at least, that is what my uncle led us to believe. He played up this non-existent rivalry in the Austrian press and he did so with such success that for a time Father was the talk of our entire country.'

Houdini nodded, but kept silent.

'As you know, he attempted the escape with considerable misgivings. But Uncle Florian had already announced a date for the first performance, had spent a small fortune — money we could ill afford, as it turned out — on publicity, and my father had no choice. He would have sooner died than disappoint his public . . . and ironically, he came close to doing just that.

'Of course, it was a terrible personal

tragedy for us. Annalise — I do not expect you to believe this, but she was not always the heartless creature Uncle Florian eventually made of her. She and I worshipped our father and to see what he became after the accident . . . was . . . truly heartbreaking.

'On a more practical level, we also lost our main source of income, at the same time finding ourselves having to pay a vast amount for my father's continued care at the *Palliativestation* in Engelhartstetten. It further transpired that many of the investments my uncle had made upon my father's behalf were . . . unwise, to say the least.

'To that end, I suggested that Annalise and I embark upon our own stage career as soon as possible. Even before we started, though, I think we knew we were nowhere near good enough and were reluctant to tarnish the reputation our father had worked so hard to achieve.

'I will not make excuses for Annalise and me, gentlemen. We could have said no when Uncle Florian first suggested that we use those few skills we *had* acquired for certain . . . criminal enterprises. He argued that, since Europe had become a hotbed of intrigue, it followed that one nation would pay handsomely for the secrets of another. In his time he had made numerous friends within the Austrian government, and that was where it started. Under his guidance, Annalise and I were soon travelling throughout Europe — even to your own country, Herr Holmes — to obtain vital papers and documents for one government or another.

'As I have already stated, I was never happy about the direction our lives had taken. But we earned more money than my poor father ever managed to earn as the King of Clubs, and so long as a goodly proportion of it went towards his continued care . . . well, we decided to continue along that path.'

'You had the potential to become the perfect criminal, Herr Eder,' muttered Holmes.

Wolf frowned at him. 'I beg your pardon, sir?'

'A few days ago an acquaintance of ours, a certain Dr Freud, told us that a man who allows his conscience to dictate his actions, as long as that same conscience also *justifies* them, has the makings of the perfect criminal.'

'I am far from that,' said Wolf. 'I have detested every low thing I have done, not least the unfortunate death of Frau Lane. That was not meant to happen. We had intended only to ask her where she went earlier that evening and then to send her back to the Royal with a message for you, Herr Houdini. But she tried to escape and . . .'

Wolf shuddered before continuing. 'Gentlemen, I fear that something in my sister changed following my father's accident. To deflect attention from his own part in my father's downfall, my uncle filled us both with the idea that this had really been engineered by Herr Houdini. Annalise accepted our uncle's version of events without question and allowed her hatred for Houdini to fester and grow until she became hard and vicious. Did she kill Frau Lane by accident? I believe she did, yes. But did she regret it? I fear not. She showed no remorse, just gathered up the . . . the body and . . . and despite all my protestations . . . disposed of it.'

Something in him broke then, and he sobbed, once, before recovering himself.

'I am just glad the whole sorry business has come to an end at last.'

'Not quite,' said Holmes. 'I should still like to know why you wanted to break into the Imperial Palace to begin with.'

Wolf shrugged. 'To understand that, Herr Holmes, you must also understand something about the House of Habsburg. For centuries it was able to expand its influence largely through a great number of arranged marriages. Through these the Habsburgs were able to gain significant political and religious influence.

'In the middle of the sixteenth century the

Habsburg dynasty split. The so-called 'junior' branch became the Austrian Habsburgs. The Spanish Habsburgs retained the status of 'senior' branch. They ruled Spain and its colonial empire, as well as the Netherlands, parts of Italy and, for a time, Portugal.

'But the Spanish Habsburgs died out in 1700. They had been able to consolidate their power by their willingness to marry and pro-create with blood relatives. Of course, this often incestuous interbreeding resulted in all manner of deformities for those who did not die at birth; of insanity and disease as well. This is what eventually killed off the Spanish Habsburgs and led to the War of Spanish Succession.

'And yet not all members of the senior branch suffered the same unhappy fate. One such family in Spain, the Adalbertos, survived and believe they can prove their claim to the Austrian throne — if only they can obtain the evidence they believe Emperor Franz Joseph keeps locked away in the Palace records.'

'Then your mission was to break into the Palace vaults and obtain that evidence,' said Watson.

Wolf sighed. 'Yes, and the Adalbertos were willing to pay a small fortune to get it. But our biggest stumbling-block was how to enter and leave the Palace without getting caught. We pored over the plans we stole from

Christie's, but could find no way that did not involve too many risks. Then, when Herr Houdini came to our country . . . well, Uncle Florian said we could use his expertise to our advantage, and at the same time take our revenge upon him for forcing my father to undertake the Underwater Box Escape sooner than he would have liked.'

Holmes cleared his throat. 'You do realize, of course, that you have just confessed to spying for and against your own country, of abduction and complicity to murder.'

'I do, sir.'

'And you understand the likely sentence for those crimes?'

'Yes, Herr Holmes,' Wolf said bleakly. 'But I will face my fate in the knowledge that I deserve it. It is the one honourable thing I will have done for some considerable time.'

Houdini sprang up from his chair. 'Wait a minute,' he exclaimed. 'You mean I risked my neck saving this guy just so he can *hang?*'

Holmes stared at him, his expression inscrutable. 'Would you rather he be set free?'

Houdini glanced down at his wife, who quickly nodded.

'Yes, dammit,' he said.

'I see. And you, Purslane? As a representative of His Majesty's Government? What do *you* think?'

Purslane shrugged. 'The choice is not mine to make, Mr Holmes.'

'But you have heard his story. You must have an opinion.'

'Of course I do. Of them all, he was the least culpable, and he has already been punished, not least by his own conscience.'

'Well said.' He turned to Watson. 'What is your opinion, old friend?'

Watson had been thinking about something Holmes had said some days earlier, something Purslane had said, too. Now he broke his long silence. 'I think for Wolf to stand trial,' he replied, 'would only tarnish the good name of Eder, and cast a shadow over every wonderful thing his father ever achieved. I believe that if we were to take the law into our own hands and show him clemency, he would spend the rest of his days caring for his father and making amends.' He looked directly at Holmes and said meaningfully, 'There are some people in this life who are evil through and through. And yet there are a great many others who, despite their mistakes, may thrive, if given a second chance.'

Holmes allowed himself a faint smile. He knew Watson was really referring to the woman he had known as Irene Hastings.

'Then we are agreed,' he said. 'The crash, and the subsequent deaths of Florian and

Annalise Eder, was a very unfortunate accident — nothing more.'

Wolf looked at him through the steam rising from his mug. 'You would let me walk free?' he asked in disbelief. 'After every hurtful thing I have done? I mean, can you *do* this?'

Holmes hesitated for a moment then said, 'We can indeed.'

★ ★ ★

Once a harried translator arrived at the border post, it took a surprisingly short time to explain matters to everyone's satisfaction. The translator — a thin, bespectacled lieutenant — and Captain Široký showed great sympathy for Wolf, once they realized that he was the son of the King of Clubs; his father's name was known and revered even in their own country. Široký assured him that every effort would be made to retrieve the bodies from the river, though it might take several days to do so.

With the matter thus concluded, Holmes and the others finally donned their coats and hats and took their leave. As Wolf accompanied them he seemed to be in a daze.

The early-evening weather was dismal with light snow. As the others headed toward

Freud's waiting Daimler, Wolf pulled Holmes to one side and extended his hand. 'Thank you, sir,' he said, his voice lacklustre, his thoughts still dominated by his uncle and his sister and all the events which had led him to this moment. 'I do not deserve your mercy. I do not deserve *any* mercy.'

'But you have it,' Holmes replied. 'And I believe you will always endeavour to justify it.'

'Then goodbye to you,' said the younger man.

Holmes frowned. 'You are not coming with us, in the car?'

Wolf shook his head. 'I shall make my own way home,' he said.

'In these conditions you may never make it.'

Wolf smiled sadly. 'Then let my fate be in the hands of a higher authority.'

And without another word he turned and started traipsing through the snow, back across the bridge and into Austria, the blanket draped around his slumped shoulders, his head down.

Purslane, seeing him go, cried, '*Eder!*'

But Wolf didn't hear him, or if he did, chose not to respond. He just kept trudging through the snow until at length he was completely swallowed by the blizzard.

The others stood in a silent line, watching,

waiting, hoping that he would have a change of heart and come back. He didn't.

After a moment Houdini put his arm around Bess and pulled her close. Watson, watching them, was reminded fleetingly of Grace, the woman he had loved and now realized could never be replaced. And yet he could hardly bring himself to indulge in self-pity. At least he — they — had survived this business, unlike poor Frances Lane.

'A heck of a day,' Houdini said to break the silence. He looked at Watson, and Watson could see that he too was thinking about his late assistant and wishing with all his might that she could also have been here at this resolution. 'You know, I was just thinking.'

'Yes, Mr Houdini?'

'Maybe we should wait until tomorrow before we drive back to Vienna.'

'I was thinking the same thing,' added Purslane. 'We aren't far from Bratislava now. It would make admirable sense to find a hotel there, and allow both you and Mrs Houdini a chance to recover from your ordeal.'

'Sounds good to me,' Houdini agreed. Then he gave in to it, because he simply couldn't pretend any longer. 'And tomorrow we'll go back and care for Frankie, right, Bess?'

His wife nodded tearfully. 'Bless her, she

was closer than family to us,' she managed. 'As such, we'll care for her and ... and prepare her for her burial.'

She and Houdini followed Purslane to the Daimler, crunching through the snow and holding each other close as they went.

Holmes was about to go after them when Watson called to him.

Holmes turned. 'Yes, Watson?'

'Thank you,' Watson said softly.

Holmes cocked his injured head. 'For what?'

'At the beginning of this adventure you promised me a chance to recapture something of our salad days. You kept your promise; thank you for that.'

'You are entirely welcome,' Holmes said with a smile.

Watson glanced up at the leaden sky. 'The new century may only be thirteen years old,' he mused, 'but the pace of change has increased so fast that it is easy for a man to convince himself that he has outlived his usefulness.'

'Never,' said Holmes.

'I see that now. And I shall let you in on what may be a terrible, selfish secret.'

'Will you, indeed? Watson, I am all ears.'

'I wish we could do it all over again. By God, I haven't felt this energetic for years.'

336

'You may well get your wish,' said Holmes. 'I must confess, I have enjoyed my retirement, but the city has been beckoning me for some time now, and I have been considering selling my place in Sussex and moving back into town — perhaps even back to Baker Street, since I understand that the late Mrs Hudson's nephew has had no luck in attracting new lodgers for our old rooms.'

Watson stared increduously at him. 'Are you suggesting what I *think* you're suggesting?'

'It was expediency that first brought us together,' said Holmes. 'I was an impoverished detective with not a single client to my name and you were struggling to make ends meet on your army pension. Though neither of us is exactly strapped for cash these days there is a bond of friendship between us that I would like to see continue . . . even flourish . . . and as we have just observed, there is no shortage of new and varied crimes that still warrant our attention. What do you say, Watson?'

'I still say we are too old for such gallivanting,' Watson said.

For an instant Holmes looked disappointed.

Then Watson grinned and offered his hand. 'But I also say that I simply cannot wait to begin our adventures anew!'

'Then it is settled,' said Holmes, adding softly and with heartfelt sincerity, 'And from this day forward may God have mercy on the criminal classes!'

POSTSCRIPT

From the Journal of John H. Watson, M.D.

29 June 1914

I have just heard the news concerning the assassination of Archduke Franz Ferdinand of Austria and it has given me cause to remember the events which befell Holmes and me in that country last October.

It appears that the nephew of the aged emperor and heir to the throne was assassinated on the streets of Sarajevo yesterday afternoon. Reports indicate that he was shot once in the neck.

I understand from the papers that two attempts were made upon the archduke's life yesterday. The first happened during the morning, while he was directing manouevres with the Austrian Army Corps. A bomb was thrown at the imperial motor car, but its occupants escaped unhurt.

Unfortunately, however, the archduke's good fortune deserted him when, later that day, a student came close enough to the car to shoot both Franz Ferdinand and his wife.

The reports present a desperately sad scene. It appears that, at first, no one even realized that the assassination had taken place. Then, seeing blood issuing from the archduke's throat, his wife at once threw herself upon him. In so doing, she herself was shot in the abdomen.

Despite his wounds, the archduke was heard to cry, 'Don't die, my Sophie! Stay alive for our children!' He then came close to passing out, but when asked by an aide if he was in much pain was able to reply, 'It is nothing.' And he was still repeating that same phrase — 'It is nothing,' — when he died a few minutes later.

It is cold comfort to know that this unhappy conclusion has for some time now been inevitable. Bosnia and Herzegovina have been under Austrian occupation since 1878, when the Treaty of Berlin authorized the dual monarchy to hold the two provinces. Austria-Hungary is, as a result of territorial divisions and constitutional differences, ruled partly by the Germans and partly by the Magyars. The Slavs, who form a great majority of the people, numbering as they do some twenty-two million or more (as against eleven million Germans and close to ten million Magyars), remain understandably hostile to such a political system. In many

Serbian quarters, the archduke was considered to be one of the greatest opponents of the pan-Serbian movement.

But it is the identity of the assassin that has chilled me to the very bone. He is a nineteen-year-old student born in the Livno district of Grahovo. He has made no attempt to deny the crime of which he is accused. Indeed, he appears to revel in his notoriety, and notoriety it most surely is, for there is talk that, should Austria-Hungary declare war against Serbia as a result of the archduke's death, it will inevitably lead to a conflict of worldwide proportions.

The assassin claims that he has been planning to kill Archduke Franz Ferdinand for some time now, and cites 'nationalist motives' for his actions. Apparently, when the archduke's car slowed down in Francis Joseph Strasse, he seized his opportunity and struck. Germany, in particular, is said to be shaken by the assassination. The papers write that its consequences for Germany are second only in significance to those that must inevitably accrue to Austria-Hungary itself. Will the dual monarchy be as trustworthy an ally without the strong hand of Archduke Franz Ferdinand guiding the army and navy? That is the question uppermost in the German mind.

For myself, I am sick to my very stomach to think that Holmes and I both knew the assassin, whose name is Princip Gavrilo . . . the very man — boy, rather — who Javor Vasiljavic of the Black Hand once said would, if left to his own devices, start a world war.

I can only pray that Vasiljavic's comment was an opinion and not a prediction. For who can tell what will happen should the clouds of war loom dark and large across the entire world?

World War I began almost a month to the day later, on 28 July 1914.

*Books by Steve Hayes and
David Whitehead
Published by Ulverscroft:*

FERAL
DEAD END
FANATICS
KILLER SMILE
UNDER THE KNIFE
CAST A DEADLY SHADOW
TOMORROW, UTOPIA
BLACKOUT!
COMES A STRANGER
SHERLOCK HOLMES AND THE
QUEEN OF DIAMONDS
NIGHT CREATURES
SHERLOCK HOLMES AND THE
KNAVE OF HEARTS
THREE RODE TOGETHER

By Steve Hayes:
GUN FOR REVENGE
A WOMAN TO DIE FOR
VIVA GRINGO!
PACKING IRON
A COFFIN FOR SANTA ROSA
TRAIL OF THE HANGED MAN
DEADLY PURSUIT
(*with Andrea Wilson*)
A HEART THAT LIES
(*with Andrea Wilson*)
LADY COLT
A CANDIDATE FOR CONSPIRACY

A MAN CALLED LAWLESS
THREE RIDE AGAIN
(*with Ben Bridges*)
DRIFTER
SHADOW HORSE
(*with Ben Bridges*)
LATIGO
SHE WORE A BADGE

By David Whitehead:
HELLER
STARPACKER
TRIAL BY FIRE
HELLER IN THE ROCKIES
THE FLUTTERING
SCARE TACTICS
BAD THINGS HAPPEN AT NIGHT